PRAISE F

## THE GHOS

"A complex, interesting story that maintains suspense and intrigue page after page after page.... Scandalously entertaining."

—Sadie Hartmann, *Cemetery Dance*

"Henry writes with a keen eye for detail, drawing readers into the disturbing world with pitch-perfect '80s nostalgia and plenty of eerie atmospherics." —*Publishers Weekly*

"A vividly visceral visit to small-town horror." —*Booklist*

"Thrills, terrifies and sends chills up the reader's spine from start to finish." —Paperback Paris

## PRAISE FOR

## LOOKING GLASS

"Mesmerizing.... These somber, occasionally disturbing novellas offer a mature take on the children's story but balance the horrors of the City with hope." —*Publishers Weekly*

"Fans will delight in discovering the unknown family backgrounds and future fate of Alice and her wild and bloody Hatcher."

—*Booklist* (starred review)

## PRAISE FOR

## THE GIRL IN RED

"An engrossing page-turner that will delight anyone who loves running through thought experiments about the apocalypse." —Paste

"With *The Girl in Red*, Christina Henry once again proves that retellings don't necessarily lack originality."                    —*Kirkus Reviews*

"Beautifully written and daringly conceived, *The Mermaid* is a fabulous story. . . . Henry's spare, muscular prose is a delight."
—Louisa Morgan, author of *A Secret History of Witches*

"There is a current of longing that runs through *The Mermaid*: longing for the sea, for truth, for love. It is irresistible and will sweep you away."                    —Ellen Herrick, author of *The Sparrow Sisters*

"A captivating tale of an intriguing young woman who finds herself in the world of the greatest showman, P. T. Barnum. Original and magical, this is a novel to dive into and savor."
—Hazel Gaynor, *New York Times* bestselling author of *The Cottingley Secret*

"Christina Henry shakes the fairy dust off a legend; this Peter Pan will give you chills."                    —Genevieve Valentine, author of *Persona*

"Turns Neverland into a claustrophobic world where time is disturbingly nebulous and identity is chillingly manipulated. . . . A deeply impactful, imaginative and haunting story of loyalty, disillusionment and self-discovery."                    —RT Book Reviews (top pick)

"Henry keeps the story fresh and energetic with diabolical twists and turns to keep us guessing. Dynamic characterization and narration bring the story to life. . . . Once again, Henry takes readers on an adventure of epic and horrific proportions as she reinvents a child-hood classic using our own fears and desires. Her smooth prose and firm writing hooked me up instantly and held me hostage to the very end."
—Smexy Books

"An absolutely addicting read. . . . Psychological, gripping and enter-taining, painting a picture of Peter Pan before we came to know him in the film: the darker side of his history. The writing is fabulous, the plot incredibly compelling and the characters entirely enthralling."
—Utopia State of Mind

PRAISE FOR

# ALICE

"I loved falling down the rabbit hole with this dark, gritty tale. A unique spin on a classic and one wild ride!"
—Gena Showalter, *New York Times* bestselling author of *The Darkest Promise*

"*Alice* takes the darker elements of Lewis Carroll's original, amplifies Tim Burton's cinematic reimagining of the story and adds a layer of grotesquery from [Henry's] own alarmingly fecund imagination to produce a novel that reads like a Jacobean revenge drama crossed with a slasher movie."
—*The Guardian* (UK)

"A psychotic journey through the bowels of magic and madness. I, for one, thoroughly enjoyed the ride."
—Brom, author of *The Child Thief*

"A horrifying fantasy that will have you reexamining your love for this childhood favorite."            —RT Book Reviews (top pick)

"Henry takes the best elements from Carroll's iconic world and mixes them with dark fantasy elements. . . . [Her] writing is so seamless you won't be able to stop reading."            —Pop Culture Uncovered

"Alice's ongoing struggle is to distinguish reality from illusion, and Henry excels in mingling the two for the reader as well as her characters. The darkness in this book is that of fairy tales, owing more to Grimm's matter-of-fact violence than to the underworld of the first book."            —*Publishers Weekly* (starred review)

# NEAR THE BONE

CHRISTINA HENRY

BERKLEY
NEW YORK

BERKLEY
An imprint of Penguin Random House LLC
penguinrandomhouse.com

Copyright © 2021 by Tina Raffaele
Penguin Random House supports copyright. Copyright fuels creativity,
encourages diverse voices, promotes free speech, and creates a vibrant culture.
Thank you for buying an authorized edition of this book and for complying
with copyright laws by not reproducing, scanning, or distributing any part of
it in any form without permission. You are supporting writers and allowing
Penguin Random House to continue to publish books for every reader.

BERKLEY and the BERKLEY & B colophon are
registered trademarks of Penguin Random House LLC.

Library of Congress Cataloging-in-Publication Data

Names: Henry, Christina, 1974– author.
Title: Near the bone / Christina Henry.
Description: First Edition. | New York, NY: Berkley, 2021.
Identifiers: LCCN 2020032331 | ISBN 9780593199763 (trade paperback) |
ISBN 9780593199770 (ebook)
Subjects: GSAFD: Horror fiction.
Classification: LCC PS3608.E568 N43 2021 | DDC 813/.6—dc23
LC record available at https://lccn.loc.gov/2020032331

First Edition: April 2021

Printed in the United States of America
3rd Printing

Book design by Laura K. Corless
Title page art: Ladakh Mountains © SIHASAKPRACHUM/Shutterstock.com;
abstract grunge texture © Nejron Photo / Shutterstock.com

# NEAR
# THE
# BONE

# CHAPTER ONE

There was a dead fox in her path.

At first Mattie only saw it as a streak of scarlet across the fresh snowfall. Her initial thought was that some predator had gotten a rabbit from the traps she'd come to check.

Then she saw the orange fur matted with blood, and the place where something sharp had torn through the fox's middle. Viscera were strewn over the snow, the scent fresh and strong despite the cold air.

There weren't many creatures that would eat a fox—a bear would, of course, a bear would eat anything. Maybe a mountain lion, sometimes an eagle, but almost no creature would take the trouble of killing an animal and then not bother to eat it at all. None, as a matter of fact, except people, but there were no people at the top of the mountain except for Mattie and William.

Mattie crouched down to get a better look at the animal, but she didn't see any prints or claw marks that would give her a clue. She stood again, brushing the snow off her heavy wool skirt, and paused for a moment, irresolute.

Perhaps she ought to go back and tell William about the fox straightaway. Then she decided she ought not to until she checked the traps. That was why he'd sent her down to the creek in the first place, and if she didn't do as she was told then she would pay for it.

Mattie stepped around the fox and paused again. There was a strange track in the snow beside the fox's body. She couldn't quite make sense of it.

The track seemed to be from a bear, but if it was a bear then the animal was much larger than any bear Mattie had ever seen— maybe twice as big as the biggest grizzly in the area. The print appeared to be a rear paw—she could make out the curve of the heel and the five toe pads. But the claw marks at the front were much longer and deeper than usual. The size of the print made her think it must be the biggest bear in existence.

Mattie glanced around the path, checking for more prints. The path she followed wasn't a man-made one but a deer trail. The trail was flanked by the trunks of tall mountain pines and the remains of scrub from the summer. She found another print—another rear paw, and some distance away from the first. That was strange, too. It was like the bear was up walking on its hind legs like a person. They might do this for a few moments, especially to intimidate another creature, but not as a general practice.

Mattie shook her head. This wasn't anything she should worry about. She could practically hear William's voice saying, "Get a move on, girl. It isn't any of your concern. You're always curious when there's no cause to be."

Yes, she should check the traps before William had to come down and find out what was taking her so long.

Mattie continued on, kicking up some of the powdery snow with her boots as she went. It wasn't proper winter yet—summer was barely over, in fact—but they'd already had several days of snowfall and unusually cold days. William worried that they might not have enough food set by if the winter was especially harsh. There wouldn't be very many animals about. They'd all be snug in their dens.

That made Mattie wonder—what was a grizzly doing, leaving fresh meat behind like that? This time of the year most of them were getting ready to bed down for the winter. Those bears still active wouldn't pass up an opportunity to put on a little extra winter fat. If the grizzly wanted to save the kill for later it would have cached the fox—though it was hardly worth caching what amounted to a mouthful.

She had to stop worrying on it. William was waiting.

They had three snares set apart in the brush by the creek. All three were full, which meant rabbit stew with carrots and potato. William would be pleased.

Mattie put the rabbits in her canvas sack, carefully reset the snares and started back to the cabin. A few flakes of snow drifted down as she walked and she stuck her tongue out to catch one—

*(holding hands with Heather with our heads tipped toward the sky, catching as many snowflakes as we can, our eyelashes coated white)*

No. She was not to think of that, either. That was only a dream. William had told her many times that it was all something she'd made up in her head and he didn't want to hear about that nonsense.

She shouldn't dwell on the dream or the strange bear print or the dead fox. She should hurry home with the rabbits, because her husband waited for her. He expected her to be a good wife.

When she reached the dead fox again on the way back, Mattie carefully stepped around the corpse and the prints in the snow. William might want to come and see them later, but she wasn't going to trouble herself about it anymore. She wasn't going to think of how strange it was, because William told her what to think and she was sure he wouldn't like her thinking on this.

William was outside the cabin chopping wood when Mattie hurried into the clearing.

The clearing was large enough to accommodate their two-room cabin, a storehouse for meat, an outhouse and a small garden in the summer. William had cleared away extra trees so that there was fifteen or so feet of open ground in front of the cabin before the forest. He said this was so nobody could sneak up to their home without him knowing.

Her husband was a tall, powerfully built man—more than a foot taller than Mattie, with broad shoulders and large hands and feet. His hair was dark, streaked with gray, but his eyes were bluer than ice on a frozen creek bed. William's back was to her but he immediately turned as if he'd sensed her presence when she stepped into the clearing, the heavy wood axe in his left hand.

He said nothing as she approached, only waited with that expectant, impatient look that told her she'd made a mistake.

"There was a dead fox," she said by way of explanation. "But the traps were full."

Mattie thought the evidence of a good night's supper would be enough to distract him, but she should have known better. "Why should the fox be any of your concern? I told you to check the snares and come straight back."

Mattie bit her lip. This was the trap. If she didn't answer, he would be angry. If she tried to explain, he would be angry.

"Well?"

She should try, at least. Maybe he would understand this time.

"Something killed the fox and left it there," she said.

His gaze sharpened. "A person? Someone in the woods?"

"No, no," she said quickly. She knew how careful he was about keeping the location of their home a secret, how upset he got if there was any sign of people nearby. "There was a track, like a bear track, but much bigger than any bear I've ever seen."

William's jaw relaxed a fraction. He did seem relieved that she hadn't found evidence of a person.

That slight unclenching deceived her, though—she wasn't braced when he dropped the axe in the snow and his fist flew out.

Stars shot across her vision and she tasted blood on her tongue. Her bottom felt cold.

*You're sitting in the snow. Get up before your skirt gets wet,* she thought.

"You know if you find anything unusual you're supposed to come get me immediately." William didn't sound angry, but then he never did. There was never any yelling, any warning that the blow was about to fall.

"I thought it would be better if I checked the traps first," she said.

She knew she ought to stand up, but if she stayed on the ground she was harder to reach.

"That's your trouble, Martha," he said, using her Christian name—always a bad sign. "It's not your role to think."

"Yes," she said. "I'm very sorry."

He stared down at her, and she could tell he was deciding whether or not he'd punished her sufficiently for her transgression.

"Take those rabbits inside and skin them," he said. "When you're finished you show me this dead fox."

"Yes," she said, pushing out of the snow.

Her stockings were wet just above the tops of her boots. It would be nice to change them when she went inside but William might come in with the firewood and find her doing something other than the task he assigned.

Mattie hurried toward the door of the cabin, her shoulders hunched. She didn't relax until she heard the whistle and thud of the axe again. That meant William wasn't following her.

She put her boots away and set about the task of skinning and dressing the rabbits for cooking later. Rabbits were small and not much work, and Mattie knew that William would expect her to finish quickly.

*Don't make him angry again. Do your job as you're supposed to.*

But her mind wandered away, as it often did, and she had to call it back so that William wouldn't find her woolgathering. Her hands made quick work of the rabbits even as her thoughts drifted elsewhere, to that place they weren't supposed to go.

William came to the door of the cabin and called in. "Are you finished?"

Mattie knew he didn't want to remove his snow-coated boots only to put them on again. This was less about saving her the trouble of wiping up the water on the cabin floor and more about saving himself the effort of lacing and unlacing.

"Just about," she called back.

"Don't take too long," he said, and shut the door again.

In truth she was finished, but she wanted an extra minute or two to wash up and compose herself. She'd been thinking about the dream again, thinking that she heard a song playing (*something about a dove, there are these big black things and the music is coming out of them, coming from a silver disc, but that seems silly. Something from a dream like William always says*)

William believed music was sinful so she knew it wasn't anything she'd heard since she'd come to live with him.

Mattie plunged her hands into the cold water in the basin and scrubbed the blood away, trying to scrub the dream away with it. William seemed to be able to sense her dreams on her, like a scent that clung. He was already irritated. If she went outside with those strange images still in her eyes, he'd be even angrier.

A few moments later she was outside again, bundled in her coat and mittens and boots. William had his rifle in his hand.

"Show me," he said.

Mattie indicated the deer path she'd followed earlier. William didn't like Mattie to walk in front of him and she was careful not to do this. Her tracks were still visible in the snow, in any case. Only a few flurries had fallen since Mattie returned home.

There were crows gathered around the fox corpse, picking at the exposed meat. William shooed them away and they flew off, cawing loudly.

Mattie stood behind him and a little off to the side, so she could see his face. She hated being surprised by his moods. He might decide she was silly for mentioning the fox to him in the first place, and that would stack on top of his earlier mood to create a fury she could not escape.

Sometimes Mattie wondered why he married her, why he'd chosen her in the first place, especially when he always seemed to find fault. He could have picked a different girl, one with more of the qualities he seemed to desire—someone less curious, more biddable.

Mattie watched her husband closely as he scanned the area around the fox. His eyes widened when he saw the paw print. "Did you find any more of these?"

She pointed toward the scrub to their right. "There."

William went to take a closer look, and it was only then that Mattie noticed the scrub was broken, like something very large had blundered through it. The bark on one of the trees had long, deep claw marks, as if the animal had scraped it as it went by. William ran his hand over the marks, a thoughtful expression on his face.

"If it's a grizzly, it's the biggest damned grizzly there ever was," he said. "I wonder where it came from. Something that big would need a lot of game."

Mattie remembered then just how sparse game had been over the last few weeks. Both she and William had attributed this to the early cold snap. But maybe it wasn't the cold at all. Maybe it was this bear, this monster of a bear that was out in the woods eating up all the moose and deer that William wanted to kill and hang in their storehouse for the winter.

"I'd like to think it's gone from the area," he said. "The footprints seem to indicate its going down the mountain, anyway. Some lucky fellow is going to shoot it and end up with his name in the newspaper, not to mention the best trophy anyone has ever seen."

Even if some man did shoot the bear, Mattie would never see his name. She was expressly forbidden from reading anything except the Bible. On the rare occasions that William went into town and returned with a paper he would always lock it in his trunk.

Mattie was not permitted to be in the bedroom when he opened the trunk, and he kept the key on a key ring that was on or near his person at all times. The keys to the cabin and the storehouse were also on this key ring, as well as two strange keys. Mattie didn't know what these were for, and the one time she'd asked about the keys he'd given her two black eyes so she never asked again.

"Big bear like that would be a lot of meat, though," he mused. "We could eat all winter on that bear."

*If you can kill it without getting killed yourself,* Mattie thought.

William glanced at her, and not for the first time Mattie had the idea that he could hear what she was thinking.

"You don't think I can kill it?" he said, and there was a glint of something in his ice-chip eyes, something that might have been humor on another man. "Well, you might be right this once, Mattie girl. I'm not going to get a bear that size with this."

He indicated the rifle, which he mostly used for deer hunting.

"It might be gone anyway, like you said," Mattie offered tentatively. "Gone down the mountain."

He looked at her, then back at the claw marks. "I'd like to be sure. But if it's still around I don't want you wandering on your own. Stay with me."

He pushed through the broken scrub, expecting Mattie to follow. She did, carefully lifting her skirts so they wouldn't snag on the broken branches.

William strode ahead without pausing, and Mattie hurried to catch up.

"There," he said, pointing to another print in the snow. "This is the darndest bear I've ever seen. Doesn't it ever go down on its forepaws?"

Mattie didn't answer. She knew he didn't expect her to do so.

They followed the prints for a good while longer. Every step they took gave Mattie a tiny thrill. She wasn't allowed to go down the mountain, only to places close to the cabin that William approved. It had taken a long time for her to earn that privilege, too. At first she wasn't allowed to go anywhere without him, not even to the outhouse.

The forest didn't look any different but Mattie was still deeply aware that she was in a place that was forbidden and new.

After some time her mind began to wander, as it often did, and the tune for that song drifted over her again, but she couldn't quite catch the words. If she knew the words then she could grab another part of the dream, a hazy thing that was just out of reach.

William halted abruptly and Mattie noticed just in time, jolted out of her reverie before she plowed into his back.

"Where did it go?" he said. "The prints just stop here."

They stood in a small clearing, the towering pines surrounding them like a fairy circle.

*(but how do I know that when I've never seen one except maybe I have there's Heather crouching in the grass pointing at the mushrooms saying it's a fairy circle)*

William stood still for a moment, his eyes darting all around the clearing, but there was nothing to see except unbroken snow.

"What did it do, fly away?" he said.

"Maybe we turned in the wrong direction," Mattie said tentatively.

"There's a print just outside the clearing and it's facing this direction," William said. "I'm not a fool, Mattie, not like you."

"Of course," she murmured. Her heart pounded faster, because when she made these kinds of mistakes he had to correct her.

But William was far more interested in the mystery of the bear at that moment. He continued scanning the area for any sign he might have missed.

Mattie backed out of the clearing, retracing her steps to the last print. It was another rear paw, and it was certainly odd that there was only evidence of rear ones. The animal was definitely not behaving like any bear that Mattie had ever seen. She inspected the trees that surrounded the clearing.

"There!" she said, pointing to the claw marks high up on the trunk of one of the trees.

William came to stand beside her, his gaze following the direction of her finger. They both looked higher, into the thick cover of pine needles. Mattie half-expected to see a bear sleeping on a branch high above, but of course there wasn't one. That was a foolish thought she'd had. The bear that went with that paw print would surely be too large to sleep on a tree branch.

William was checking nearby trees now for any other signs. "Nothing," he said, and then seemed to come to a decision. "That's enough of this foolishness. There's work to be done."

That meant William had decided Mattie had wasted his time with her information about the fox, and that if she didn't do her chores exactly right the rest of the day she would pay for it.

Mattie thought of her sewing basket, filled with William's clothes that needed mending, and felt a little thrum of anxiety. She was not a natural seamstress. Her stiches were neat but she took a long time about them. William blamed Mattie's mother who, he said, "should have taught you the proper arts of a woman instead of leaving them to me."

Early in their marriage William had given her some ancient pattern books, their edges yellowed and frayed. By painstakingly following the directions, Mattie was able to slowly teach herself how to make and mend their clothes. She remembered spending many nights hunched over scraps of cloth, the tips of her fingers raw and bleeding, while William watched her in the flickering candlelight.

He always watched her, even when she thought he wasn't.

They started back toward the cabin, following their own boot prints in the snow. Mattie could tell from the hunch of William's shoulders that he was irritated. He hadn't been able to solve the mystery of the print and now he was realizing just how long they'd wasted on this fool's errand.

*Because of me*, Mattie thought resignedly. *Maybe I shouldn't have told him about the fox after all. But if I hadn't then I would have been in more trouble for taking too long checking the snares.*

There wasn't any correct answer for Mattie. There never was.

All she could do was gnaw on her thoughts like a nervous little chipmunk.

A strange cry shattered the still air.

It wasn't quite a bear's roar, or a mountain lion's call, or an eagle's screech, but a nerve-shattering combination of all three, mixed with another sound—something almost, but not quite, human.

Only then did Mattie realize they'd heard no sounds since the call of the crows William had shooed away from the dead fox—that is, nothing except their own voices. No bird cries, or skittering of little things searching for one last nut for the winter. No crack of falling branches, no whisper of wind.

All the forest had been a hushed and waiting place, and she and William had fumbled into it like two clumsy bulls. She felt eyes on her then, the eyes of the trees and birds and squirrels and rabbits, eyes that watched in pity at the two foolish humans in their midst.

The cry sounded again. It echoed in the air, bouncing off the trees, making it impossible to tell exactly where it was coming from.

"William, we should hurry," she said, tugging at his sleeve. "We shouldn't be out here."

He'd stopped dead again when the first cry came, his body still but alert, searching for signs of his quarry. Now he brushed Mattie's hand away, too preoccupied to hurt her for presuming to tell him what he should do. That was almost always a punishable offense.

"Quiet," he said in a low voice. "Get away from me so I can get a clear shot."

He was going to try to kill it, whatever it was, and Mattie was certain now it wasn't a bear. No bear sounded like that. No bear acted the way the animal that made those prints acted. But if it wasn't a bear, then what was it?

Whatever the creature was, William would fail. It was too big for her husband to kill with a rifle. Even she, with her limited knowledge, could tell from a print in the snow.

Terror washed over her, cold and sure. What would happen to her if William were killed? She'd be all alone on the mountain. She didn't even know how to reach the nearest town, for she'd never been away from their cabin since they came here.

William took a few steps away from her, raising the rifle to his shoulder. "It's somewhere ahead of us. Stay behind me."

She nodded. Her lips and tongue were numb—not with cold, but with fear. Her body shuddered underneath her coat.

*Don't let anything happen to him, Lord. Don't let me be left alone.*

Then she realized that if the giant bear-creature killed William, it would kill her, too.

Relief shot through her body like a jolt of lightning. No more trying and failing. No more questions without answers. No more dreams. No more pain.

Mattie walked in William's footsteps, calmer now. Whatever happened would be God's will, just as it had been God's will for her to be chosen by William in the first place.

Branches cracked somewhere in front of them—many branches breaking in quick succession like a gun going off, *pop pop pop.*

Mattie glanced over her shoulder, a part of her expecting to discover the creature had dropped out of the sky and loomed behind them. But there was nothing behind, and nothing ahead, either, at least that they could see.

William crept forward for several more minutes, the rifle braced at his shoulder. For the third time that day he came to a sudden halt, and this time Mattie did run into him.

He was too distracted to scold her. "What in God's name?"

Mattie peeked around his arm and gasped.

Before them was a scarlet pool of blood, sinking into the powdery snow. Something very large had been killed, and recently. There were no remains, however, and no sign of the thing that killed it. The only prints nearby were their own.

"It doesn't make any sense," William muttered.

Mattie tilted her head back, saw the bent branches overhead, and thought that perhaps it made more sense than William thought. But she wouldn't say that aloud. It was never a good idea for her to contradict him.

*But I do wonder what it might be. Even if I'm not supposed to wonder about anything at all.*

William was preoccupied for the remainder of the day. He appeared to hardly notice what Mattie did—and this was certainly a blessing, since the only time he ever cared about her work was when she did it wrong.

He brooded all through supper, saying not a word, shoveling the rabbit stew into his mouth without seeming to taste it. After supper he stared into the fire while she carefully mended a ripped sleeve and a torn trouser hem and darned two pairs of socks.

She began to hope that he might forget about her daily duty, that he might be so lost in thought she would be allowed to go straight to sleep. But the moment she put away her needle and stretched her cramped fingers he seemed to waken.

His ice-chip eyes caught hers as sure as a rabbit in a snare. "A man has to have sons, Mattie."

She stood silently and went into the bedroom.

Mattie woke some hours later with the song she'd been trying to remember on her lips. *A dove sings . . .* she thought, but she couldn't catch the rest of it and it slipped away again.

William snored beside her. The noise must have woken her—it often did, though she'd never dare complain about it. She slowly climbed out of bed so as not to disturb him with sudden movement.

Mattie went into the main room of the cabin, closing the bedroom door behind her. The room was freezing. She hadn't stopped to put a dressing gown over her nightgown. She wrapped a quilt over her shoulders like a shawl. Her breath made a cold fog in front of her face.

She didn't feel tired anymore, though she knew she ought to sleep. There would be more work in the morning, and if she was tired or slow or clumsy then William would notice and . . .

*And the same thing will happen that always happens,* Mattie thought, tears pricking her eyes.

Once, when she was younger, Mattie asked why he had to hit her so often and so much. He'd hit her again for this impertinence and then explained that it was his duty as a man and her husband to discipline her, that he did it so she would learn the proper obedience of a wife.

Then he handed her the Bible and told her to read aloud from Ephesians.

She did, though there was blood in her mouth and her cheek swelled and tears streamed out of her right eye. "Wives, submit yourselves to your own husbands as you do to the Lord. For the husband is the head of the wife as Christ is the head of the church, his body, of which he is the Savior. Now as the church submits to Christ, so also wives should submit to their husbands in everything. Husbands, love your wives, just as Christ loved the church and gave himself up for her."

He'd taken the Bible from her then and knelt before her, gently cradling her head in his big hands. "God wishes for you to obey me. I don't want to hurt you, Mattie. I get no pleasure from it. If you would only listen and perform your duties properly, I wouldn't have to. Do you understand?"

She nodded, even though she didn't, even though she thought William should do some more contemplating on the part about husbands loving their wives.

He'd kissed her forehead and said, "I chose you out of all the girls in the world to be my bride. You're my special, special girl."

William didn't celebrate birthdays, and the days seemed to run into one another here, but Mattie tried to keep track of the years as best she could. She thought she was about twenty, maybe a little older. William was older than her, but that was because it was right and proper for an older man to guide his younger wife.

She went to the window that faced the woodpile and the storage shed. There was a long narrow table under the sill where Mattie prepared food and did other tasks. Earlier she'd skinned and dressed the rabbits there, all the while keeping a wary eye on William as he chopped wood.

Mattie kept a jug of water and a cup for drinking on one end of the table. There was a thin crust of ice on the water. She broke the crust with the handle of a spoon and poured out a little water. It was so cold it made her gasp.

She stared blindly out into the shadows of the forest. What would happen if she just pulled on her boots, opened the door and ran out into the night? William would never know. He slept so hard these days that he might not notice she was gone until hours from now. She might be able to make it as far as the town by then.

Mattie wasn't certain where the town was but surely she could find it. It was at the bottom of the mountain, and William always managed to go there and back in the same day.

But . . . Mattie's thoughts stuttered to a halt, her momentary hope dying on the vine. The people of the town knew her husband. They would only send her back to William.

He had always told her that if she tried to run away they would return Mattie to him, for she was his property and they knew where she belonged.

*Besides,* Mattie thought hopelessly, *you can't run away in just your nightgown and a blanket. You'll freeze to death.*

The cry of the bear-creature came out of the woods again, distant but still close enough that she shrank from the window.

*And if you don't freeze to death you'll get eaten by that thing.*

It wasn't a bear. It didn't sound right, the way a bear sounded. But it almost didn't matter what it was. Mattie didn't need to see it to know it was a killer.

She knew she should go back to bed, that sometimes William woke up in the night and reached for her. If she wasn't present there would be hell to pay.

Her feet wouldn't move, though. She stayed there at the window until the first pink light of dawn showed above the treetops.

# CHAPTER TWO

After breakfast William said, "I'm going out today to see if I can track that bear."

Mattie's surprise must have shown on her face, for William did an uncharacteristic thing and explained himself.

"I'm worried about it coming close to the cabin. We've got meat in the storehouse and if the bear depletes all the hunting around here it might just decide it's easier to take our stores than go down the mountain in search of more. You know that bears have gotten into the storehouse before."

Mattie nodded. Two black bears—or maybe the same bear twice—had managed to break the door handle and push inside, gorging themselves on the stores.

The first time this happened Mattie was alone in the cabin. William was out on one of his trips to town. She'd stood helplessly at the window, unable to do anything about the bear because

William had refused to teach her how to fire a rifle. Mattie listened to it blundering around inside the storehouse for hours, until the bear finally trundled out the door again and wandered away.

The only consolation on that occasion was that it was late spring and there hadn't been much meat left in the storehouse. They'd used up much of it over the winter and the summer hunting hadn't yet begun in earnest.

The second consolation, at least for Mattie, was that William blamed himself and not her. That was a rare enough occasion that she never forgot the moment.

"I ought to have put a different kind of handle on the door. I knew they could open doors. And I should cover the window, too."

Mattie didn't ask how he'd come by the knowledge that bears could open doors but she believed it. She'd seen the animal that had gotten into the storehouse do that exact thing—press down on the handle with its paw until the mechanism unclicked and the door swung open.

A bear returned a couple of days later, before William had an opportunity to fix up the storehouse. This time William was at home, and in short order that bear had been dispatched and was hanging up in the storehouse himself.

After that William had boarded up the window and resealed any holes in the storehouse. "I'm sure it just looked in the window and saw the meat hanging there. Those bears are smart as anything."

He also changed the door handle to a knob that would be harder for the bear to turn and added another lock.

There hadn't been any other incidents since then, but now

William was worried. A groove formed between his eyes, one that only appeared when he was particularly troubled.

Mattie was hesitant to speak—when she criticized William (*or even appeared to criticize him*) he always got so upset. But since he seemed in an uncharacteristic mood today she dared.

"I thought you said that rifle wouldn't kill a bear that size," she said.

"It won't," he agreed.

That's when she knew he was really worried, because it wasn't like William to let any comment of hers pass without censure.

"I don't necessarily want to kill it, at least not today. But I'd like to see it, maybe track it to its den. It's getting colder, so it will have picked out a place for the winter even if it isn't spending all its time there yet. We know it is big, so there are only a few places it can go. I'd like to get a better idea of just how big it really is. It's eating up all the game around here, that's for sure."

"Yes," Mattie said, then added, "please be very careful," because this was what wives were supposed to say when their husbands went out to do something that might be dangerous. She was still confused about how she ought to feel if something bad happened to William.

Part of her longed for it (*a wicked part, you know that's a wicked thought, to wish your husband harm*), but the other part was afraid of what would happen to her if he was gone. He'd kept so much knowledge from her that she wasn't certain she could survive without him.

"You're going with me," he said.

"Me? Why?" She'd assumed she would stay home and perform

her regular duties. That's what she always did while William was out hunting.

William gave her a long look, as if trying to decide if he should tell her the answer. Finally he said, "I could use an extra pair of eyes, and yours are the only ones available. If I had a son, now . . ."

He trailed off meaningfully. Mattie flushed with shame, as she was meant to, and she felt the familiar pierce of grief under her ribs, grief that would sneak up on her and make her lungs seize.

She'd tried and tried to do her duty as his wife, but none of her pregnancies would keep. Twice she'd bled out the baby. William had beaten her terribly after the second time, incandescent with rage and accusing her of using witch's arts to rid herself of her children. Her left arm had never really healed properly. It ached most cold days, and when she held her hands in front of her she could see the knot in her left forearm, the not-quite-straightness of it.

The third child had come too early, far too early, so that when he slipped from her body there seemed hardly anything to him at all. She'd held him in her arms even though he never cried, his body cold before she even had a chance to name him. That was the only time Mattie had ever seen William weep.

"I'm sorry," Mattie said, for she knew the fault was with her, with her defective body, and also because if she apologized it always put him in a better mood.

*Though even if our son had lived he'd hardly be old enough to go hunting. He'd still be small enough to hold on to my apron strings, and then where would you be, William? You wouldn't have an extra pair of eyes at all, because I would be home with the child.*

Mattie stood and quickly cleared the table, because that was a very rebellious thought and William could always see those in her eyes, could sense when the spirit he'd tried to grind out of her reasserted itself.

"When you're done with the breakfast dishes put on your trousers," he said. "Your skirts aren't good for running, and anyway they make so much noise."

Mattie only had one pair of trousers, which she wore very rarely because William said they were not decent. Despite this, he had conceded the occasional necessity of them, particularly when he needed her help with some strenuous chore.

It was much easier for Mattie to move without the weight of a skirt and two petticoats. Her legs felt lighter, freer when she wore her trousers. She felt light enough to fly.

*(or run away)*

Mattie hunched over the water basin and scrubbed the dishes, not looking at William. He'd definitely see "run away" on her face, even if it was only a passing thought. Even if she didn't really mean it.

*(although you sort of meant it you really did)*

She had to quash these rebellious thoughts. They weren't becoming of a good wife, and William reminded her constantly that her purpose was to be a good wife to him.

A short time later they were back in the woods. They moved up the mountain this time instead of down. William said there was a small meadow at a slightly higher elevation than their cabin, and at the edge of the meadow was a cliff face with several caves.

"I've seen big grizzlies go in and out of there sometimes," he said. "And a bear as big as this one we're after—there's not a chance it's going to dig out a den. It's going to look for something ready-made. But you keep your eyes open just the same, Mattie girl. We might find he's gone to ground somewhere else."

Mattie didn't understand why William was fixated on the creature, not really. He said it was because of their meat stores but that didn't seem to be the actual reason. She didn't think the vague way he wanted to go about finding it was very useful, either. Why didn't they go back to the place where they found the tracks yesterday and start from there? It was so unlike William, who was normally very ordered and logical.

*He's afraid of something,* she thought as she trudged along behind him. *He's afraid of something, but it isn't this creature getting inside the storehouse or eating all the game.*

Mattie stared at the back of his neck, trying to think on what it might be. She felt there was a clue in something he'd said the day before, but she couldn't quite grasp it.

She was supposed to be his extra pair of eyes, in any case, and if she spent all her time looking at William's back and thinking about yesterday then she wasn't doing what he'd told her to do.

The woods were more pleasant today, less close, less silent and watchful. The sun emerged from the cloud cover and made the snow glitter a fierce and brilliant white. Birds darted between the trees, chittering and chattering their many thoughts to one another. Squirrels and chipmunks watched them pass from branches or from beneath bits of brush, tolerant of the bumbling humans in their midst.

Mattie didn't think the creature (she didn't know when she'd stopped thinking of it as a bear, but she was somehow sure that it wasn't quite a bear, whatever William said) was anywhere nearby. The forest felt different than it had the day before. Now that she thought about it, the woods had felt that way from the moment she'd gone out to check the traps. It hadn't been because of the fox, either. She'd been uneasy from the start, though she hadn't recognized the feeling.

William walked without speaking, pausing only to inspect markings that meant nothing to Mattie—broken bits of twig, a disrupted bit of snow, a piece of cracked bark. None of these things appeared to be the work of the creature. The signs they'd seen the day before had been much more obvious.

Mattie sensed William's increasing frustration and wished he hadn't insisted that she accompany him. It would be her fault, somehow, if he didn't find any sign of the animal.

After an hour or so they reached the meadow. It was about four times the size of the clearing in which they lived. Mattie imagined that in the summer it would be filled with the colorful bobbing heads of mountain flowers—aspen daisies and harebells and blanket flowers and golden banners. William had taught her the names of the flowers, and how to find edible herbs and berries.

She had a sudden memory of William leaning down to point out some columbine. She'd been very small when he did that. In her mind's eye she could see her hand reaching out to stroke the petals, a little girl's hand.

The field was brown now, all the flower petals blown away or dried up. Above the meadow was a sloped rock face, several openings dotting the cliff.

"That's where it will be if it's anywhere up here," William said.

Mattie eyed the slope. It was very steep, and there was a great deal of loose scree. It looked dangerous—unnecessarily dangerous, since there was no sign this meadow had been crossed recently by anything larger than a rodent. And if there were bears bedding down for the winter up there, then it would be foolish, even treacherous, to go poking around. What was William thinking?

"If there are bears asleep up there—" Mattie began, but William cut her off.

"Think I don't know there might be? We're not going to wake them if there are. We're only going to look around the entrance to see if any of the prints are like the one we saw yesterday." His fist curled, but he didn't raise it. "Don't try telling me my business, Martha. Now stay close and keep quiet."

*Stay close and keep quiet.*

Something twanged deep inside her brain—darkness, a rough hand over her mouth. A whisper. "Stay close and keep quiet."

William realized she wasn't following and turned around, a muscle in his jaw twitching. Mattie hurried after him before he could speak again, or remind her in another way that he'd given her an order and she was supposed to obey it.

He strode easily up the slope while Mattie struggled behind. She rarely had to do any kind of strenuous climbing since William insisted she stay so close to the cabin. He stopped by the first entrance to check the ground. Mattie rubbed at the stitch in her side, her breath coming in hard pants.

"You'd better quiet yourself," William warned. "You sound like a bellows."

Mattie nodded, trying to catch her breath. "Maybe I should stay here while you go on? It's very difficult for me, William."

She tried not to sound like she was pleading, because that always irritated him.

"You will stay with me," William said between his teeth. "Now keep up."

He went on toward the next cave entrance without checking to see if she would follow. He knew she would.

*Why is he acting like this, insisting I stay with him? He would normally leave me behind in a second if I impeded his progress in any way. It's not practical for me to try and keep up.*

When Mattie first came to live with William he'd been like this—insistent that she stay with him every moment—but it had been a long time since he'd behaved in this manner.

*Back then he was afraid I'd sneak off if he took his eyes off me for a moment. He's afraid of that again, and it's because of the creature.*

Mattie couldn't piece together why she thought this, though. There was a step she was missing. She only knew that something had changed since yesterday, and that was the presence of a new animal near their home.

But she shouldn't think on it. She shouldn't try to solve the puzzle of William's mood, because she never seemed to solve it right, and anyway, William always told her she should let him do the thinking.

The second cave entrance was much higher on the slope than the first, and by the time they reached it Mattie felt dizzy and a little sick to her stomach.

William crouched down, peering closely at the patches of dirt interspersed between the rocks. Mattie breathed in deeply, trying to settle her racing heart.

She caught a whiff of something rotting, the thick wet stench of decay, and felt the blood drain out of her face. Cold sweat poured down her temples as she covered her nose and turned her head away. *Don't get sick, don't get sick,* but there was nothing for it, she'd already felt nauseous and the smell undid her.

Mattie stumbled away, trying to put a few feet between her and William. He was always deeply revolted when she vomited. He seemed to think that if only she had better control of her body then she wouldn't get sick.

"I told you to stay . . ." he started, but by then she was heaving out her breakfast behind a boulder. "Disgusting."

When she was finished, Mattie lay her cheek against the cool rock and wished for some water. Her throat felt scorched and her mouth was filled with a sour tang.

Then William grabbed her by the back of her collar and yanked her up, dragging her back by her heels. Her coat was buttoned up high against the cold and it pressed against her throat, making her choke and gag as he pulled. He tossed her roughly to the ground on her back a few feet away.

He climbed on top of her, kneeling, his knees holding her in place on either side. He grabbed the front of her coat with both fists and yanked her up halfway, shaking her.

"Are you expecting, Martha? Are you carrying my son and trying to keep it a secret?" William's face was red, his mouth a curled snarl, spit flying from it onto her face. "Don't think you can hide it from me! Don't think you can use your witchcraft to bleed him from your body again."

"No," Mattie said, her voice a thin little thread. She couldn't breathe, couldn't think, couldn't make the words come out. "No, I wouldn't."

His weight pressed down on her middle and all her organs rattled in her rib cage with each shake.

"I didn't—I wouldn't—the smell—"

"What smell?" William said, shaking her again and making her teeth rattle.

"I can't," she said, clawing at his hands. "I can't—"

*Catch my breath. I can't breathe.*

He released the front of the coat abruptly and her head crashed back to the ground. Sharp rock bit into the back of her skull and warm liquid flowed into her hair. Stars shot across the vision of William looming over her.

"Explain," he said in that voice that made Mattie think of frozen rivers, of icicles with long sharp points.

She tried to draw in a deep breath but the bottom of her ribs was trapped beneath William. If she didn't explain soon his fury would crash over her, more terrible than before.

"Wasn't . . . feeling . . . well . . . the climb," she panted. "Then . . . smell from the cave. Rotten."

His gaze sharpened. "I didn't smell it."

"I . . . check again."

"You're not hiding a pregnancy from me?"

Mattie shook her head, but this made her vision go crazy again. "I . . . wouldn't. Wouldn't."

He leaned close, which took the pressure off her lungs, but his breath was hot on her face and made her stomach jerk again. She hoped to God that she wouldn't be sick with him this close because he would really hurt her if she threw up on him.

"You'd better not be lying. You know what happens to girls who lie."

*Cold darkness. The sound of a door slamming closed. Fists swollen from beating desperately against the wood.*

"The Box," she whispered. "I'm not lying. I wouldn't."

He seemed to see what he wanted to see in her face because he abruptly climbed off. Mattie lay there for a moment. She felt blood trickling down her skull and hoped the wound wasn't deep. Infection was always a risk with any open wound, and William became irritated when he had to look after her.

"Get up," William said.

Mattie did, slowly, because the world tilted crazily and she still didn't have her breath back. William watched her dispassionately, making no attempt to assist her.

*He doesn't cherish you. He doesn't love you,* she thought, but the same despairing thought followed that always did—*Where can I go? What can I do?*

She was completely dependent on him in every way.

As soon as Mattie was on her feet, William jerked her toward the cave mouth. Almost immediately they were bathed in the waft of fetid air. Mattie turned her head away, covering her mouth and nose with her scarf. Even William, normally so self-mastered, made a gagging noise.

Mattie couldn't help a tiny little smile of satisfaction at that, and since her mouth was covered she allowed herself to have it. William would never know.

He pulled up his own scarf and took a few steps inside the cave. The cave's deep shadow swallowed him up immediately.

"Smells like a cache," he said. "But bears don't usually keep a cache where they sleep, or in places where they can't cover up the food."

"If it is a cache shouldn't we stay out?" Mattie asked.

She did not want to go inside where it was dark and stank of dead things. Her legs felt wobbly and off balance and her vision still hadn't righted itself. Everything would blur, then clear, then seem like it jumped up and down, then go blurry again and the cycle would start all over.

"If it was in the cave we would know. It would have rushed out the second you started making all that noise. I didn't come all this way just to turn around because you're so weak you can't climb a hill."

He pulled two candles from his pocket and handed both to Mattie. He lit each one with a long wooden match.

"You stay right next to me so I can see. I can't hold a candle and the rifle at the same time."

Mattie nodded. William wanted to go inside, so there wasn't any point in arguing any more even if this was the most foolish idea he'd ever had. Her throat felt clogged up with her fear, a tangible thing that she couldn't swallow down.

They shouldn't go into the cave. Even if the bear (*or creature*) wasn't there at the moment it could return at any time. When it did they would be fish in a barrel, trapped with no way to escape.

Mattie kept pace with William as they entered. Hot candle wax dropped onto her mittens, but she'd knitted them thick and tight to keep out the cold. The wax settled and cooled quickly without burning her.

The smell was much worse just a few paces into the cave. The walls took a sharp turn and grew narrower, the ceiling much lower. Mattie and William were able to walk side by side, but only just.

"There," William said, pointing to the ground in front of them. He tucked the rifle under his arm and took one of the candles, crouching down to peer at the dirt. "Do you see?"

33

Mattie stepped closer, squinting down. The flickering candle allowed her to just make out two of the prints they'd seen yesterday, side by side and about a foot apart.

"It must have to bend over to get through here," Mattie said.

"I knew it was up here. I knew it," William said, triumph ringing in his voice. "Now I can kill it before anyone comes looking."

"Comes looking?" Mattie said. "Why would anyone?"

"An animal that big will attract trophy hunters and other types," William said darkly. He didn't elaborate on what those "other types" might be. "All that has to happen is for one fool to catch a glimpse of it somewhere down the mountain. They'll all swarm up here like a bunch of ants, stomping through our woods and killing our game. They'll come knocking at our door, asking idiotic questions and wanting water and food. But if I can stop it all before it starts—"

He seemed to realize then what he was saying and whom he was saying it to. He stood, thrust the candle back into her hand and said, "Come on."

"But why are we going farther in?" Mattie asked before she could stop herself. She cringed away as he leaned toward her.

"Because I said so. You listen to me now or you know what will happen." His tone was all cold fury. He marched ahead and she followed, because she did know what would happen if she didn't follow.

*He's angry because he explained too much. He's angry because now I know that what he's really afraid of is people. He doesn't care about the creature in the woods or what it might do. He just doesn't want anyone else to come looking for it and find us.*

*(No. Not us. Me. He doesn't want anyone to find* me.*)*

Before Mattie could explore that idea further, the stink, which she'd grown somewhat accustomed to, became abruptly unbearable. Then her boot found something round and slippery and she flew forward, crashing onto her elbows. The candles slipped from her hands and rolled away, their meager light winking out.

"Clumsy idiot," William said. She heard him fumbling in his pockets for another candle and matches.

The darkness was too close, pressing all around her, making it impossible to breathe. There was something under her, several somethings, things that poked at her at odd angles and clacked together like beads.

*Bones.* The word streaked across her brain like a panicky firefly. She scrambled back and away, swiping desperately at the front of her coat to make sure nothing had stuck.

William struck the match and for a moment all she saw was his face illuminated by the lit match head. Then the candlewick caught. William lifted the candle high, and Mattie shrank away from what the light showed.

They were in a large chamber, the ceiling several feet higher than the passage, and stacked all around the walls were piles of bones. The bones were enough to send Mattie fleeing but she didn't dare, as William went closer with the candle, muttering, "What in God's name?"

She saw then that the parts were sorted—skulls in one place, ribs in another, leg bones next to that and so on. They were from all kinds of animals, large and small—Mattie recognized deer and elk and mountain lion, and also chipmunk and squirrel and fox and coyote.

"It's not natural," William said. Mattie heard a quaver in his voice that had never been there before. She wondered if he was even aware of it. He seemed completely fixated on the bones. "No animal acts like this. No bear acts like this. But if it's not a bear, what can it be?"

Mattie inched away from the chamber as far as she dared. She wanted to flee into the passage, to run back down the mountain until she was back in her own cabin, where there were still things to fear but these were things she knew and could understand. She didn't understand this. She didn't understand an animal that kept the bones of its victims.

"Let's leave, William. Let's go before it comes back."

He ignored her, pacing around the chamber, inspecting each bone stack. When he reached the far side of the room, his head jerked back, as if in shock.

"Found out why it smells so bad in here. Come look."

Mattie did not want to look. She wanted to leave the cave, not head in deeper, but she knew an order when she heard one.

She shuffled slowly forward, her heart in her teeth. *We need to leave, we need to get out of this terrible place, it's not natural, it's not normal, the creature is going to return at any moment and kill us and our skulls and ribs will be sorted with all the rest.*

"Look," William insisted.

Mattie covered the scarf over her mouth and nose with her mittened hand. The reek was unbearable as she peered around William. A moment later she gasped and stumbled back.

It was a pile of organs, hearts and intestines, again in different sizes and from different creatures, all in various states of decay.

"Don't you dare faint," William snapped as Mattie swayed on the spot, her hand clutching his shoulder so she wouldn't fall.

"I can't breathe in here," she said. "Please, William, please."

He turned away, clearly uninterested in her distress and intent on his investigation.

"Please," she whispered, or maybe she only thought it because William didn't even twitch.

*What would he do if I ran? If I just went to the cave mouth he would be angry, but maybe not too angry, especially if he saw I wasn't trying to run from him, just the cave. He couldn't be too angry, could he?*

No, he could be very angry about it. Mattie knew that.

Still, she wanted to be as far from the rotting organs and eerie piles of bones as possible, even if it meant leaving the circle of light provided by William's candle. Mattie backed away carefully until she was at the chamber entrance again. The darkness swallowed her up, squeezed tight around her ribs.

"Please, please," she whispered. "Please let's leave this terrible place, let's just go."

Then she heard it. The strange cry they had heard in the woods the day before—a furious roar that was nothing at all like a bear.

# CHAPTER THREE

t was far off still—not on the slope yet, not about to enter the cave, but it would very soon. Mattie knew that for certain.

It would come home with its kill and find them in its cave, like Goldilocks sleeping in the little bear's bed, except they wouldn't be able to escape like the small girl in the story. They'd be trapped.

Which was exactly what Mattie had feared would happen.

William peered around the chamber, moving the candle here and there, completely absorbed in his task. It was apparent he had not heard the monster's call.

*I could bash the back of his head in with one of these bones. I could leave him here and the creature would find him and rend him to bits and make all of those bits part of its collection.*

Then the roar came again, and Mattie couldn't be sure but she thought it was closer, and there was no time for anything she might want to do but hadn't the courage to actually do.

"William," she said. "It's coming."

"What?" He turned around, blinking in the candlelight, his mind returning from somewhere very far away. Mattie recognized the symptoms.

"I heard it roar," she said. "Outside. It can only be on its way here."

"This is my chance," he said, crossing the chamber in just a few huge steps. He thrust the candle at her and said, "Stay behind me. If you get in my way, you'll wind up getting shot."

Then he pushed by her, hurrying toward the exit without waiting for Mattie. She hurried after him, afraid to see what the creature looked like, afraid to see it running at them with an open maw ready to devour.

And it would devour them. William's flimsy rifle was no match for the thing that made that horrible roar.

They were just at the cave mouth when the cry came once more, long and furious. It echoed strangely around the meadow, reverberated off the rocky cliff so that Mattie couldn't tell if it was nearby or not. It might break through the trees below them at any moment.

William quickly scouted the immediate area and found a boulder that provided both cover and a view of the tree line below.

"Blow that candle out, idiot girl," he snarled. "Do you think it won't smell the fire?"

*Do you think it won't smell* us? Mattie thought, but she blew out the candle and crouched low beside him.

They heard branches cracking, the sound of something huge blundering through the trees.

*Or traveling through the branches*, Mattie thought. Yesterday the creature had seemed to disappear high above them, even if William didn't believe it.

The noise was tremendous, and the echo made it impossible to tell exactly where it was coming from.

"Just how big is it?" William muttered, training his rifle below.

*I don't care*, Mattie thought. *I want to go home.*

But the place she saw in her mind's eye wasn't the spare two-room cabin where she'd lived for the last twelve years. It was the place she always dreamed about, the place William said didn't exist.

*Heather*, she thought. The two of them holding hands and spinning across the carpet and laughing to the music, a woman wailing, "Just like a white-winged dove sings a song . . ."

Mattie heard William suck in his breath, felt the growing tension that emanated from him. She realized then that everything had gone quiet, just like the previous day, and right after that they'd found the huge strange pool of blood.

The birds had fled.

*All the little creatures are still and huddled and so are we. I wish I could fly away like a bird instead of crouching behind a boulder like a scared little mouse waiting for the swipe of a cat's paw.*

William curled his finger around the rifle's trigger. Mattie listened hard. She thought there might be something approaching, but it wasn't anywhere near as large as the creature. It sounded like it was picking its way carefully along the trail, trying to be as silent as possible.

She heard the twitter of sparrows then, and whispered, "It's gone. The crea— the bear, I mean. Whatever's down there, it's something else."

"Quiet," William said.

A moment later, a man emerged from the trees.

Mattie stared at the stranger as William cursed under his breath. He paused for a moment, seemed to come to a decision. Then he said in a low tone, "Don't talk to him. Don't you say one blessed word or you'll pay for it later."

He put the rifle on his shoulder and stood up. William strode down the slope toward the man, who hadn't appeared to notice them yet. The stranger had paused in the meadow, crouching down with a small black box near his face.

The box was familiar to Mattie, but she couldn't remember quite why. The word was on the tip of her tongue.

*A camera*, she thought. *He's taking a photograph.*

She remembered having a camera herself, an old-fashioned one that belonged to her mother. When you pressed a button, the photo would come right out and you wouldn't have to take it to the photo lab for processing.

She remembered standing next to Heather, both of them shouting, "Cheese!" and making silly faces while Mom took photo after photo.

She remembered taping those photos to the wall of her bedroom, deliberately tilting them this way and that so that the overall effect was a huge jumbled collage.

As they approached the man, Mattie felt her stomach roil, watery nausea clogging her throat. It had been many years since she'd seen any person other than William, and part of her recoiled from the contact. She wasn't supposed to talk to strangers. That had been her mother's rule, and it was William's, too.

The stranger's clothes also made her feel uneasy, for while they were completely different from her own, they were also somehow familiar—part of the echoing memory that had been pounding in the back of her mind since the day before.

He wore a bright coat with blocks of color on it—blue and orange, and it was made of a very shiny material. *A windbreaker,* she thought. *I used to have one, but it was red. Heather's was bright pink, like a glowing raspberry.*

Aside from the windbreaker he wore gray pants with many pockets and brown leather boots with pine-colored laces. The stranger carried a very full pack on his back, the same bright orange as his jacket, with a bedroll (*no, a sleeping bag*) tied to it. As they got closer, Mattie saw he wore fingerless gloves with a mitten top buttoned back.

Every part of his appearance sparked something in her—curiosity, a memory, an unfixed kind of longing. She glanced up at William and hoped he wouldn't see any of these things on her face. They would only make him angry.

The man appeared to hear them approach, for he dropped the camera back to his chest (where it was attached by a strap), glanced around, then stood, smiling. His teeth seemed very white and even. Mattie self-consciously pressed her lips closed in reply. She was missing a tooth from her lower jaw—it had gotten infected and William had to pull it out.

She shuddered, remembered the way William had strapped her head to a board with his leather belt so she wouldn't move, remembered the horrible wrenching as the tooth pulled free of the gum, the blood gushing everywhere. The rest of her bottom teeth had moved around as a result of the empty space, some of them tilting crookedly like broken tombstones.

"Hello there!" the stranger called, waving.

Mattie felt she ought to wave back, but William had told her not to speak and she was certain waving counted as speaking.

William didn't wave back, either, nor did he call out a response. He marched toward the strange man, so brightly colored against the faded meadow. The stranger's smile wobbled, then receded as it became apparent that William was not approaching for a friendly chat.

Mattie struggled along just behind William, still feeling sick and dizzy, but she could tell the expression on his face just by the set of his shoulders and the stiffness in his walk. His eyes would be fixed in a cold glare, his lips compressed, a muscle in his jaw ticking like a bomb.

The stranger took a quarter step backward as William stopped a few feet away from him. Mattie came to a halt near William's left elbow, half of her body hidden behind her husband. She saw the stranger throw an uneasy glance at the rifle held loosely in William's arm.

"What are you doing here?" William barked.

The stranger had brown eyes, and now they flared in annoyance. Mattie expected him to yell at William, to respond to William's aggression with some of his own, but the stranger only said, "It's public land," in a tone that was mildness itself.

"It's public land, yes," William said, "but it's dangerous up here this time of year, especially if you don't know what you're doing. The weather can turn in a second, and there are a good many bears, and they can be aggressive."

The stranger gave William a half smile that did not reach his eyes. "Thanks for your concern, but I've had plenty of experience.

What are you and your daughter doing up on the mountain so late in the season?"

He glanced at Mattie, who quickly turned her gaze to the ground. The stranger had dark curly hair that peeked out from under his knit cap. She saw that just before she looked away.

Mattie felt William swell up beside her, his anger a palpable thing.

"She is not my *daughter*. She is my *wife*," he said through his bottom teeth.

If William had spoken to her like that, Mattie would have shrunk away, because that tone was a warning of what would come next. But the strange man didn't seem to feel the danger, because when Mattie dared look up again, she found him watching her curiously.

He seemed to take in their clothing for the first time, for he asked, "Are you Amish or something?"

"No," William said, and Mattie thought, *Oh, stranger, please run away, can't you tell that my husband is about to explode and when he does he will hurt you, he will hurt you like you've never been hurt before.*

The stranger then looked from William to Mattie and back again, and said, in a very skeptical tone, "Your wife?"

He didn't wait for William to respond but instead addressed Mattie directly. "Do I know you? You look so familiar."

Mattie froze, because William had said not to talk to the stranger, but the stranger had asked her a question and if she didn't answer, it would be rude. William might punish her later for being rude but he also might punish her if she talked to the stranger. Her jaw felt stuck in place, paralyzed by indecision.

"You don't know her," William said, shifting so the stranger could no longer see Mattie's face. "We aren't from this area."

This was a lie, of course, a bald-faced lie. Mattie knew William didn't want the man to know they lived on the mountain.

"What high school did you go to?" the man persisted, trying to see around William's shoulder. "Your face—"

"You should move on from here as soon as possible," William said, and something about the way he shifted the rifle in his arms made the stranger go still. "There are bears."

"Bears," the stranger repeated, his voice flat.

Mattie didn't need to see his face to know he didn't believe William.

"Let's go," William said to Mattie, grabbing her arm and pulling her away.

She felt her husband's anger in the clench of his fingers around her arm.

"Don't you dare look back at him," William growled. "Don't you tempt him with your wiles. I know you wanted him. You're nothing but a whore, Martha, like all women are whores."

Mattie didn't protest, didn't say that she hadn't thought of the man that way. No matter what she said, William wouldn't believe her.

*He's mad because the stranger thought I was William's daughter and not his wife.*

She knew William was much older than her, of course—she wasn't certain exactly how much, but there was at least twenty years' difference between them. His hair was more than half gray, and he had wrinkles around his eyes.

*That stranger, though. He was young like me. Close to my age.*

*And he thought he knew me.*

Mattie risked a quick look backward, wanting to see the stranger's face one more time. He wasn't looking at Mattie and William, though. He stared up at the cliff face, at the place where Mattie and William had come from just before they'd met the stranger.

*Don't go in the cave,* she thought. *The creature will catch you.*

Mattie looked back just in time, for when they reached the cover of the woods again, William thrust her away roughly and turned again toward the stranger.

"I ought to shoot him right now," William snarled, raising the rifle to his shoulder. "A man ought to know better. He ought to *respect* another man's property. He oughtn't have looked at you like that when you belong to me."

"No, don't!" Mattie cried, curling her hand over his arm.

"What, you don't want me to shoot your lover? Get your hands off me, Jezebel. I have every right to kill him and you. You're mine, Martha. Mine to let live or let die. Mine in every way. And if any other man thinks his plow will sow your fields, he will by God *pay* for that disrespect."

Mattie knew William would beat her when they got home—knew because the man had glanced at her and she glanced back, knew because William felt insulted, knew because William was already angry and worried about the creature, knew because the stranger had been in the wrong place at the wrong time. All of these sins would be Mattie's fault, as all the things were always her fault. The pain was coming. She knew that.

And because her punishment was inevitable she dared to defy him, to keep her hand curled around his arm just above his elbow.

She dared to say, "I don't care about him, William, truly I don't. I would never look at any man but you—"

"Liar," he spat. "You're a bitch in heat, like all women are."

"—but if you kill him, then people will come, lots of people, they'll come searching up the mountain to try and find him and you don't want that, do you? You don't want lots of people crawling all over the mountain because of the bear, that's what you said, but if that man goes missing, then there will be even more people, there will be . . ."

She trailed off, trying to think of the right term. It was something she knew from long ago, but couldn't quite recall.

"Search parties," William said.

"Yes, search parties," she said. She ought to have known that term, *search parties*. There was something about them that was important, important to her, but she'd forgotten. "So you shouldn't kill him because of that. I don't care about him at all, William, not at all, but you don't want search parties here, do you?"

Mattie didn't dare look anywhere except William's face. He still had the rifle trained on the stranger. Mattie saw death in William's eyes, a longing to pull the trigger, to avenge his insulted manhood.

A muscle twitched in his jaw. Then he abruptly dropped the muzzle toward the ground. Mattie hastily released his arm and took a step back.

"Search parties," William said, glancing at her. She thought she saw something move across his face, something like fear, but it disappeared in an instant and Mattie decided she must be mistaken. "This has been a wasted day. There are chores to finish. I should have been out hunting stores for the winter instead of wasting my time on this bear that frightened you yesterday."

The creature *hadn't* frightened Mattie the day before—at least not right away. She'd only thought the death of the fox had been odd. But it was going to be her fault that William had wasted his time today, and she was sensible enough not to remind him that he'd decided that very morning that the bear was a threat.

That was why they'd spent the day away from their usual tasks—because of William's decision, not hers. She didn't remind him, either, of the creature's strange behavior—the cave of bones, the pile of organs. She wanted to go home and forget all of it. She hadn't shaken off the nausea completely and she wanted to lie down.

Not that William would allow her to rest, of course. Resting was for when her chores were finished. Resting only came after she'd done her nightly duty for her husband.

William stalked away from the meadow, taking huge strides. As always, he moved forward without checking to see if Mattie was behind him. He expected her to follow, and that was that.

Mattie looked back at the stranger one more time, and found he wasn't where they'd left him. He was climbing the slope toward the caves.

*What if the stranger finds the bones and is interested in the creature? What if crowds of people come up to the mountain to find out about it?*

William would be furious if that happened. Though perhaps one of those people would take Mattie away, if she asked.

*William said you belong to him and nobody could take you away. A wife belongs to her husband.*

But what if somebody did take her away? What if somebody with a kind face, kind eyes like that stranger had, what if somebody like that helped her? What if she could find the place again, the place where Heather was?

*William said that place isn't real, it's a dream, a dream sent by the devil to tempt you away.*

She stared at the back of his jacket, at the graying hair he kept cut close to his head, at the huge hard hands that swung at his sides. One of those hands held the rifle, and Mattie had a sudden burst of insight.

*He never taught me how to use the rifle because he doesn't want me to use it on him.*

Mattie would never do that. She would never hurt her own husband. Would she? She didn't think she would do that. She didn't want to hurt him. She only wanted William to stop hurting her.

What would have happened if she'd asked the stranger in the meadow to take her away?

*William would have shot you both dead on the spot, that's what.*

He was going to beat her when they got home. Probably worse than he had in years, Mattie knew. He was angry about so many things at the moment, and all of those things would be attributable to her somehow.

She heard his breath, harsh and fast, and knew without seeing his face that he was remembering everything that happened earlier and arranging it to his liking.

Mattie turned her eyes up to the trees, wanting to see anything except William's back, the angry set of his shoulders, the corded veins in his neck.

She halted, her mouth suddenly dry, shaking her head because it didn't seem possible that she was seeing what she thought was there.

Up above, hanging from nearly every tree, were animal corpses. Most of them were small animals—chipmunks and squirrels and possums and field mice—but some were larger. She saw at least two foxes and even a lynx.

Each animal was arranged neatly over the path that Mattie and William followed. There were one or two animals per tree, each one tied to a branch by a bit of its own viscera.

*Like Christmas ornaments*, and the thought made her sway on her feet, for a memory pushed through the fog in her brain.

*The enormous Christmas tree in the living room, far too big for the space, and all the pretty colored lights winking, the silver star on top and the piles of gifts underneath wrapped in red and green paper.*

*Christmas, and one pile is for me and one is for Heather. There are our stockings with our names on them. One says HEATHER and the other says SAMANTHA.*

"Samantha," she whispered. "Not Martha. Samantha."

"Mattie!" William roared.

She looked at him, not really seeing him, still seeing the blurred outline of a name on a stocking, and it wasn't the name he'd called her all these years.

"Mattie!" he yelled again.

She shook away the stocking, the ornaments, the girl who might have been called Samantha. William had gotten much farther along than she, and he beckoned to her so that she'd catch up.

Mattie remembered the animals then, all the little rabbits and rodents hung in a row, like strange breadcrumbs showing the way to the meadow.

"William," she croaked, her throat hardly able to say his name. "William."

He stomped back in her direction, and she knew she should be afraid, because his face said that he wasn't going to wait until they got home. He was going to punish her right then.

She swallowed, pointed up, tried to make the words come out as he closed in on her.

"The trees, William," she said, but her voice was so small and far away, it had dried up in her throat, and half of her was still under the Christmas tree, staring at the name on the stocking.

Then his fists were on her, and she didn't remember any more.

# CHAPTER FOUR

Mattie woke coughing, a cough that became a choke, and she'd swallowed enough blood in her time to know her mouth was filled with it. Her head bumped along the ground, snow in her hair and seeping down her neck and under her coat. She'd lost her hat. A cruel hand clamped around her ankle, yanking her along on her back like she was a sled being pulled by its string.

William halted, looked back over his shoulder at her, his eyes full of contempt. He released her leg, letting it drop to the ground. Mattie cried out.

"Get up, you useless little bitch. Now that you're awake you can walk yourself home."

Mattie stared up at him, then past him to the trees overhead. There were no more animals. William must have dragged her out of the creature's territory.

*Or maybe it just hasn't finished marking all the trees. Maybe it's trying to mark every one in the forest.*

"Get up, I said." He kicked her in the ribs, and she rolled to one side, every bit of her aching. "Sun's going down in a couple of hours and I'm not carrying you home."

Mattie spit a mouthful of blood into the snow. It looked shockingly red—like a bull-flag, like lipstick, like a stop sign.

*Red means stop,* she thought. *Red means I can't go on anymore.*

But she tried to rise up anyway, tried to push her rubbery legs into place. She couldn't manage it and fell back into the snow again.

William grabbed the front of her coat and pulled her up so that her feet dangled somewhere near his knees. His face pressed very close to hers, all his bright burning anger gone now, replaced with ice.

Mattie would rather have had the burn. The ice always hurt more.

"You listen to me now, Martha. You only got what you deserved, and since you deserved it, you will walk home on your own two feet. If you don't keep up with me I will not return for you. If you are not home by bedtime it will go worse for you when you do arrive. You are my vessel to do with as I please. Do you understand? Now walk."

He dropped her and there wasn't a chance in the world she'd catch herself, as broken and disoriented as she was. Mattie crumpled to the ground.

She felt like she had no bones anymore, and everything around her spun in all directions at once. That's when she noticed she could only see out of one eye.

Mattie carefully probed the area with her fingers. Her left eye was a swollen mass, so tender to the touch that she cried out.

"I said *walk*," William said.

Mattie looked up at him, pushed vaguely into the snow to help herself stand, but only managed to make little snow piles on either side of her body. Tears pricked at the corners of her eyes. They made her swollen eye sting.

"I can't," she whispered. "I can't stand up. Please help me. Please."

She reached for him, her hand trembling.

He glared down at her for so long that she thought he might relent. Then he spun on his heel and strode away.

"Wait," Mattie said, but her voice wouldn't get loud enough for him to hear. It was only a tiny thing that whispered.

She touched her neck, whimpered at the slight pressure. *He must have choked me,* she thought. *I don't remember.*

William was disappearing quickly. He seemed very distant to her already, his brown coat and trousers blending in with the trees.

Mattie felt the first stirrings of panic.

*Don't leave me, don't leave me, I don't know the way home.*

She'd never come this far before, never been allowed to. The cabin was down the mountain from where she was, that was all she knew. William had set the pace and the path.

Why, oh why hadn't she paid more attention? Why had she let her mind wander? She'd never been like that when she was young. When she was young she'd drink in everything around her greedily, tucking every sight away in her mind so she could remember it later.

(*They were moving through the dark woods fast, so fast, but what she could see she promised herself to remember. She'd remember so that she could find her way home.)*

But where was home? That she couldn't remember.

*Home is the place where they called you Samantha.*

*Samantha,* Mattie remembered. *Samantha.*

Samantha struggled. Samantha fought back. Samantha ran away.

Yes, she ran away from William but he caught her and put her in the Box. The Box was where bad girls went.

"If I don't get home soon he'll put me in the Box," Mattie said to herself.

She had to stand up. She had to. *But how will you find your way home?*

Stand up first. Just stand. Then walk. Then worry about how to get where she needed to go.

But it was no good. No matter how she rolled and pushed and struggled, she couldn't get on her feet. After several minutes she lay in the snow, panting, unable to do anything except gaze up at the too-bright sky and the dark silhouettes of the branches against it.

*Trees,* she thought. *The animals in the trees. William doesn't know.*

*(It doesn't matter because William is going to be safe in the cabin with the warm fire and you're going to be out with the night and the cold and the creature that strings animals up like decorations)*

The creature. She needed to get away, get inside before it found her. It wouldn't even need to hunt her in the state she was in. It would just scoop her up and take her back to the cave and rip her to pieces and sort all those pieces like a child organizing its building blocks by shape.

**Get up, Mattie. Get up before it finds you.**

She rolled to her stomach, propped herself up on her elbows, then used her elbows to dig into the snow and pull herself forward, dragging her legs behind.

It was painfully slow going. Her body felt like it wasn't attached to her brain, like it wouldn't respond to the orders she gave it. Every few inches she stopped, her breath hard and fast. She felt the throb of her heart against the snow, thought sometimes it might beat right through her ribs and stay there, an offering for the thing in the woods.

After a long while she was close enough to a tree trunk to grab it. She threw both arms around the tree, pushed up with her knees, and by very slow degrees managed to kneel. Her face rested against the tree bark, her arms trembling.

"Keep going, Mattie. Keep going."

Somehow she got one foot on the ground, and then the other, and then—hugging the tree for dear life—she rose up until finally, *finally* she was standing.

The next tree wasn't too far away. Mattie unwrapped her arms, used both hands to brace against the trunk. Then she pushed off, using the momentum to stumble into the next tree.

She was up. She could walk—if you could call it walking. She just needed to find her path home now.

A second later she laughed, though she stopped quickly because laughing made her throat hurt and because it was a horrible barky sound that echoed strangely in the deep silence of the forest. She didn't need to find the way back. William's footprints were right there in the snow.

Mattie glanced anxiously up at the sky. The footprints were

only useful as long as she had light. William had said it was only a couple of hours until sundown. She didn't know how much time had passed since then.

*Every minute you stand here dithering is a minute of sunlight wasted.*

She vaulted off the second tree as she had the first, but the next trunk was farther away and she nearly missed it, only just grabbing one of the low-hanging branches to stay upright.

Mattie staggered from tree to tree in this way, always keeping the trail of William's footprints visible. Too soon she realized that the trail was growing more difficult to see. The shadows had deepened. The sun was setting.

A bubble of alarm bloomed in her chest. She didn't have any light. William had the candles and matches.

She took a good look around her for the first time since she'd awoken from her faint. Nothing appeared familiar. There were only trees and rocks and snow, and she had no notion of how far away the cabin might be.

Her stomach twisted. It had been hours since she'd eaten. Her mouth and throat were parched, too.

Mattie knew how to find edible berries in the woods but it was well past berry season. She gripped the tree hard with one arm and cautiously lowered into a crouch. She inspected the snow for animal droppings and, finding it clear, scooped large handfuls into her mouth.

It was so cold against her bruised throat that it hurt. A second later she felt a sharp pain in her temple and behind her left eye.

*Brain freezy!* she heard Heather say. *I got a brain freezy!*

Mattie almost saw Heather there, waving a dripping ice cream cone around while she held her head with her free hand.

*I got a brain freezy,* Mattie thought, and pressed her tongue to the roof of her mouth. Her mother told her once that was how to stop an ice cream headache.

*Mom,* she thought, but there was no face or voice to go with the name. There was only a vague sense of a person Mattie might have known once, a shadow that she called *Mom.*

The snow did nothing to fill her stomach or to fix her light-headedness, but her throat was less parched and that, at least, was something.

Mattie didn't know what to do about the growing dark, though. William never let her carry or keep matches. She wasn't even allowed to use them unless he was present, and she didn't know how to start a fire without matches.

*That man might, though. The stranger by the cave. If you asked him, he might help you.*

William would be so angry if she did that. Maybe angrier than he'd ever been.

*Look how he was just because the stranger talked to you.*

"It doesn't matter anyway. You're too far from the stranger now."

But it would be nice if he were near. It would be nice if she weren't alone in the creeping dark, hungry and hurt and exhausted. The stranger had kind eyes. Mattie thought he would be kind to her.

*That's fairy-tale nonsense, Mattie. That's the sort of thing Heather always liked, stories about princes who saved girls from towers and witches and curses and glass coffins. That's not the kind of thing that happens in real life.*

*In real life you never see the stranger again, and no one comes to rescue you from the tower.*

*(or the cabin)*

Mattie pushed off the tree, staggered to the next. William's footprints in the snow were nearly impossible to see already. How could the sun set so quickly? What would happen if she wasn't at home when William wanted to go to bed?

*"A man's got to have sons, Mattie."*

Yes, it was her duty to give him sons and she had failed thus far.

If she wasn't home when he said she should be, would William come looking for her? Or would he leave her out in the night and cold and find some other vessel to bear his children?

*"I've invested so much time in you, Martha. I hope you appreciate how I've worked to make you a good life."*

"Yes," Mattie said as she tossed herself from tree to tree, clinging to trunks and branches like bits of driftwood in the ocean. "Yes, I know how hard it is for you."

William had to work so hard, had to discipline her so often. She wasn't a good listener. She forgot that she wasn't to criticize him. She forgot to be grateful.

"I'll be a good wife to you, I promise," she whimpered.

She was so tired and hungry and it was so dark. She never knew until she came to live on the mountain how dark the night could be.

"I'll be good, only come and find me, don't leave me alone out here, don't leave me."

Mattie didn't know where she was going anymore, couldn't see anything except the vague shapes of trees and the shifting shadows in the snow.

The night moved all around her, the secret wind and the silver sliver of moon, the rustling of branches, the scurrying of night creatures, the trickle of water.

*Water.*

There was water nearby.

"The stream," she said, hurling her body in the direction of the sound.

If she found the stream, she'd know her way home. The deer path was easy to find from there, even in the dark. Mattie knew that path by heart. It was the only place she was allowed to go on her own because it wasn't far from the cabin.

She wouldn't be home too late and William wouldn't be furious. The sun had only just gone down, hadn't it? Soon, so very soon, Mattie would be back in the cabin, fed and safe and warm.

**You'll be warm there, but you won't be safe. Not safe at all, and only fed if he lets you eat. You should keep going, keep heading down the mountain, keep running until you find Heather and Mom again.**

She stilled, thinking, wondering. Did she dare? Could she?

**You can. You don't have to stay. He left you. He left you out here to die.**

Mattie didn't know who that voice belonged to, but it didn't sound like her.

*It might be Samantha. Samantha is a girl I used to know. Samantha was never afraid until William.*

The faint trickle of the stream was just ahead. She heard it. It was very close now.

*Just get to the stream. Just get there and you can decide.*

A moment later she was on the bank, stumbling down to the water's edge.

The thumbnail moon cast just enough light here, away from the canopy of pines, for her to see that she'd emerged almost directly across the stream from the deer path.

*That's a sign, isn't it? A sign from God?*

William would say it was. He'd say it was a sign that she should return to his side where she belonged instead of running away.

**Run away,** Samantha whispered. **Run away while you still can.**

"But I can't," Mattie murmured. "I can't run. I can hardly walk."

She knelt—if she was honest with herself, it was more like a collapse—by the trickle of stream, pulled off her mitten and scooped water in her mouth. It was so cold her fingers froze instantly, and the liquid hurt her parched throat instead of soothing it.

Mattie rubbed her hand on her trouser leg to dry it before putting her mitten back on. Then she stared at the water, trying to decide which way to go.

If she crossed the stream then the deer path would take her directly to the cabin. The cabin was where she belonged. William had told her that every single day since he'd taken her there.

If she followed the course of the stream it would take her down the mountain. William had told her many times *not* to do that very thing, for the stream led to a river and there were often strangers by the river, strangers that might hurt her or try to take her away from her rightful place at his side.

*The stream will take me to the river. The river will take me away from him.*

But she couldn't make herself move, couldn't make a decision. She was so tired. Now that she'd stopped moving her body didn't want to cooperate until she'd had some rest. Maybe she could go to sleep on the bank and decide in the morning. Her eyelids drooped.

**William might find you in the morning. Get up, get up, the time to run is now.**

Something else moved in the darkness.

Mattie heard the crunch of snow beneath huge and heavy paws, a thick snort, the crackle of branches.

*The creature. It's here. It's here. It's going to eat me and I'll never see Mom or Heather again.*

She turned her head very slowly in the direction of the noise, not wanting to attract the creature's attention. She was hidden in the shadows of the bank, and the very faint breeze was blowing upstream, away from the sounds.

The creature emerged from the woods several feet away downstream from where she knelt, barely breathing and hoping desperately not to give herself away.

She didn't have any sense of it except that it was huge, bigger even than she'd thought based on the size of its prints. The dark made it impossible to determine any trait other than its size—an enormous silhouette, something powerful barely suppressed by the shape of its skin.

The creature was seemingly unaware of her presence.

*That's because you're upwind. Just keep still and wait for it to go away.*

The animal lumbered toward the stream on its back legs, its movement oddly quiet considering its size. As it bent its head down to drink, Mattie looked away, her heart slamming against her ribs. She did not want to attract its attention by staring. She wanted to fade into the landscape, just another rock or tree or hummock of grass.

**But what is it?** the very curious part of her asked. **It's not really just a bear.**

That curious voice in her head didn't sound like Mattie. Mattie was never curious, because when she was, William made her stop. Curiosity was not a quality becoming of a good wife.

She thought it might be Samantha. Samantha was a trouble-maker. Samantha wanted to know about the creature. Samantha wanted Mattie to run away down the mountain.

If Mattie ran away then the creature would chase her. She was safer, much safer, going back to the cabin. Going back to William.

The creature slurped at the stream and every moment it stayed Mattie's tension ratcheted tighter. When would it go? How could she escape if it just sat there, directly in her path? She didn't think she'd be able to sneak away quietly in the state she was in, not even if she took a very long way around the animal.

Even if she chose the cabin she was in danger. Just crossing the stream would attract the creature's attention.

*Keep still like a little mouse. You know how to do it. You do it all the time, when you don't want William to notice you.*

Yes, it was a skill she'd perfected—shrinking inside her body, her thoughts receding so they weren't visible, so that she was nothing but a body and everything about her that mattered was hidden away.

She did it when William was looking for an excuse to punish her, or when he did punish her, or when she lay in bed with him grunting on top of her, doing her duty as his wife. She took part of herself away and kept it safe where he couldn't see.

If she did that now then maybe the creature wouldn't notice her, wouldn't sense the spark of something living.

The animal growled, snorted out several short breaths, pawed at the ground.

Mattie didn't know if it was wise or not but she had to look. She had to know if it had spotted her and was preparing to charge. She risked a glance in its direction. She still couldn't make any sense of it other than size, but it seemed to be settling down on the bank.

*Is it going to sleep there?* Mattie thought in alarm. *No, it can't. I have to get home.*

**(no, you have to get away)**

It didn't matter what she wanted or didn't want. If the animal went to sleep, she'd be trapped until it woke and left the area.

Her stomach made a long keening sound, as loud as a gunshot in the still night.

The creature paused. Mattie heard it sniff the air as she hunched over, her face in her knees, trying to make her body as small as possible, trying to make herself invisible.

After a moment she heard it grunt and resume its pawing and shifting.

*Oh, please go. Please, God, if you're listening, please make it go.*

But God never listened to Mattie's prayers. No matter how often she begged God to make William stop, He never listened. He never helped. He never struck William down the way He ought to do.

Mattie stayed hunched over her legs, trembling, as the animal's breath settled into the deep, even rhythm of sleep. There was nothing for it now. She would have to go back to the cabin. The plan to follow the stream was impossible with the creature in the way.

Even if it woke up in an hour or two the plan wouldn't work. If Mattie wanted to leave William, she needed time, all the time she could manage. She needed a head start, especially now that she was barely able to walk.

*It's a sign, a sign that you're not supposed to leave William.*

What else could it be? Why else would every obstacle appear in her way just as she considered (for the first time in years, so many years she couldn't count them) getting away? God hated her. He must. She must be as bad, as sinful as William always said, or else this wouldn't happen. Mattie squeezed her eyes tight so the tears wouldn't come, but this only made her swollen left eye hurt more, and the tears came anyway.

She stayed there a very long time, weeping, listening to the sound of the monster sleeping a short distance away from her, close enough for it to wake up and kill her if it wanted.

Mattie slept, though she hadn't meant to.

She woke with a start, her breath a sudden exhaled *whoosh*, her right eye flying open in panic. How could she have slept with danger so near? It was well past bedtime, and William would be furious.

She checked the place where the creature slept. The sliver of moon was hidden by a bank of clouds, and the stars were, too. The sky was an unyielding field of black.

Mattie squinted in the direction of the creature and listened hard. She didn't hear it breathing or shifting in its sleep. She couldn't make out its deep shadow against the other shadows.

It was gone. It had gone while she slept.

Mattie uncurled her stiff limbs, stretching her legs out in front of her and her arms overhead. Everything hurt, and the renewed blood flow after sitting for so long made all her aches worse, made her bruises throb with fresh energy. Her left eye, when she touched it, seemed just as swollen as it had been hours before. The thin layer of snow hadn't seeped through her clothes, which were wool and sturdy, but the cold had, and her bones felt brittle.

Mattie didn't know if she'd be able to stand but she had to try. She couldn't stay on the stream bank forever, waiting for William or the creature to come and scoop her up.

After a great deal of pushing and struggling and wobbling she managed to get on her feet, though she swayed as all the blood rushed out of her head. She was so hungry she thought she could eat anything—even the pine needles looked appetizing. Mattie took a few deep breaths until she felt steadier. While the hunger-weakness didn't go away, she did feel less dizzy than she had earlier, and she attributed that to rest.

*Just how long did I sleep?* she thought, slightly panicky. If it was long enough to feel that much better then it was probably far too long.

Mattie took a tentative step forward, testing her balance. It was harder to walk when she couldn't see out of one eye. Her body listed to the right side—the side she could see out of—like a ship with a breach in its hull.

*Slow, slow,* she told herself. She had to cross the stream, and she couldn't see well enough to pick out dry rocks to hop on—not that she had the agility at the moment to do so in any case.

There was nothing for it. She'd have to wade through and hope it was shallow enough that only her boots would get wet.

Mattie flinched as she splashed into the water. Every sound seemed magnified a thousandfold, designed to draw the attention of the very creature she wanted to avoid. There was every chance the animal was still nearby. It might have woken only a moment before she did.

Freezing water seeped through the tongues of her boots and over the tops, soaking her heavy knitted socks. Mattie never did such a good job with her own socks as she did with William's, for it was a chore that she greatly disliked. As a result there were a great many loose holes for the water to pour through and chill her bare skin. By the time Mattie reached the opposite shore she was shivering all over and couldn't feel her feet. She still didn't feel entirely sturdy on her legs, either. They wobbled uncontrollably with each step, the steps of a baby toddling for the first time, not the steps of a grown woman.

Mattie climbed the bank, using her hands to steady herself as best she could, scrabbling in the snow. After what seemed like a very long time, she made it to the top. She was on the same side with the deer path that would lead home.

*Home. Not my home. William's home.*

She trudged forward, hardly able to lift her feet. They felt like two heavy blocks of ice attached to her ankles. It was even darker under the trees, with the moon still hidden by the clouds and the branches crouching over the path like giants' arms.

*They might grab me up and take me away, take me to a place far from here.* She knew she was on the verge of hysteria, that exhaustion and terror and pain had sapped her so that she didn't know how to think in a straight line.

*All that nonsense about Samantha. That's a fantasy, a dream. There is no Samantha. There's only Martha.*

Her left eye throbbed. There was a faint buzzing in her ears and just under it she heard the crunch of her footsteps in the snow and her own labored breath.

A branch broke nearby, the crack of wood as startling as thunder.

Mattie stopped, listening hard, biting down on her lower lip to keep herself from exhaling.

*It's out there,* she thought, and there was no doubt, no attempt to convince herself that it was a deer or a squirrel. The sound came from the creature. She knew it with every terrified beat of her own heart.

She peered into the trees, trying to detect any shape that wasn't a tall, slim tree trunk, but it was hard to see anything properly with only one eye.

*It could stand right next to me and I wouldn't know. I'd never see it until I turned my head.*

Mattie didn't move for several moments. There was no other sound so she cautiously started forward again, trying to make less noise. She was conscious of every rustle of clothing, the swipe of her long braid against the back of her coat, the squeak of her leather boots, the rough exhale of her breath.

Something else was breathing.

# CHAPTER FIVE

M attie stopped again, terror making her whole mouth numb. This time she heard the sound of its claws against the snow for just a half second before it, too, paused.

*It's stalking me.*

Panic bloomed inside her. Sweat trickled over her ears.

*It's stalking me. It's* playing *with me.*

Mattie had no doubt that an animal that large could kill her with one disinterested swipe. It had no need to hunt her.

*Unless it wants me to be afraid first.*

But it was impossible that an animal would think like that, or that an animal could really even think.

*Only humans enjoy the fear of others, Mattie, don't be stupid. It's only being cautious, the way predators will be, making certain of their prey before they strike. You need to get away before it does.*

But how? She didn't know exactly how far she was from the

cabin. The path to the stream and the traps from the front door normally took about a half hour or so round trip, but she wasn't going at anything near her normal walking pace. The cabin couldn't be too far from where she stood, but would she reach it in time? Would the creature allow her to get that far?

*Just walk forward. Just move forward and try. If it attacks then you can . . . what? What can you do against a thing that size? You can't even stop William.*

She stifled a crazy laugh, the kind of laugh that only emerged when a person was at the end of their rope.

*You won't be able to stop it if it attacks.*

*(but I don't want to die)*

That stiffened her spine, because it was comforting to realize that despite everything, she didn't want to give up and die right there. She still wanted to live, no matter how painful life was, no matter how much God had forsaken her.

Mattie moved forward again. Now that she knew the creature was near, she heard its subtle movements, the way it carefully mirrored her pace.

*It's not a normal animal. It's not natural.*

The creature was on her left side, the blind side. If she turned her head she might catch a glimpse of its shape out of her right eye but she didn't need to see it to know it was there.

She felt it, felt the way it disturbed the air between them, felt the intensity of its stare—its watchfulness.

Mattie was so frightened she could hardly feel her body. Her limbs seemed both stunningly heavy and light as air, and she felt caught in a kind of slow-motion haze. Her head throbbed, especially the left eye, and her mouth kept filling up with saliva, forcing her to swallow convulsively over and over. All the while she felt the shadow moving in time with her, smelled the rank scent of its fur and the blood on its breath.

*The blood in the snow and the animals hanging from the trees. Why does it do those things? Why does it not eat its prey the way an animal is supposed to? Why is it following me? Does it want to eat me or add me to its collection?*

The atmosphere seemed to shift, the quality of the creature's attention changed. She sensed it, the way she could smell a storm approaching on a sunny day. Mattie's heart beat even faster than it already was doing—a little rabbit sprinting away inside the hollow of her body.

*It's had enough of this game. It's going to attack.*

She curled up her fists, though she didn't know what to do with them, didn't know how she might hurt the creature, didn't know if she'd even have a chance. Her hands seemed like tiny, pathetic things—weak and useless.

*You're useless.* That's what William always said.

And then the clouds shifted and the tiny sliver of moon was revealed and she saw the end of the path just ahead of her. The end of the path, and the clearing and the cabin beyond.

"William," she said, and a surge of energy she didn't know she still had pushed her into a run.

William had the gun. William could shoot the creature. He'd wanted to anyway—that was what the ridiculous, exhausting trek was supposed to be about earlier. And now Mattie was bringing the terror right to their door. All he had to do was stand on his porch and shoot it and she wouldn't have to be afraid anymore, wouldn't have to spend any more terrified nights out in the woods.

Her sudden movements must have surprised the animal, for she didn't hear it follow as she half-ran, half-staggered to the cabin.

The lights were out—of course they were out. It was the middle of the night and William was asleep. The door seemed so far away, then it abruptly jerked closer, like time and space had suddenly shifted.

*Almost there,* Mattie thought. *Almost there.*

The creature hadn't followed. She sensed its hesitation, its reassessment of potential threats. It snorted and pawed the ground, much like it had before it settled down to sleep, except this didn't sound like settling. This sounded more like it was deciding to charge or not.

The cabin door was suddenly before her, though she didn't know how she'd managed to get there. A thrill of triumph shot through her as she grasped the knob, turned it, and pushed. The door rattled, shifted, stopped as it met the pressure of the bolt on the other side.

William had locked the door.

"William!" she called, pounding the wood with her fist, but her cries were small and feeble things just like her fists. He'd squeezed her throat too hard and she couldn't scream even though she wanted to.

"William!" she cried again, banging her forearms against the door. It rattled the bolt but stayed fast.

She threw her body against it with all the strength she had left, calling her husband's name, all the while thinking, *How could he? How could he lock the door against me? How could he leave me out here?*

He was a heavy sleeper, so it was possible he hadn't heard her knocking, but she had to wake him. If she didn't wake him she'd be out in the clearing all night, and sooner or later the creature would come out of the trees. She didn't think it would wait much longer.

And when it did, it would open her up, take her bones, string her to one of the branches that lined the path to its cave. All William would find in the morning would be a splash of scarlet in the snow.

*Like the fox, except it didn't take the fox. I wonder why.*

She wondered, too, how part of her was still wondering about the fox when she was about to meet its fate.

"William," she called. "Please, wake up. I'm sorry. I'm so sorry. Please let me in."

She thought she heard movement in the cabin—the creak of a floorboard, the faint rustle of clothing.

"William, please, I'll be good, I'll do anything you say, only let me in because the monster is out here with me, it's been following me, please, please let me in."

She scraped at the door with her mittened hands, slumping to the ground. "Please," she whispered. "Please, please."

Another creak. Mattie was suddenly certain that William stood on the other side of the door, perfectly awake.

*He never went to sleep. He was sitting there in the dark, waiting for me, waiting to punish me no matter when I got home.*

"William," she said, but she couldn't yell any more, or try to. She didn't even know if the word actually came out of her mouth.

A third creak. She knew he was deciding whether or not she deserved to stay out all night for coming home later than he'd said to do.

*I'm going to die. Everything I've done to get here has come to nothing, because William is not going to open that door.*

She knew it with the same certainty that the sun would rise in the morning. He wanted to teach her a lesson, and he probably didn't believe her when she said the creature was following her.

William was not going to let her into the cabin. Mattie should save her energy, stop banging away at the door. She needed to find somewhere to hide. But where?

The storehouse was just as bad as the cabin—William locked the storehouse and kept the key hanging on a special key ring, the one Mattie was never allowed to touch. The only other shelter was the outhouse, and "shelter" was a hopeful word at best.

The outhouse was much less sturdily built than the storehouse and the cabin, being, as William once said (with uncharacteristic crudity), "Only a place to shit out of the wind."

It wasn't falling apart, but Mattie had much less confidence in her safety if she hid inside it. On top of everything else, there was the ignominy of hiding for her life inside an outhouse.

The creature roared, and it was as if Mattie had never heard the sound properly before. The deep strangeness of it, the sense that it was many animals' cries merged into one—those qualities were magnified by the closeness of the monster and the open clearing. Mattie couldn't wait for William any longer.

*He's not going to let me in anyway. It's more important that he proves to himself that he's right about me. If I die out here, it will only be divine punishment in his eyes.*

She clawed at the doorframe, using it to pull up to her feet again. Branches cracked in the woods that surrounded the cabin.

Mattie heaved herself around the cabin, past her little garden, past the grave of her child and up to the very edge of the clearing and into the outhouse. The door was inclined to slam shut, so she pulled it closed behind her as silently as she could, wincing at the squeal of the hinges.

There was no lock or latch, nothing to make her feel safe even though she knew a creature of that size could tear the door from its hinges. She half-wondered why she was even bothering to hide, except that she felt she shouldn't stop trying to live—not yet, anyway.

The smell in the outhouse was not as extreme as it would be in summer, but it was still unpleasant. Mattie had a vague idea that it might cover up her scent and the creature wouldn't be able to find her, though she didn't truly believe it could be fooled by such tricks. It wasn't a regular sort of animal.

*What an embarrassing way to die, hiding in the toilet.* She covered her mouth with her mittens, trying not to giggle. Why, oh why, was she about to laugh when her life was in danger?

*It's because you're scared, so scared you're on the verge of hysteria.* Then she heard it outside, the huffs and the snorts, its enormous bulk moving slowly toward the place where she hid.

Mattie backed away from the door, but there was nowhere to go in the tiny space. William had put a wooden lid over the hole ("because we're not animals, Mattie"), and she sat down on the lid very quietly, and made herself as still as possible.

She heard the creature sniffing outside, very close, and thought now would be an excellent time for William to come charging out of the cabin with the rifle. But of course there was no sound of the cabin door opening and closing, no crack of a shot to shatter the night.

There was only Mattie, cowering in an outhouse because her husband refused to open the door to her, and the monster crouched outside.

A few of the boards had small knotholes in them. Mattie could have peered through to see the creature, to know precisely what it was doing, but she was afraid to move, afraid to look, afraid that if the creature felt her eyes upon it that it would strike.

*It doesn't matter. It has to know where you've gone. It's smart enough to follow you through the forest, sneaking all the way. It's got some plan of its own, one that you could never hope to understand.*

The creature roared again, long and loud. It was right outside the door, sure to strike. Mattie closed her right eye and braced for the blow, the way she always did.

The blow never came. After several agonizing minutes, Mattie opened her eye. She no longer saw the shadow of the animal through the cracks in the wall. Had it left? But why would it do that?

The animal had followed her all this way, had known exactly where she was hidden. Why wouldn't it strike while it had her cornered?

*Maybe it has moved away from the outhouse but is still waiting out there, waiting for you to walk out into its arms.*

Mattie didn't hear it any longer, didn't hear its snorts and huffs or the sound of its claws scraping through the snow. But that didn't mean anything. She knew that it could sneak, could be silent when it wanted. She didn't dare go out again, even if she had to sit there all night, her anxiety stretched thin and tight.

But why would morning be any better? It was during daylight when she'd found the fox, and when she and William had heard the noise in the trees. The creature wasn't limited to nighttime hunting.

*Though my discovery of the fox was late in the day.* She couldn't think why this mattered. Her thoughts were going in crazy circles again. It just seemed that the light of the morning should make everything better, that a new day ought to wash away the terror of the night.

*I don't know why you think that, Mattie, it never has before. Every day only brings fresh terrors.*

Something broke inside her then, the thing that had kept her scurrying, head bowed, anxious to please a husband who never wanted to be pleased but only hunted for faults to correct.

William had locked the door against her, chosen his pride over her safety. He'd been awake—Mattie was certain of that. He must have heard the roar of the creature outside. He'd know she wasn't lying, that her life was in danger, and he didn't care.

He didn't care what happened to her as long as she learned a lesson—his lesson. If she survived then William would consider it divine providence, a sign that God had preserved her for the benefit of her husband.

As soon as she thought this, she felt the second string that held up her life snap, the empty threads falling away inside her. There was no God. There was only William, and the stories he told to control her.

Something flailed inside her—the terrified little mouse that she had been. It scrabbled for purchase, grasped desperately for those broken strings.

**No,** Samantha said. **You don't have to be that mouse anymore.**

Mattie remembered standing on the edge of a picnic table in

her mother's yard, leaping into the air, absolutely confident that she could fly if she just believed that she could do it. She'd do it over and over, and every single time she'd feel something—a push, a lift of air under her feet—and know that she was nearly there, that the next time she'd fly for sure, soar away like a beautiful falcon.

**Who do you want to be?** Samantha whispered. **A falcon or a mouse?**

Mattie didn't know if she could be a falcon or not, but she didn't want to scurry along the ground any longer.

She stayed in the outhouse until she saw the light of dawn brightening the interior of her foul hiding place. Then she pushed open the door, wondering what the day would bring, wondering what she ought to do next.

*How can I even look at William now? What am I to do?*

Mattie stopped, staring at the snow before her. There were marks scratched there, almost like symbols, carved with a bloody claw.

She couldn't make sense of them, felt overwhelmed by the very idea of them—an animal making shapes in the snow, shapes meant for her to see.

Then the meaning of the symbols suddenly snapped into place, and she understood why the creature had followed her the night before, why it hadn't killed her.

It wanted to know where she lived—her and William—because they'd gone into its lair. And it wanted to warn them to stay away. The writing in the snow was a warning.

Mattie didn't think that they would receive a second warning.

She caught movement at the bedroom window and saw a flash

of William's face there before it disappeared. A moment later she heard the cabin door slam.

He strode around the building. She could tell by the look on his face—the compressed lips, the ice-chip gaze—that he was gearing up for a lecture on the Proper Behavior of an Obedient Wife. But Mattie didn't want to hear his lecture.

*No*, she thought. *Samantha doesn't want to hear it.*

Mattie didn't want another beating, though. She was sick and sore and exhausted from the last one and her ordeal of the night, so she pointed mutely at the symbols on the ground and hoped that William would be sufficiently distracted to forget about whatever he had in store for her.

William halted, following the line of her finger with his gaze. The blood drained from his face, and she felt a small and very petty sense of glee at seeing him so wrong-footed.

A moment later all sense of delight was gone when he said, "What is this devilry? More of your witchcraft?"

"No!" she said, holding up her hands in front of her body, as if to ward him off. "I didn't do that. It was that creature—the bear. It followed me last night."

She had to get his mind away from any thought of witchcraft. If she didn't, then he might decide she was performing some spell to keep from getting pregnant, and he might kill her this time.

"How could a dumb animal do this?" William said, his voice made of ice and fury. "This is some vengeance of yours for last night."

*So you know it was wrong to leave me outside,* she thought, but there wasn't time to dwell on it. She had to move him away from witchcraft.

"Look," she said, crouching halfway to point at the deep gashes in the snow. "They're claw marks. You can see they're just like the marks on the trees we saw two days ago. I don't think it's just some dumb animal. There were all those strange bone piles in the cave, remember? It sorted them all. Normal animals don't do that."

William's eyes moved from Mattie's face to the symbols and back again. He was thinking about it, she could tell. She considered mentioning the animals tied to the trees—the ones she'd seen just before he'd knocked her out. She decided against it. If she interrupted his train of thought, he might find it was easier to conclude it was her witchcraft, after all.

"What could it mean?" he murmured.

She knew he wasn't talking to her, didn't expect an answer. She waited while he walked all around the symbols, bent down to peer more closely at them, ran his fingers over the gashes. Mattie wished he would hurry. Hunger gnawed at her, and she desperately wanted as much water as she could drink.

William stood up. "Go inside and wash yourself. You smell like the outhouse. Then make eggs and bacon for breakfast."

Mattie hurried away, leaving him there to contemplate the markings in the snow. He'd have to get the eggs and bacon from the storehouse, which meant she'd have a few moments to herself.

The fire wasn't lit when she entered the cabin, which meant she'd have to wash in cold water. *Exactly as he meant for me to do. More punishment.*

She took the jug of water from the table by the window, poured it into a basin, and carried the basin into the bedroom, careful not to slop water on the floor. William hated it when she did that.

*What if he slipped on the water and got hurt? What if he*

*knocked himself on the back of the head and wasn't able to get up?*
*You could throw him out in the snow and leave him there for the*
*creature to find.*

Mattie shook her head. No, she couldn't do that. She didn't
want to hurt William. She only wanted to get away. She didn't want
to be hurt anymore.

**(He did it to you. He left you out there in the snow to die.)**

She had to stop thinking about it or he would see it on her
face—her resentment, her anger. If he saw those things in her eyes
then she'd never escape him. He'd make sure of it. He'd break her
legs, starve her, watch her every moment of the day. So she had to
be good and keep her head down and reveal no spark of rebellion.

*And wait for my chance.*

Mattie stripped off her trousers and shirt, soaked a cloth in the
cold water, then wet her skin all over. As she did, she discovered
new bruises—a band of screaming purple around her ribs, a swollen mass in her thigh, the clear outline of his knuckles near her
belly button. She rubbed a sliver of soap every place, trying not to
cry out when she touched a tender spot. Then she rinsed herself
with the cloth.

She heard William stomp into the cabin, followed by the clatter of wood. He was building the fire for breakfast. She'd have to
hurry.

Mattie wrapped her long braid around her head and pinned it.
There was no time to wash her hair, which was thick and heavy
and fell to her hips—William never allowed her to cut it. She
pulled on her thickest woolen stockings, a flannel dress and a
sweater over it.

She was shivering all over, desperate to get in front of the fire—even though she wouldn't, strictly speaking, use it for warmth. William needed his breakfast, so she'd be near the fire to cook. Any benefit to her was incidental.

William had gone out again by the time Mattie returned to the main room carrying the washbasin. She arrived at the front door just as William returned. He put the eggs and a slab of bacon on the table and took the basin from her to dump outside. This wasn't kindness to spare her an extra chore, she knew. It was because he was hungry and wanted her to start cooking.

Mattie quickly sliced the bacon, laid it in the pan, and slid the pan onto the metal grate over the fire. Then she scooped coffee grounds into the mesh basket of the percolator, added water to the pot, and carefully put the pot in the hot coals near the edge of the fire. It was then time to turn the bacon. When that task was done, she set out plates and forks and cloths for napkins. William returned just as she took the bacon out of the pan and put the plate of still-sizzling meat on the table.

She cracked the eggs into the bacon grease while William took off his boots. He sat down at the table and waited. Mattie pulled the perking coffee pot out of the coals, her hand wrapped in a towel so she didn't burn it on the metal handle. She poured out William's coffee, turned the eggs, and a moment later she was at the table holding the hot pan, scooping eggs onto their plates.

"Four for me, one for you," he said.

*Don't rise,* she thought. She didn't say anything, even though she was so hungry she could have eaten everything on the table herself. She gave him four eggs, keeping the smallest one for herself, and didn't complain when he ate the lion's share of the bacon, either.

*Keep your head down and wait for your chance.*

"I'm going into town today," he said.

She looked up in surprise. After leaving her in the woods she'd been certain he'd stand at her shoulder all day long, dogging her every move.

"You will not leave the cabin for any reason," he said.

She nodded. This was a standard instruction.

"You may have half the remaining bread while I'm gone. No butter. No coffee or milk. Only tea."

Mattie knew there was only about a quarter-loaf of bread left. He was saying she could have a slice or two for the remainder of the day.

*So I'm to be put on prisoner's rations, then.*

"I may be gone into the night. It depends on how long it takes me to find what I need."

This was the most surprising thing he'd said yet. William always went to town and returned quickly, well before sundown.

"What are you going for?" Mattie asked, then bit her lip.

William hated questions. He always said that if he wanted her to know something, he would tell her. She was certain he'd respond that way, in his frozen-river voice, but instead he was silent.

She risked a glance and found him staring at his empty plate.

Then he said, "That bear is no bear. It's a demon come to earth."

Mattie was shocked by this conclusion, but she didn't respond. She'd already spoken once when she hadn't meant to.

"Those bones in the cave, the markings in the snow—no animal behaves like that. It can only be a demon. And if it is a demon, then God sent it here to try me."

Mattie realized something then, something she'd always been

vaguely aware of but never able to fully articulate. William was insane. He *believed*, truly believed, that whatever was out there in the woods was a creature from the pit and that he had a holy mission to destroy it.

There were so many things about her life, about William, that she'd never seen clearly before. Every time she'd shown a spark of spirit, William crushed it beneath his boot heel before she could think or question her circumstances. The only reason she was able to see him clearly now was because he'd left her alone to die, and therefore left her time to think for herself.

"I need traps," he continued. "Traps big enough for a monster like that, and a rifle with bigger shot. And other things. They may not be easily available, so it may take some time for me to acquire them. You will not leave the cabin. You will not eat more than I have allowed you to eat. You will spend the day scrubbing every surface until it shines."

"Yes, William," she murmured.

Mattie would do whatever she had to do to lull him into believing she was as broken as she'd always been.

*He shouldn't have left me out in the woods.*

*That's his mistake. Now you just have to make sure he pays for it.*

# CHAPTER SIX

Mattie cleared the plates from the table and washed them while William collected all the things he would need for the trip. He took his key ring and went into the bedroom, closing the door firmly. A moment later she heard the click of a lock and the sound of rummaging.

*He's gone inside the secret trunk,* she thought as she took out oil and rags for cleaning. *I need to know what's inside there.*

She was certain that he kept his money for buying supplies in the trunk, and she would certainly need money once she escaped. She couldn't rely on the kindness of strangers—strangers who might know William, who might not believe her, who might deliver her back to him like a naughty child gone astray.

But how could she get into the trunk in the first place? William never left the house without taking the keys. There had to be a way to break the lock, but she wouldn't be able to try until she was ready to leave forever. If William returned home and found Mattie there and a broken lock on his trunk then . . . well, it didn't bear thinking about.

When he emerged from the bedroom, Mattie was polishing the floor.

"Just where you belong," he grunted.

She kept her head down, rubbing the oil into the hardwood. She sensed his sudden flare of interest, the same way a small animal senses the presence of a predator. Mattie knew he was thinking of the previous night, how she hadn't been home for the nightly ritual to get sons on her.

*Just leave. Just go.*

She didn't think she could bear it just then, didn't think she'd be able to pretend she was pleased by his attention. After what seemed like decades but was probably only a few moments, William huffed out an impatient breath, pulled on his boots and said, "I'm leaving."

He slammed the door behind him before she even had a chance to turn around.

Mattie spent the morning scrubbing and polishing every surface, not because she wanted to please William (as she might have before he locked her out of the cabin to die) but because it was only sensible to keep from angering him.

If he got angry, he would punish her. If he punished her, she would be weak. She wouldn't be able to escape if she was starving or beaten half to death.

With one of the sudden bursts of insight she'd had so many times in the last day she realized this was exactly why William did punish her so often. It had nothing to do with her behavior. It was because if she was physically weak she couldn't run away. Every beating took more of her heart away so that she wouldn't have the guts to even try.

And every time he told her the memories of her life before were false, he narrowed her world to the mountaintop, the cabin, to him alone.

*But I'm not going to stay. I'm going to find Heather. And Mom.*

She wished she could remember their faces. She could see Heather if she tried hard, though the image was blurry—round cheeks, a nose covered in freckles, brown eyes with pretty flecks of gold in them, all framed by brown hair.

"Brown eyes," Mattie murmured, her hand fluttering in the direction of her swollen eye. "Like mine."

*"Pretty little girl with pretty eyes,"* she heard someone say, and it sounded like William, a younger William, a William she'd known long ago.

Mattie stopped, her heart pounding.

She'd remembered something—just a flash, not enough to grasp, to take out and examine.

William—he must have been in his late twenties, maybe thirty at most, at any rate much younger than he currently was. He sat across the table from Mattie, but it wasn't their rough-hewn wood table in the cabin. This table was smooth and white and she was much, much smaller (though she'd never really gotten tall; she might still be mistaken for a child if you didn't see her face).

Over William's shoulder was a female figure in a yellow sweater with her back to Mattie (*no, Samantha, I was Samantha then*), a woman with the same dirty blonde hair as her own, except it was curly and ended in the middle of her neck.

*Turn around,* Mattie thought, *turn around so I can see your face.*

But the image slipped away, a cracked and broken thing, and she found herself on the floor weeping, unable to stop.

After a long while she made herself get up and finish her chores. By the end of it her whole body throbbed, but especially her left eye. The swelling seemed worse than the day before, and when she touched it she felt a great pouch of fluid pushing against the top of the eye socket.

*I can't run anywhere until this is better. I'm at a disadvantage with one eye. Especially with that monster out there.*

She knew she couldn't run with William gone to town in any case, though at first that might seem the best time. If she ran down the mountain while he was coming up she could run right into him. The idea of him catching her in the act of escape made her shudder. Who knew what punishment he might inflict if he found her in the woods trying to get away from him?

But trying to leave when he was at home wasn't the best idea, either. Perhaps she could sneak out at night, when he was sleeping. She'd have to drop a bag of supplies out in the woods somewhere beforehand.

Mattie pressed her hand to the side of her head. She wasn't sure how she would do it. There had to be some way, but she wasn't up to considering all the options at the moment. Her eye needed some relief.

There were several long icicles dangling from the front eaves of the cabin. If she could reach one she might break off a piece and wrap it inside a cloth and press it on her eye.

*But I mustn't leave the porch because if I do William will see the footprints in the snow and then he'll be angry.*

Mattie didn't care that he would be upset, not in the way she'd cared the day before. She only cared that he would hurt her, and if he hurt her she couldn't escape from him.

She peered out the front window. It wouldn't do to have him return and catch her breaking his edict. He'd said he would be gone until after dark, but he might only be testing her.

All appeared still and silent.

Mattie opened the door slowly, half-expecting William to stride out from behind a tree, his ice-chip eyes frosted over.

**You're still afraid of him.** This was Samantha's voice.

*Yes, I am. I might always be,* Mattie thought.

That was a hard and terrible thing to acknowledge, the idea that even if she managed to get away, that he would haunt her always—the boogeyman in the closet, the monster under the bed, the creature tapping at her window.

*Tapping at her window. There was someone tapping at her window and she was rubbing her eyes and there was William, waving at her from the dark.*

She stopped, frozen, feeling she was on the verge of understanding something very, very important.

Then she heard the voices. Male voices in the woods, approaching fast.

*Oh, god, no,* she thought, fleeing into the cabin and throwing the bolt. She hurriedly drew the front curtains and then did the same for the other two windows at the back of the cabin—one in the main room, one in the bedroom.

*Don't come near. If William sees your footprints in the snow he'll blame me and you'll ruin everything, don't come near, don't.*

She wasn't strong enough to take another beating so soon after the last one, and she wasn't strong enough to run away on her own yet, either.

*Please leave, don't come near,* but of course she heard their voices draw closer and closer, closer and closer, until she could make out the words.

"Do you think your Amish girl lives here?" A man's voice, young, full of laughter.

"I told you, she wasn't Amish. It was just some dumb thing I said because their clothes were so old-fashioned." This was the second voice, also young. And familiar. The stranger from yesterday.

"No, not him," she breathed.

William had half-killed her because the man had *looked* at her. If he discovered that the man had actually come to their cabin door—and he would discover it, of this she had no doubt—he might *actually* kill her.

Kill her and find some other happy, pretty girl to grind beneath his boot, because a man needed sons.

*No. No, I can't let it happen to anyone else.*

**(If you can't let it happen to anyone else then you'll have to kill him, because if you run then he'll find another girl. You know he will.)**

"Go away, Samantha," Mattie whispered. Her head hurt and her eye hurt and she was so terrified that the men outside would find her that she could barely suck in a lungful of air.

*Please leave. Please go.*

**(But they might help you)**

*Or they might hurt me. They might be just like William. I can't trust them. I can't trust anyone.*

She heard the clatter of their boots on the porch. Mattie backed away from the door, crouched down in the middle of the room, made herself into a tiny ball.

*I could disappear if I wished hard enough. I could turn into a mote of dust.*

A hard knock sounded at the door.

Mattie bit her lip to keep from crying out.

"Nobody's home," the first man said. "You can see the footsteps in the snow leading away from the door."

"Only his. Not hers," said the second man, the man Mattie thought of as her stranger.

*No, don't think of him that way. You don't know anything about him. You don't know if you can trust him. And if you think kindly of the stranger then William will see it in your eyes.*

"She must be here," the stranger said.

Mattie saw his shadow at the front window, knew he was trying to see inside, but she had pulled the curtains tight and she wasn't moving. He'd never see anything in the cabin that way.

"Come on," the second man said. Mattie heard impatience in his voice, like he'd already had enough of indulging his friend's whim. "She's not here. This might not be where she lives, anyway. There's something more interesting here. Come look."

"It's got to be where she lives," the stranger said. "Where else could they have come from?"

"Who cares?" The second man's voice sounded farther away.

Mattie wondered what had caught his attention. Could he be interested in the storehouse? That was the only other building in front of the cabin.

*If he tries to break in there, I must go outside, because I can't just huddle here while someone steals our winter stores. I'll have to say something, stop him somehow. Though I haven't the least idea how.*

"Obviously I care, C.P.," the stranger said. He knocked again and Mattie just barely managed to stifle a scream.

"I can't believe we're wasting this much time looking for some weird *married* girl you bumped into on top of a mountain. You could just ask out a girl from work, like everyone else. Or go to a club. Or a bar. Or sign up for one of those singles adventure groups."

"Stop being dumb. This isn't about sex."

"Then what is it about, Griffin? I thought we were up here to investigate a sighting, not hunt around for some girl."

*Griffin. His name was Griffin.*

"You didn't see her," Griffin said. "She was scared. And . . ."

"I know you think you saw her somewhere before." C.P. sounded skeptical.

"I did," Griffin said. "I just can't put my finger on it."

"Listen, I think we should get out of here. If she is home she's clearly not welcoming visitors. Besides, there were all those private property signs posted."

Mattie's eyes widened. There were private property signs around their cabin? How had she never noticed them? She knew how to read.

*William probably doesn't let you go anywhere near the signs. The signs are only important to keep away people who might drift in this direction, and he's always made certain that you won't accidentally encounter anyone. But the whole mountain isn't private. Griffin and William both said something about the clearing and the caves being public land.*

"You said that guy had a gun, right?" C.P. continued. "Anyone who lives alone in the middle of the woods with a bunch of 'keep out, private property' signs posted is not going to welcome unexpected visitors. We should move on before he comes home and decides to shoot us on principle."

"Yeah," Griffin said.

He still stood very close to the door. His voice was so close that Mattie almost imagined he was inside the room with her.

*Maybe I could trust him. Maybe I could. He seems kind. He sounded worried when he talked about me. Maybe . . .*

"And the property is marked on the map, so we don't even have an excuse. Anyway, come and look at these prints in the snow," C.P. said. "These look a lot like the ones you took pictures of yesterday."

Mattie heard Griffin move off the porch. She unwound her coiled body and slid her stockinged feet over the floor cautiously, so as not to make a sound. She wanted to see the two men. She wanted to know what they were doing.

She twitched the curtain aside, just a fraction of an inch, just enough to make a slit to peer out between the curtain and the window frame.

The two men were crouched in the center of the clearing inspecting the prints in the snow. They had their backs to the cabin and all she could see were their caps and their large backpacks—Griffin's orange, C.P.'s blue. Their voices were low and Mattie couldn't make out what they were saying. Her stranger—*Griffin, his name is Griffin*—took several photographs with the camera that was still slung around his neck.

Both men stood, their eyes on the ground, and carefully crept around the clearing, stopping occasionally to take more pictures.

Mattie released the curtain and inched back when she realized that they were going to follow the creature's tracks around the cabin. She didn't want them to accidentally catch a glimpse of her. They passed within a few feet of the window, and she caught some of their conversation again.

". . . have to hurry because Jen is going to meet us on the trail in about an hour and we don't want to miss her," C.P. said.

She hadn't seen his face yet, this friend of Griffin's, just the back of his head covered by a red knit cap with a large fluffy ball at the crown.

*I had a hat like that once. Except it wasn't red. It was blue and white and maroon stripes with a blue puffy ball at the top, and there was a big "A" on the front.*

Mattie couldn't remember what the "A" was for, though. She had a flash of men swooping around on ice, holding sticks in front of them, but she couldn't quite remember what they were doing or why.

She shook her head. That wasn't important right now. She had to know what the strange men were doing, and if they had moved on. Mattie had a vague notion of going outside to sweep away the evidence of their prints, and then her own. Then William would never know they had come and she wouldn't have to face his wrath.

Mattie stepped silently into the bedroom. She knew of old where the boards creaked and how to avoid them. This was practically second nature now, as she never wanted to wake William if she got out of bed in the night. And she didn't want the two men outside—if they were still there—to know she was inside.

She inched away the curtain and peered out.

Griffin's camera obscured his face and Mattie saw his finger depressing a button over and over. C.P. was gesturing excitedly at the symbols in the snow, the ones the creature had left the night before, the ones that had convinced William that the creature was a demon come to try him.

Mattie couldn't quite hear what they were saying, but their intention was very clear. They were interested in the creature, like William was. And they were going to follow its tracks.

*No,* she thought. *They can't.*

If Griffin and C.P. followed the creature from the cabin, then the animal would think that she and William had ignored the warning. The creature would kill Griffin and C.P., and it would come back to the cabin for her and William.

It sounded crazy, even in her head—the idea that an animal could think and reason like a person. And maybe it didn't think and reason exactly like a person, but it clearly wasn't simply made up of instinct like every other animal in the woods. Mattie couldn't let the two men outside risk being sorted into piles like the creature's other victims.

*And I don't want it to come back for me, either.*

But what should she do? Go outside?

*No, I had better not. It's not safe. It's not just about William, either. I don't know if I can trust them.*

But she couldn't just allow the strangers to wander blithely into danger.

She stood, irresolute, unable to warn them, unable to force herself to break William's dictate.

**How will you ever run from him if you can't even do this?**

Samantha again. She was very sassy for such a small girl.

*"You've got a sassy mouth on you."* William's voice, one of those long ago and far away threads that seeped forward from the back of her mind, followed by a memory of pain—a great swipe of his hand across her face.

**Just go. Just tell them before it's too late.**

*But I can't go outside.*

Mattie's hands moved, seemingly without her own thought or consideration, but they were trembling. They pushed the curtains back, lifted the window. Cold air rushed into the cabin, stinging her face.

Both men turned as the window scraped in its frame.

Mattie opened her mouth, tried to say, "You can't follow it," but nothing came out except a little croaky sound.

"What the hell?" C.P. said, but Griffin was already moving toward the cabin.

He must not have had a clear view of her face, for when he drew closer she heard his quick indrawn breath. His dark eyes snapped with anger as he rushed closer.

"It's you! My god, what did he do to you?"

Griffin reached through the open window but Mattie retreated a few steps in shock. No one ever touched her except William. She hadn't even spoken to another person in years.

Mattie tried to steady herself, but she couldn't stop wringing her hands and her heart was beating so hard she felt sick. The back of her throat was clogged with acid and her legs shook.

"I'm sorry," Griffin said, holding up his hands in surrender. "I didn't mean to scare you. I was just so . . ."

He trailed off, and she saw him making an effort to hide his surprise and anger.

*William never does that. Once his anger bubbles up he lets it spill over, lets it burn me.*

"My name's Griffin Banerjee. This is my friend C.P. Chang."

C.P. approached the window, peered in. His eyes widened but he gave Mattie a little wave. "Hey."

Mattie swallowed. She didn't realize how frightened she would be, how strange it would feel to speak to new people.

"I—" she managed, but then the gorge rose in her throat and she had to stop and swallow it down. "I need to tell you . . ."

Why was her voice such a whispery thing? Why couldn't she just be firm and strong and tell them what needed to be told?

"Do you need help?" Griffin asked. "We could help you. You look like you need a doctor."

C.P. frowned at Griffin, and Mattie could read the thought behind his gaze—*We don't have time for that.*

"N-no," she said. "No doctor. But you can't go up the mountain."

There, she'd gotten it all out. Sweat pooled at the base of her spine. Now that she'd told them, she wished they would leave, go back to where they came from, cease staring at her like she was an animal in a zoo.

C.P. turned his frown from Griffin to her. "Why not?"

Mattie gestured out the window in the general direction of the symbols. "The creature. It came to warn us. Don't disturb it or it will hurt you."

"You've seen it?" C.P. asked, his frown abruptly replaced with excitement. "When? What happened? Can you describe it for us?"

The sudden barrage of questions made her step backward again, like she could escape his interest if only she moved far enough away.

"You can't go up the mountain. It left a warning," she said.

"You saw it do that?" C.P. asked, gesturing behind him at the symbols traced in the snow. "When?"

She wasn't explaining this correctly. If she had then they wouldn't be asking more questions, acting excited instead of frightened. If they *knew* then they would leave. And they would be safe.

*And I will be safe, too, because then the creature won't come back and punish me for their behavior.*

Mattie turned her good eye on Griffin, who was watching her intently.

"Y-yesterday," she said, and had to stop because her mouth was so dry. She wished for a glass of water. Why was this so difficult? Why was it so *hard* to get the words out? "Yesterday when we saw you . . ."

She trailed off, because the intensity of his stare was making her forget what she wanted to say. She wished she could cover up her swelling left eye, because he seemed fixated on it. In another moment he'd ask her again if she needed a doctor, she was sure of it. Mattie hurried on before he could.

"Yesterday, when we saw you, did you go into any of the caves?"

"No, I didn't. It's not a good idea to go into a cave alone—too many things can go wrong and there was no cell signal up there. C.P. didn't come up until today," Griffin said.

"I had finals, and I couldn't get off work until today," C.P. said. "The project deadline was Tuesday but I couldn't finish *my* job until other people finished *their* job . . ."

He trailed off, realizing that Griffin was glaring at him and Mattie was simply confused.

"Project?"

"I've got a work-study project . . ."

"It's really not the time, C.P." Griffin said.

"Right," C.P. said, and subsided.

Mattie hadn't understood anything that he'd said. "Cell signal" and "work-study"—it was like he was speaking a foreign language.

"Anyway, I didn't go into any of the caves. I was curious about what you and your husband were doing up there. I couldn't believe it when I saw the tracks." There had been a demonstrable pause between "your" and "husband," like Griffin couldn't quite believe that William actually was her husband.

"But why do you care about the tracks?" This wasn't what she meant to say. She meant to tell him about what was in the cave so he would know, he would understand and then he would leave.

Griffin and C.P. exchanged slightly sheepish grins.

"Well, we're cryptozoologists," Griffin said. "In our spare time, you know."

Mattie must have appeared as blank as she felt because C.P. said, "It means that we go hunting for evidence of supposedly mythical creatures. You know, like Sasquatch and chupacabra, things like that. We heard there was a sighting of something big up here—some campers saw it in the woods, and later found some tracks. We thought maybe it was a Sasquatch sighting but these prints are like nothing we've seen before."

"Sasquatch?" Mattie felt that she'd completely lost the thread of the conversation. This was some kind of fun for them, a lark with their friends. They didn't understand. She had to make them understand.

"Sasquatch, yeah. Like Bigfoot."

"Bigfoot," Mattie said.

The word—such a strange and funny word—twanged another deeply hidden memory. Mattie (*no, Samantha*) and Heather and Mom were on a trip somewhere, and in the gift shop there were these funny shaped keychains like really big feet. *Gift shop. Keychains.* She'd forgotten what those things were. She could almost smell the shop again—it smelled like the new T-shirts hanging on the rack and the row of candy sticks by the cash register and the woodsy undertone of cabin walls because the shop had been in a tiny cabin.

"Candy sticks," she said, remembering peeling the plastic wrap halfway down the stick, the taste of blueberry on her tongue.

"Candy sticks?" C.P. said.

Mattie shook her head. "Nothing. Sasquatch. The thing in the woods is not a Sasquatch."

"So you *have* seen it?" C.P. asked.

"Yes," Mattie said. "It's not what you think. And you need to get off the mountain."

"You keep saying that," Griffin said. "But you won't tell us why."

Mattie hesitated. If she told them what was in the caves they would probably want to go look, and that was dangerous, so dangerous. But if she didn't tell then they wouldn't understand and they would go fumbling around and then the creature would tear them open.

"In the caves, in one of the caves, there are bones. Lots and lots of bones, piles of them. And they're all sorted—skulls in one place, ribs in another, that kind of thing. And there are organs, too, a pile of organs. The creature did that. It killed all the animals and it made—" She stopped, because she'd forgotten the word. She looked at Griffin. "It's a word, like a prize?"

"Trophy?"

"Yes," she said. "Trophy. It has all these trophies. And William and I went into the cave and saw these things. The creature knew we'd been there. It knew even though it wasn't in the cave when we were there. It followed me last night. It stalked me through the woods until I came to the cabin and then it left that warning in the snow."

Griffin tilted his head to one side. He'd been watching her fixedly throughout her narrative. She couldn't tell if he believed her or not, or if he understood how strange and frightening it had been in the cave. She didn't think she'd communicated this properly.

"How do you know it's a warning?" he asked.

"What else could it be?" Mattie's frustration was mounting. She had to make them understand. "It didn't hurt me, though it could have. I was all alone and had no weapon. I couldn't do anything against it. But it just followed me and then it left those marks in the snow, so that we would know it had been there, so we would know that it knows where we live."

"Why were you alone in the woods?" Griffin asked.

"I . . . Because William . . . It's not important," she said.

This wasn't something she could explain to a stranger. And it wasn't important. They needed to leave. That was the important thing. Leave the mountain so that they would be safe. Leave the cabin so that she could find some way to eliminate the evidence of their visit. She peered out at the sky. The day had started off sunny but a heavy bank of clouds had moved in. It might snow.

*Snow would be wonderful. Snow would cover everything up and make it clean and William would never know.*

"Did your husband leave you out there?" Griffin asked. "In that state?"

There was something in his voice, something Mattie had never heard before, at least not on her behalf. *Outrage. He's not angry at me. He's angry for me.*

Something warm and new bubbled up inside her, something dangerous. *I can't feel this right now. I can't be pleased that he wants to defend me just because no one ever has before.*

"I want to know more about this cave," C.P. said. "Do you remember exactly which one it was?"

Panic replaced the warm feeling. "You can't go there. Don't you understand? You can't go up there at all. It's not a Sasquatch, or some harmless made-up thing for you and your friends to play at hunting. It's a monster. A real monster."

Both Griffin and C.P. looked insulted.

"We're not playing," C.P. said. "We're serious. We're trying to find solid evidence of a cryptid."

"You don't need to find evidence. You need to go home before something terrible happens to you."

Her teeth chattered. The cold air coming in through the open window was even colder. Mattie smelled snow on the air.

*It will cover the proof of them, and I'll be safe from William. It might even send them off the mountain. They can't want to sleep outdoors in a snowstorm.*

"You don't look so good," C.P. said.

"I'm just c-cold," Mattie said. "I have to shut the window."

This was clearly meant to send Griffin and C.P. on their way, but they both hesitated.

"I really think we should take you to a doctor . . ." Griffin began.

Something exploded out of Mattie then, something she didn't even recognize.

"I told you I don't need a doctor. I don't want a doctor. *Why* won't you listen to me? Why are all men the same? You're just like William, who never listens to a thing I say, never thinks I have anything important to say. I talk and I talk and I tell you that you need to leave, to get off this mountain before you're ripped apart like those animals, but you just ignore me and only think about what you want, what you think should happen. Stop talking about a doctor and start talking about collecting your friend before something terrible occurs."

She stalked toward the window and yanked it down in front of their stunned faces.

## CHAPTER SEVEN

Mattie pulled the curtains together so she could no longer see the men outside. There was something burning in her, an over-bright feeling that half made her think she could shoot flames from her eyes.

One of the strangers (*that's right, they are strangers, they aren't your responsibility*) immediately banged on the window, shouting something, but Mattie backed away and out of the bedroom. She didn't think they would break through the window or try to hurt her, but she didn't want to take a chance. And she didn't want to listen to them shouting, either.

She shut the bedroom door to trap any lingering cold air in there and went out to huddle by the fire, which was low. William had left some firewood for her and she carefully placed two logs with trembling hands.

What had made her scream like that, made her behave in such a way? That wasn't like her at all.

*If you acted that way around William, that would be the end of you.*

They weren't the sort of men who would hit her just for losing her temper. At least, she didn't think they were—how could she really know? She was pretty certain, though. And because she felt safe, felt that they wouldn't beat her senseless for speaking her mind, she'd vented her feelings on them—and more than just her current feelings, too. She'd vented the feelings that she'd been tamping down for years.

*I shouldn't have done that. They were only trying to be kind.*

Mattie felt a little guilty then, felt that she ought to apologize, but then decided against it. She didn't want to be drawn into another conversation with them. Despite their kindness, there was nothing else to say. She'd tried to convince them that it would be dangerous to stay on the mountain. She didn't think she'd succeeded, but she could hope. Perhaps they would consider her words later and escape before they were harmed.

A pounding at the front door startled a little scream out of her before she could swallow it.

"Miss? Miss? I mean, ma'am. Listen, I'm sorry about what happened. I didn't mean to . . . Well, could you come out and talk to us again? Maybe at the door this time? We could really use your help."

They knew she was inside the house, so she couldn't pretend not to be at home.

*But you aren't required to answer them. You aren't.*

**(You're being a fool. They could help you. They could help you run away.)**

*Except that they aren't leaving the mountain. They're going to stay and tramp around and try to find the creature, and what good will it do you to trail after them while they do that? William will come after you and if the creature doesn't get you then he'll shoot all of them and it will be on your head.*

No, Mattie realized that she couldn't trust anyone to help her. If they helped and were hurt because of it, she'd never forgive herself.

"Miss? Miss?"

Mattie wondered why Griffin was calling her "miss." Then she remembered that she'd never told them her name.

**(What is your name, anyway?)**

"Go away, Samantha," Mattie whispered. "I don't have time for you right now."

Griffin pounded a few more times.

Mattie heard C.P.'s voice. "She's not coming to the door, man. And we gotta meet Jen. And there's no cell signal here so I can't text her and tell her why we're late. She's going to leave us if we don't get going."

"I know. I just . . ." Griffin's voice trailed away.

"I know, I know. You've seen her somewhere before."

"I wish I could remember."

Mattie heard Griffin's tread on the porch, then the crunch of his boots in the snow. C.P. said something she couldn't make out, and a few minutes later all was silent.

She crept up to the front window and peered out, making certain they were gone. The clearing was empty except for their footprints.

The tracks were everywhere, and Mattie felt a flare of panic. What if there wasn't enough snow, or it didn't start falling soon enough? A few lazy flakes were drifting down but those flakes were hardly enough to fill the footprints that crisscrossed the clearing and wrapped around behind the cabin.

Mattie went to the back window and checked that the two strangers weren't behind the cabin, either. There was no sign of them. She wondered if they'd gone back the way they came, or if they'd taken a different route. She wouldn't know unless she followed their tracks, and she didn't want to follow their tracks. She didn't want to have anything to do with them.

*I don't,* she thought, but it was like she was trying to convince herself. Part of her wondered why she hadn't gone with them. It would have been the easiest way to free herself of the hell of this cabin.

*You know why. Because you can take any risk to yourself, but it's not fair to place it on other people.*

No, her original plan was still the best one—to get better, to heal so that she could sneak out under cover of night and disappear before William ever realized what had happened. She should forget about C.P. and Griffin. She'd tried to warn them, tried to save them. Maybe they would survive the creature's fury. There wasn't much she could do about it.

*Why does Griffin keep saying he knows me?*

Mattie wondered if she'd known him Before. But even if she had . . . she'd been a small child when she came to live with William on the mountain. Griffin never would have recognized her after all these years, and it wasn't realistic for her to try to dredge up some potential memory of a boy from her very spotty memory.

*Did I know you?*

There were no boys in her thoughts, no memory of any other child except Heather.

She realized she was standing at the back window, woolgathering. The snow had begun to fall in earnest. It was like that on the mountain. There was no snow and then suddenly there was more snow than you could imagine.

Mattie remembered standing at the front window with Heather, their hands and noses pressed against the glass, wondering if there was enough snow for school to be called off.

"Snow day," Mattie murmured.

Sometimes it was just a few flakes, not enough to hold up the bus. Sometimes the weatherman would predict snow for the morning that wouldn't arrive in time to disrupt the school day. The girls would rush to their bedroom windows in hopes of seeing a proper blizzard outside, and instead there would be bare sidewalk and bright sun, no hint of snow anywhere. Then they would drag themselves downstairs, heels slamming against the wooden stairs, their bodies seemingly made of dripping rubber and their voices to match.

*"Whhhhyyyy do we have to go to school today?"*

And their mother would tell them that it was hard luck but that was the way it was. Mattie knew their mother would tell them this but she couldn't hear it, not the same way she heard her own voice or Heather's.

*Why can't I remember my own mother?*

A thick fall of snow was coming down. Mattie saw it filling in the marks made by the creature and the telltale footprints of the strangers who'd violated William's mountaintop sanctuary. She realized just how lucky the two strangers had been that William hadn't been home when they arrived. William would have chased them off with the rifle instead of pretending not to be at home.

**You're still more of a mouse than a falcon, you know.**

She ignored that voice, the one that sounded like Samantha. Samantha had never been scared, not really, so it was easy for her to be fearless. Samantha had never lost a part of herself in a deep well.

"But I'm trying," Mattie whispered, turning away from the window. "I am trying."

She made tea and cut off a slice of bread. She was half-tempted to sneak a little butter, just a scraping, but William was sure to have noted the precise shape and amount of butter left in the dish.

One day she would be away from him and she would eat all the food she wanted, eat until her stomach was stretched tight and she felt like she could hardly walk.

*And I'll have . . .*

Her thoughts ground to a halt there, because she didn't know what she would have. The only food she could think of was the food that she and William ate—stews made from animals hunted in the woods, or fish fried in the cast iron pan, or vegetables she took out of her garden. The only things that they ate that weren't made by their own hands were butter and eggs and milk, which William collected from town. He said that chickens were too much trouble to raise and would attract too much attention.

Mattie had never questioned this, the same way she'd never questioned anything that William said, but she realized now that it was true. Chickens made noise—roosters especially—and might attract the attention of anyone wandering nearby who'd ignored the private property signs that C.P. and Griffin had mentioned.

*If I manage to get away from here alive* (and this was not a certain concept, not at all, when she stopped to think about how many things could go wrong it was enough to paralyze her), *I'm never eating venison or rabbit or fried fish again. I'll eat all the foods that people eat in the other places.*

She still couldn't imagine what those foods might be, though. The only food she remembered was ice cream.

Mattie stared down at her plate, now empty of its meager bread slice, and tried to imagine it filling with some food that she'd eaten with Mom and Heather. But the tin plate remained the same, a blank space scattered with a few crumbs.

She glanced at her work basket. There were many things to mend in it—there always seemed to be more clothing to mend— but she couldn't dredge up the energy at the moment. All the shocks of the last twenty-four hours—the cave, the stranger, the beating, dragging herself through the snow, the creature stalking her, William locking her out, the two men showing up at her door—seemed to suddenly press on her, and all she wanted was to go to sleep. She hadn't slept in ages.

Mattie lay down on the couch with a blanket rolled up for a pillow—the cushions were hard, and not very good for sleeping, but she wanted to be near the fire. It didn't matter that the couch wasn't comfortable, though—she was asleep almost before her head touched the blanket.

*William at the window.*

*He was knocking, knocking very softly, like it was a secret he only wanted her to hear.*

She sat up in bed and rubbed her eyes, and saw him there, waving at her.

"Open the window," he said, his voice faint through the glass.

If it had been anyone else she never would have, but it was William, so she hopped out of bed and dragged her wooden desk chair over the carpet and up to the window. She climbed onto the chair—she was very small for an eight-year-old, and Heather always teased her about it, but Mom would hug her and say good things came in small packages so Samantha didn't mind.

It was hard for her to push the window all the way open, but once she got it partway, William helped her lift it the rest of the way.

"Good girl, Sam," he said.

"Where's the screen?" she asked.

"It's right there," he said in a whisper, and she peered out and saw it leaning against the house. "Let me through, Sammy girl."

"What are you doing?" she asked as he climbed into her bedroom. "Why don't you knock on the door like a regular person?"

He wasn't dressed the way he was usually dressed. His clothes were all black.

"You look like a ninja," she said, and a giggle escaped her.

"Be very quiet," he said, holding a finger to his lips. "Be very, very quiet."

"Like Elmer Fudd," Sam said. "Hunting rabbits."

"Exactly," William said, and swiped at her nose with his thumb. "Like Elmer Fudd. I need you to stay so quiet and so still in here, just like you're still asleep. I'm going to surprise your mother."

"Oh!" Sam said. "Can I help?"

"You already did," he said, and rubbed the top of her head. "Just wait here for me until I get back and I'll tell you all about it."

There were arms underneath her, someone carrying her with surprising tenderness. She surfaced from sleep just long enough to open one bleary eye.

"William?"

"Don't you worry now, Mattie girl. I've got you," he said.

He placed her on the bed. She felt him pulling her stockings down but she was too tired to do anything about it.

"A man's got to have sons, Mattie," he said. "I've been waiting for them."

There was an astonishing array of gear laid out in the main room of the cabin. Half of the table was taken up with boxes of ammunition, giant knives, brown bottles with warnings and skulls on them, strange round objects that were . . .

*Grenades? Are those grenades? Is he hunting the creature or starting a war?*

Mattie had never seen a grenade in real life, only on television.

Thinking about television made her stop for a second, because she had only remembered it properly just then. A box with moving pictures inside it, and she and Heather used to watch cartoons and laugh.

*Every Saturday morning, and Mom would let us eat cereal with marshmallows in front of the TV.*

As soon as she thought "cereal with marshmallows," she could remember the taste of it. The cereal was like sweet oats, soft and crumbly from being in the milk, and the marshmallows were not like the marshmallows that she ate around a campfire but small and hard and gritty, crunchy underneath her teeth. She liked the strange texture of the marshmallows best and saved them for last, let them float in the milk while she picked around them, scooping up the cereal with the spoon.

*Cereal. You remembered a food that you had before. Cereal.*

A gun leaned against the wall next to the door, the largest rifle Mattie had ever seen—the barrel seemed enormous. A chipmunk could disappear inside that barrel and never be seen again.

Next to the gun was a giant trap, gleaming silver in the faint morning light. It had huge shiny teeth, the kind that snapped together over an animal's leg. Mattie shied away from it, not wanting to come too near even though the trap wasn't set yet.

Her eye felt even worse today than it had the day before, the pouch of fluid larger and harder. She hated not being able to see out of one eye. It gave her the feeling that something was always lurking in the blank space where she used to be able to see.

William's boots stomped across the porch. She heard him kicking his feet against the side of the cabin to get rid of the snow, then the door opened.

He dropped the load of firewood by the door. "Better get the fire going, Mattie. It's a cold one out there. Going to have to keep the fire on all day."

He shut the door again. Mattie knew he was going out to the storehouse to get the eggs for breakfast. She heard him whistling as he did, and she froze in shock.

*Whistling? William whistling?*

He must have had a very good day in town. Mattie couldn't recall the last time she heard him whistle, even though he was good at it. He could whistle a tune and it actually sounded like a song, not just a random series of notes.

*He stopped whistling a long time ago, when he decided that music tempted the devil close.*

She decided not to say anything about it. If she drew attention to it then it would be her fault that he made music and attracted evil to them.

There were still large hot embers in the fireplace. William must have put wood in when he returned home the night before. Mattie stoked up the fire again so it would be ready for cooking. In the meantime, William returned with the eggs, removing his boots at the door.

"Going to catch that demon today, Mattie my girl," he said as she made the coffee. "It doesn't stand a chance."

"What are you going to do?" she asked, going about her usual breakfast chores.

"First thing is to set up that trap on the trail between here and the stream. If it comes down for water and decides to head up this way again, the demon will walk right into it."

*I don't think so,* Mattie thought. The creature seemed too smart to step into a trap, but she didn't tell William this.

"Then I'm going to take some of those grenades up to the caves and toss 'em inside," William continued. "If it's in there when I do, all well and good. If it isn't, then I'll have blown up its home base. It won't have anywhere to hide, and if it doesn't have anywhere to hide, it will be easier for me to shoot."

He gestured toward the rifle leaning against the wall. "And that gun, Mattie my girl, is strong enough to take down an elephant. It will take down that demon for sure."

"What's the knife for?" Mattie asked, as she placed his food in front of him.

William shrugged. It was such an uncharacteristic gesture that Mattie had to stop herself from staring at him. He really was not acting like himself today.

*He's lighter, freer than he has been in years. He's more like the old William, the one who used to laugh and play board games with me and Heather.*

For what felt like the millionth time her brain came to a halt, caught on a memory that had just surfaced. William used to play board games with her and Heather. She could almost see his hand holding a red gingerbread man, moving it over colored squares on a board and stopping when he reached a candy cane.

This recollection in addition to the one she'd had of her mother standing behind William in the kitchen made her wonder. She wondered just who William was to her, because she had a feeling that he wasn't just her husband. Something roiled in her stomach, something that burned and bubbled like acid. She stared at the man she'd lived with for more than a decade as he picked up the knife on the table, weighed it in his hand.

*Who are you?*

"The knife is a last resort, you might say," William said.

Mattie started. She'd completely forgotten she'd asked him about the knife. She'd even forgotten for a moment where she was—no, *when* she was. These memories that surfaced piecemeal were dangerous. They stopped her clock, made her drift away. When she drifted, she made mistakes. When she made mistakes, William got angry. Mattie was determined not to let him get angry at her again, especially not when he was in such a strangely cheerful mood.

"A last resort?" she asked, giving all of her attention to him. She couldn't afford to think about anything else right now.

"In case it gets close," William said.

William would never be able to kill the creature that way. Never. She hadn't been able to see its body clearly in the darkness but she knew it was enormous. The chances of William, say, slashing its throat were practically zero. He wouldn't even be able to reach the creature's throat. And then it would rip him up with its claws and that would be the end of William.

*The end of William.* Her heart leapt when she thought of it. The end of pain. She almost couldn't imagine it, a life without pain.

*But should you be thinking thoughts like that? Should you be thinking about William dying?*

**(Yes)**

William placed the knife back on the table and frowned at her. "That eye looks bad, Mattie girl. Does it hurt?"

This was sometimes a trick question. Sometimes he wanted to know for certain that he'd hurt her because she deserved it. And sometimes he wanted her to say her wounds didn't hurt because it was insulting that her own husband would harm her. She studied his face for a minute, tried to divine the correct answer in his eyes.

"Yes," she said, pretty sure this was what he wanted to hear, and it was also true. Her eye hurt so bad it was getting difficult for her to move around. It throbbed constantly, and the fluid under the lid seemed hard now, like it had taken on a new form.

He grasped her chin with his fingers, turned her bad eye toward the light. Her stomach muscles tensed, braced for a sudden change in mood. Occasionally the sight of his handiwork would increase William's fury.

"Going to have to drain it," he said. "Sit down."

Mattie waited while William collected two clean cloths from the small basket under her worktable. Then he took out needle and thread from her sewing kit. Finally he took his small knife—the one he always carried at his hip for little tasks throughout the day—and the needle, and heated up the tips of both in the fire.

She knew what would happen next, because he'd had to do this before. That had been many years ago, and it had been the other eye. Mattie had a little scar on her browbone from the stitches. It had mostly faded.

*How old was I? Twelve? Thirteen? It was before I started having my courses, I remember, because he was angry about that. He said I looked like a woman and it was about time I started bearing children, but I hadn't started bleeding yet and that meant he couldn't touch me. And I didn't really understand about having my courses, my "woman-time" as he called it, and when I asked him about it, he hit me and later my eye swelled up, though not as bad as this time. He'd seemed sorry about it, too.*

**(Just like he seems sorry now but don't you fall for it, Mattie. You know what he's like, what he is underneath the skin.)**

William cradled the back of Mattie's head with one hand and raised the knife with the other.

"Don't you move," he warned.

Mattie wouldn't, knew she wouldn't, because she was afraid of the knife coming near her eye. For a moment she even thought it was all a trick. She watched the knife descending, the sharp blade coming closer to her face, and thought, *He knows. He knows about Griffin and C.P., he knows they came to the house and he's going to cut out my eye in retribution.*

Then the tip of the knife slashed across the top of the swollen mass. Fluid gushed out and ran over her eye and down her cheek. Mattie whimpered.

"Hold that cloth underneath it," William said, shoving one in her hands. "Let all that stuff come out."

She pressed the cloth against her eye, underneath the wound, which felt like a flowing waterfall on her face. More and more fluid ran out, a deflating balloon. Her eye, relieved of the intense pressure, already felt better.

William had taken the other cloth and was dipping it in cold water. He returned to the table holding a sliver of soap and the wet cloth.

When it seemed like Mattie's eye was mostly done running, he gestured for her to take the cloth away. He dabbed at the cut with the wet cloth, then rubbed the sliver of soap over it. Mattie cried out as the soap touched the open wound.

"I know it stings," he said. He almost seemed gentle then, almost like he cared about her. "But we've got to get it clean or else it will get infected. And what will I do if my girl is sick?"

William hated it when she got sick. He hated it when she couldn't take care of herself, when she couldn't cook or clean or look after him. He never hit her when she was ill—she thought that some part of him considered it unfair to strike her when she was already weak—but he would stomp around the cabin growling like an angry bear until she was back to normal.

He rinsed out the soap by holding the wet cloth over her face and squeezing water into it. Mattie bit her bottom lip hard while he was doing this. Then he fetched a fresh cloth to dry it.

"Press that against it," he said, and started preparing the needle.

William had big hands, and he was often rough with them, so Mattie was always a little surprised that he could do careful, delicate work like stitch up her eye. He could have been cruel about it, could have tugged the needle through any which way, but she could feel him neatly and precisely stitching the thread in an orderly line. She tried not to think about the needle going in and out, pushing through her skin, pulling the thread along behind it.

It seemed like forever, but she knew it was only the work of a few moments. Finally he said, "That's all done."

"Thank you, William," she said, because she knew that she was supposed to.

Then she collected all the dirty cloths and the needle, which was bright with slicks of her own blood, and took everything away to clean it.

William moved around the room, sorting all of his new gear and adding some of the old. Then he sat down at the table to clean and check over the new rifle he'd bought.

As Mattie washed the dirty cloths and hung them up to dry, she wondered where William had gotten the money to pay for all of those things. She knew he must have money in the trunk in the bedroom, but how had he earned that money? He didn't work any kind of job that she could see, and they didn't make anything on the mountain that he could sell. Could he really have years and years of money to support them in that trunk?

*I have to get inside it. I have to, without William knowing.*

The keys that he always took with him when he left the cabin were hanging on a hook near the door now. They seemed to call her, to tempt her.

*If you touch the keys, he'll know. You can't do anything that will make him angry, that will make him hurt you so that you can't escape.*

She wondered if there was a way for her to jimmy the trunk lock without using a key. She'd have to be careful, though—so, so careful. If there was a scratch on the lock or any sign that she'd been inside it . . .

She put thoughts of the trunk away. There was laundry to be washed, which was always a tiresome task in the winter as the clothes would have to be strung near the fire to dry instead of outside in the sunshine.

Her eye no longer throbbed, but it hurt where William had made and stitched the cut. The lid was slowly peeling back, however, and she could see faint, cloudy shapes again. This was slightly disorienting, as one eye could see clearly and the other couldn't.

William put on his boots and then took one of the bottles from the table, tucking it in his pocket. "Going to take that trap out and lay it now."

Mattie glanced at the heavy-looking metal object. "Do you need me to help you carry it?"

He snorted a little laugh. "You've got no muscles to carry something like that, Mattie my girl. I bought a sled when I was in town, in any case. How do you think I carried all those things up the mountain by myself?"

She didn't answer, because that little laugh had made her pause. When was the last time she heard William laugh? Years. It had been years.

*He's never been so happy as he is right now, preparing to go out and kill an animal he's never seen and doesn't understand.*

He opened the cabin door and pointed out into the snow so Mattie could see the sled he'd bought. Its runners were shiny and clean. William lugged the trap out and placed it on the wooden platform. Then he waved at her and went off, pulling the sledge behind him, whistling as he went.

# CHAPTER EIGHT

Mattie watched through the front window until he disappeared into the woods. Then she abandoned the washtub and hurried into the bedroom, kneeling down before the trunk to examine the lock. It looked like an ordinary lock to her, but she couldn't imagine how she might get it open.

*You have to pick the lock.*

Pick the lock—a strange phrase. It meant something, something just out of reach, but she couldn't grasp it. It wasn't something she'd ever done, she was certain of that. No, it was something she'd seen, but the person she pictured in her mind wasn't familiar and appeared distant—physically distant, like Mattie was watching the person from a long way away.

In her mind's eye Mattie saw the person—a woman—inserting a pin from her hair inside the lock. The woman moved the pin around carefully, her ear pressed against the door so that she could hear something.

*The pin catching the lock.*

Would that work on this trunk? Mattie thought it might, but whether or not she was skilled enough to actually open it was another matter.

She decided to leave the trunk for the moment. William had only gone out to lay the trap and would return soon. She was supposed to be washing the laundry.

Mattie collected the pile of dirty clothes from the corner of the bedroom and carried them out to the washtub. She pushed up the sleeves of her dress and used a cake of soap to scrub one of William's shirts against the washboard. After she completed washing and rinsing each item, she squeezed out the cloth and then clipped it on the short line of rope that William had strung in front of the fire for her.

She checked the pockets of William's pants for any forgotten items. He was always leaving things in his pockets and then blaming her when they were ruined by the wash water. She felt a thin roll of paper in one and pulled it out.

It was a roll of money.

Mattie hadn't seen money for a long time but as soon as she saw the tightly wrapped bills she recognized them for what they were. The bill on the outside had a "100" printed on it.

Her mouth went dry. She should give this to William the moment he came home. She was afraid to unroll the bills and see exactly how much was there but it appeared to be a great deal. He'd surely notice that it was missing. He might even have left it in his pocket to test her.

The idea made her heart gallop in her chest. Could William know—could he suspect that she wanted to leave him? He always seemed to know things about her, secret things that she tried to hide in her heart. Had he looked into her eyes yesterday morning, after she emerged from the outhouse where she'd hidden all night, and *known* that she was going to escape?

*No, no. You're being ridiculous. You're crediting him with powers he doesn't have. If William thought you were going to leave him, he never would have left you alone yesterday.*

Mattie took a deep breath to calm herself. She needed to stop panicking, stop acting the way she used to act around William. If she was scared or if she acted like she was guilty, then he *would* know that she was up to something. It was so important that he not know. It was so important that he was perfectly happy with her right up until the moment she slipped out the door and into the night.

*With money I could go far, far away. I could pay someone to take me far from this mountain and William would never find me no matter how hard he looked. I would change my name—*

*(change it back, change it back to Samantha)*

*—and he'd be furious but he wouldn't be able to reach me.*

But what to do with the money in the meantime? These were the pants William had worn the day before, so he'd simply forgotten about the roll of bills. But he wouldn't forget forever.

Mattie's hands were damp and the water from her fingers was seeping into the top layer. She put the roll down on the kitchen table and wiped her hands dry with a cloth.

What she needed to do was hide the money, but in such a way that it wouldn't appear to be hidden in case William came across it. It had to look like the roll had accidentally dropped from his pocket.

It would be easier if Mattie knew exactly where he'd walked the night before, but she'd been asleep when he came home.

*Asleep in front of the fire. William picked me up and carried me into the bed.*

She grabbed the money and hurried over to the couch, kneeling down in front of it. There was a space of about two or three inches between the bottom of the couch and the floor. Mattie stuck her arm into that space up to her elbow. She felt the thick grime of dust there (*I never clean underneath here, William would be so angry if he knew*) and carefully placed the roll of bills about halfway under.

When she pulled her arm out it was covered in dust. Some of the dust emerged in balls, little tumbleweeds rolling, leaving evidence of her crime.

*What if he sees?*

"Stay calm, don't panic. All you have to do is sweep it away and he'll never know."

She heard William whistling as he entered the clearing.

Mattie dashed to the broom, grabbed it, ran back to the dust on the floor, swept it into the dustpan and dumped the dustpan right into the washtub. Normally she would empty the dust outside but that was impossible with William nearly at the door. The whistling was right up to the porch.

She leaned the broom in its corner as he stomped across the porch. He kicked his boots against the doorframe to loosen the snow from the treads. She darted back to the washtub, submerging both arms in the water just as William opened the door. When he glanced at her, she was energetically scrubbing his pants along the washboard.

"It's all set, Mattie my girl," he said, stepping out of his boots and closing the door. "If that monster approaches from the river, he'll regret it."

"What if it doesn't?" she asked.

Her voice was a little breathless, but she was washing the clothes so vigorously that surely he would only attribute it to work. Sweat trickled between her shoulder blades.

*Stay calm, stay calm. If you act like something's wrong, he'll know something's wrong.*

"Oh, I've got plans for that demon," William said. "Don't you worry. If it doesn't take the trap then I've got other ways of making it pay."

Mattie thought then of Griffin and C.P. and their friend Jen, the one they were going to meet. What if they were still on the mountain? What if one of them got stuck in William's monster trap?

*You told them to leave. You warned them. If they don't go, it's not your responsibility.*

It wasn't her responsibility but she worried just the same. They were foolish, those boys—for that was what they were, for all that they looked like men. Tromping around in the woods looking for made-up creatures? They were like children searching for unicorns or fairies.

*You have to make the house just right or the fairy won't come live in it.*

Heather's voice. Heather's hands, carefully arranging tiny pieces of twig and rock and leaf, building fairy houses in the backyard.

*But how will we know if the fairy came to live here?*

Her own voice—no, Samantha's—tiny, childish, full of doubt.

*The fairies will leave something for us—an acorn or something like that, so that we'll know they used the house and want to say thank you.*

And the next morning they'd gone out—still wearing their pajamas—and ran in their bare feet over the damp grass to the edge of their lawn. The lawn went right up to the woods—they didn't have a fence, like some other people did—and they had been careful to build the fairy houses in the grass because Mom didn't let them go into the woods alone.

Mattie remembered flattening herself against the grass—the morning damp seeping through her favorite My Little Pony pajamas—and peering inside the fairy house.

*"There's something here! Heather, look!"*

Her own hand reached carefully inside to pull out a tiny, perfect pinecone.

Of course, no fairies had come. Mattie knew that now. Her mother must have gone out to the yard in the night and put the pinecone inside so that her girls could hold on to their belief a little longer, so that their world would stay dusted with magic.

Griffin and C.P.—they were like Samantha and Heather when they were small, still believing in the possibility of something, hoping for it with all their hearts.

*But they think they're going to find some benign creature, something that will wave at them while they take photos and sketches. They don't know there's a real monster out there.*

William had been walking around the cabin stuffing objects into his pack while Mattie drifted away in her mind. She was lucky he was so preoccupied with the creature in the woods, else she surely would have been punished for woolgathering.

She squeezed the water out of William's trousers and pinned them to the line, trying very hard not to think about the roll of money that had been in the pocket. If she thought about it, she might look at the place where she'd hidden it, and if she looked then William might wonder what she was looking at.

*Keep calm, keep safe. Hide in plain sight.*

Mattie noticed William stuffing some of the grenades into the backpack.

"William," she said, very carefully, very respectfully. "If you detonate those bombs, won't people hear and come investigate?"

"Don't worry," he said. "The only place I'm going to use them is up in that cave."

That got Mattie worrying about a cave-in, or a landslide. It didn't seem like a good idea to set off a grenade in the side of a mountain.

*What if Griffin and C.P. are up there and William blows them to pieces? Surely they have families that will come looking for them, and those families will find us.*

**(If they do then you can tell them that William killed their children and then the police will take William away and you'll be free, free, free)**

No, that was a terrible thought. Mattie didn't want to build her freedom on the bodies of people who'd only tried to be kind to her. But she was concerned that the group would run into William while he was out hunting the creature, and that the strangers would come to harm.

*If the creature hasn't killed them already.*

"I can tell you're worrying, Mattie girl," William said.

He stopped what he was doing and put his hand on her cheek, a gesture that nearly startled her into stepping away. William was never tender, or he hadn't been in so long that she didn't think he knew how to do it.

"I can see by the way your brow is furrowed," he continued. "But I don't want you to worry about me. I'm going to take care of that demon and keep us safe, and then I'll come home to you just like I always do."

*Don't come home,* she thought, but she made sure that the words stayed behind her eyes, deep inside where he couldn't see them.

"Of course," she said, and pushed a smile out so that he would know she believed him.

"Things are going to be better for us after this," William said. "I see that now. God sent this demon to try me, and when I defeat it, He'll finally bless us with sons as a reward. All things are as He means them to be. And when we have sons, Mattie—when you're finally a mother as you're meant to be—I won't have to punish you so often, because your heart will be content as all women's hearts are when they fulfill their purpose."

"Yes, William," she said, and lowered her eyes modestly to the ground and hid the fierce and burning sickness that had suddenly bubbled up in her throat. She didn't want his sons. The idea of being chained to him by another human being was repugnant. And she didn't want to think about how he might raise such a son, how William might train the boy to be just the image of his father.

*I must get away before he manages to get me pregnant again.*

"You're a good girl," William said, and kissed her forehead. "I know that God will bless us soon."

"Yes."

"I'm going to go set a few other traps in places where we saw its tracks," he said.

"Like snares?" Mattie asked, doubtful that a feeble piece of rope could capture such a monster.

"No, I'm going to dig a few pits," William said. "It will probably take me most of the day. I'll do one close to the cabin, back behind the outhouse, in case it decides to come back that way. The tracks led away in that direction after it left its unholy message in the snow. After that I'll head up the way we went yesterday and dig out another one."

*Pits*, Mattie thought. Pits were dangerous to people walking in the woods, people who didn't know that there was a madman living on the mountain trying to catch a demon.

She didn't have any way of warning them. There was nothing she could do.

"I brought some fresh bread and cheese yesterday," William continued. "You could have it as a treat for your lunch today."

Mattie half-wished there'd been a monster on the mountain always, for William had probably never been so nice to her as he was today.

"Thank you," she murmured. "You're always so good to me."

"I'll bring the food in from the storehouse and then I'll head out," he said, slinging his pack over his shoulder.

Mattie watched through the window as he went out to the storehouse. He unlocked the door with the key on his key ring, went inside, and emerged holding a loaf of bread and a hunk of yellow cheese wrapped in a cloth. Mattie went to the door to take the items from him so he wouldn't have to track snow inside.

"Eat as much as you like today," he said. "You need to get strong so my seed can take root."

And then he went off around the back of the cabin. Mattie closed the front door, placed the food on the table and went to the back window. William took his gardening spade out of the small wooden trunk that held their tools and slung it over his shoulder. He went off behind the outhouse. Mattie wondered how far he'd go, and if it was safe to try to fiddle with the lock on his special trunk again.

She cracked the window despite the cold, in hopes that she would be able to hear William working. Sure enough, the sound of the shovel scraping through snow drifted in. He wasn't far enough for Mattie to feel safe trying the trunk.

She placed the bread and cheese on the table.

*I used to love cheese sandwiches. American cheese on white bread with yellow mustard. I wouldn't let Mom pack anything else for me.*

She had a sudden, distinct memory of unzipping a hot-pink lunchbox and inside was a cheese sandwich wrapped in waxed paper and an apple and a Twinkie.

"A Twinkie," she murmured. "I'd forgotten about Twinkies."

She'd forgotten about so many things, and all those forgotten moments would emerge so abruptly that it sometimes made her feel sick and dizzy, the past lying over her present like two pieces of a puzzle that didn't fit together.

Mattie could almost taste the soft yellow cake with the cream in the middle, that first burst of sweetness on her tongue. She'd take very small bites to make her dessert last for as long as possible.

William never bought sweet things. They never had a cake or a pie because Mattie didn't have the flour or sugar to make them. She'd never asked, never thought to ask because after a while she'd forgotten about sweets, but she was sure that the reason they didn't have dessert was because it was not godly.

The sounds of William digging nearby continued, so Mattie busied herself with various chores around the cabin. She tried not to think about the money she'd hidden beneath the couch. How long would it be before William discovered it was gone? Would he even say anything to her about it? He generally seemed to pretend that money didn't exist, or at least that Mattie didn't know about it.

William had told her to eat as much as she liked, and the previous day Mattie would have, but now she was so nervous about the money she'd discovered that she didn't have much of an appetite. She forced herself to swallow a slice each of the bread and cheese, because he would be upset if she didn't eat when he told her to do so.

After a while the sounds of William's shoveling ceased. Mattie wondered if he'd moved on to another location yet, and if so, how far he'd gone. It wasn't safe for her to try to open the trunk if he was on his way back for lunch or to take a nap. He might have changed his mind altogether and decided not to dig the second pit today.

*He didn't tell me not to go anywhere. He didn't say I shouldn't leave the cabin.*

*(It's implied, though. You know it's implied. You're not supposed to leave when William isn't at home.)*

She could make him a cheese sandwich and wrap it in a cloth and go out to the place where he'd just been digging, and if he was resting there she could say that she thought he might be hungry from his work. Surely he couldn't be angry with her then. She was only trying to be a good wife, to look after her husband as she was supposed to do.

Mattie sliced off two thick pieces of bread and several slim pieces of cheese. William usually preferred sandwiches with meat in them, but any meat they had was in the storehouse and the storehouse was locked.

*No it isn't.*

Mattie's hands stilled. She'd watched William unlock the storehouse that morning and emerge holding the bread and cheese. She hadn't seen him lock it back up again.

*I could get some food and hide it somewhere for the night I escape.*

But where could she hide it? It would have to be somewhere outside, where it could stay cold. She couldn't put food underneath the couch. And it would have to be something she could eat without cooking—slices of ham and cheese and bread. It wouldn't do her any good to hide a hunk of venison. That kind of food would only attract a bear, anyway—a real bear, not the thing in the woods that was pretending to be a bear.

*Pretending to be a bear. Is that what the thing is doing? Is it copying other animals it has seen?*

That didn't make any sense at all. Why would a creature copy animal behavior?

"And where did it come from, anyway? It wasn't on this mountain with us all along. We would have known."

136

Griffin and C.P. said they were on the mountain because of a "sighting." Who had seen the creature besides Mattie and William? The animal must have migrated from somewhere nearby, and Griffin and C.P. had followed its trail somehow.

She tried to think about what all of this information meant, but she couldn't pull it together. Anyway, it wasn't time for her to worry about the creature or the strangers on the mountain. She wanted to leave William. She had to have a concrete plan.

Chance had given her that roll of money, which would help her when she reached a town. William's own preoccupation with the animal he called a demon had given her a second opportunity—to take food out of the storehouse and hide it away for the day she escaped.

She wanted to rush out to the storehouse right away, but she needed to think this through. First, she should continue with the plan to bring William a sandwich. Whether she was opening the storehouse or opening the trunk, she still needed to be certain that he was gone from the immediate area.

It had taken him at least two hours to dig the nearby pit, so if he'd moved on she would have at least that long to make her preparations. Mattie finished assembling the sandwich, wrapped it in a clean white cloth and tied a knot in the top. Then she pulled on her coat and wrapped her scarf tightly around her neck. Before she went out she made certain to close the cracked-open window, because even the small amount of cold air coming in had chilled the cabin. If William found the window open he would be annoyed, especially since he'd built up the fire and left enough wood for the cabin to stay warm while he was gone.

Mattie put on her boots and stepped outside the cabin. As she pulled the cabin door closed she noticed her hands were trembling. She'd never defied William so openly before.

*You can't be afraid. You have to be brave, or at least try. William's in such a good mood today that he's unlikely to punish you if he finds you outside.*

But finding her out of the cabin might cause his mood to change. And she knew his mood could change without warning, could flare up like a summer storm.

*You're only taking him a sandwich. You haven't done anything wrong. Not yet, anyway. If he finds you in the storehouse . . .*

Mattie would have to come up with some excuse for the storehouse. She could say she wanted to make him a special dinner. As long as she was behaving like a good wife then it would be all right.

*And what if it isn't? What if he beats you so badly that you can't walk or run?*

"Then I'll have to get better, and try again," she whispered. "I have to try."

She followed the path of William's footsteps in the snow, past the garden, past the outhouse and on. There was a little clearing after the outhouse, the fresh snow broken only by her husband's boots. Mattie continued in his steps until she reached the cool dark of the pines.

Her eyes took a moment to adjust, especially the left one, which still wasn't focusing as quickly as her right. She could still see William's trail in the snow. A little farther ahead she discovered the pit.

He'd chosen a place where there was already a depression in the ground—Mattie could see the shape of it in front of and behind the pit. Then he'd dug through the layer of snow and into the hard earth to make a hole about five feet long and the same distance deep.

Mattie knew that the creature was much, much larger than this tiny pit, and she wondered how William expected to catch it. Perhaps he only wanted it to stumble, to break a limb. She supposed that the pit was close enough to the cabin that William could run out and shoot the creature if he heard it fall in.

The dirt from the pit had been spread all over the path, covering the snow. Mattie thought this was to obscure the pit at night, when the snow seemed to glow white. If there were several feet of dark earth before the creature reached the hole then it was more likely to fall in.

She supposed that he might put some meat out to lure it, and then would cover the hole with pine boughs or some such thing. It seemed very cruel to her, almost as cruel as the shiny silver trap with its snapping mouth. Both were meant to hurt, to cause suffering before death. Mattie was afraid of the creature in the woods but she didn't think it should suffer. She didn't think they ought to be bothering with it at all, really. It had warned them and they should take that warning seriously.

It was clear that William had moved on from this area. She should go back and investigate the storehouse while she had the opportunity.

*But what if he's only gone a little way farther? You'd better be certain.*

She would walk only a little bit more, just to be sure that William wasn't just around the bend of the path. She knew she only had a short amount of time and she needed to use it.

Mattie followed the trail William had broken in the snow, the cloth-wrapped sandwich gripped tight in her hand. She didn't see any sign of him except his footprints, and after about a quarter of an hour she decided it was safe and she could turn around.

That was when she heard the voices.

# CHAPTER NINE

t wasn't just voices. It was men shouting—no, William shouting, and two others speaking loudly, but not as loudly as William.

*Griffin and C.P. Oh god, what are they doing so close to the cabin? Didn't I warn them? Didn't I tell them they needed to go far from here?*

Mattie didn't want William to see her, so she stepped off the path and into the cover of trees, moving slowly and carefully between the trunks until she was close enough to see. She was just behind the group, with William's back to her and the strangers' faces visible.

William stood in the center of the path, the shovel in his hands, and it was clear from his posture that he might swing it at one of the other men any moment now.

Griffin and C.P. stood side by side, and at C.P.'s shoulder was a woman nearly as tall as he was. She had long black hair spilling out of a red cap and her lips were pressed together so tightly that they were practically white.

*That's Jen,* Mattie thought. *Their friend. The one they were going to meet.*

"I'm saying it for the last time. You get off this mountain if you know what's good for you," William said.

Griffin had his hands up in a placatory manner, but his eyes and voice were hard. "And I'm telling you that you have no right to drive us off. This is public land. Your land ends back there. We saw the signs. You don't have the right to dig like this out here. It's dangerous for anyone passing through."

"I have the right to do whatever I want. This is my mountain, and God has given me a mission," William said.

Mattie saw Jen and C.P. glance at one another, their eyes saying that William was a crazy person.

C.P. gave Griffin's arm a little tug. "Maybe we should just go."

"No," Griffin said. "He doesn't have the right to send us off. He doesn't have the right to do any of this. And when we get back down to where there's cell service, I'm going to report him. Someone ought to report him for what he's done to that girl he calls his wife, anyway."

Mattie saw the muscles of William's back bunch up, his hands tighten on the handle of the shovel. His voice, when he spoke, was low and icy cold as the river in winter.

"What," he said, "do you know of my wife?"

*Oh, no,* Mattie thought. Panic bubbled up inside her. Why had Griffin said that? William would kill her if he knew that she'd seen two strange men at the cabin and not mentioned it to him.

"We saw what you did to her," Griffin said.

"Griff," C.P. said, and there was warning in his tone.

*No, no, don't say anything else, don't make it worse, you need to run, you need to run now before William hurts you, he's going to hurt you.*

Mattie knew she ought to run herself, ought to run back to the cabin and grab the money and anything else and fly down the mountain now, before something terrible happened. But she was frozen with fear, with indecision. Should she run, thinking only of herself? Or should she stay, and try to stop William?

*And how are you to stop him? You can't stop him from hurting you.*

"I don't know how you could have seen my wife," William said. "Because my wife has been in our home for the last two days, and if you saw her there then you came onto my private property. And if you came onto my private property and looked at my wife, who is also my property, then I have every right to defend what is mine."

Mattie saw it before Griffin did, because she knew it was coming. The flat end of the shovel swung out and connected with Griffin's ear. Griffin stumbled to one side of the path as C.P. and Jen shouted. William raised the shovel again.

*He's going to beat Griffin to death,* Mattie thought, and then she was running before she knew what she was doing, but running toward the fight instead of away from it as she knew she ought to do.

"William! William! Stop!" she shouted.

William turned at the sound of her voice, the shovel ready to swing. His eyes were colder than she'd ever seen them, the deep freeze of winter settled there.

"Have you come to defend your lover, little whore?" William spat. "Did you let him inside our home to plow your fields while I was away?"

"No," she said. "No, that didn't happen. But William, listen, you can't hurt them. If you hurt them then the police will come. You don't want the police to come, do you? You don't want anyone on the mountain. You told me so yourself."

He hesitated for a moment. She saw him thinking, considering. Mattie eased around him, staying out of swinging distance of the shovel, and peered at Griffin. The side of his face was coated in blood, and Mattie was sorry for it, sorry he was hurt.

Jen and C.P. helped him up and dragged him backward, so that they, too, were out of William's immediate reach.

*Good,* Mattie thought. *Run. Run away now.*

"William," Mattie said. "Please. Let's go home. Leave these people alone. They haven't done anything to you."

"He dallied with my wife. Is that not an offense?"

"No, William, he didn't. They came to the cabin but I didn't open the door. I didn't do anything."

"She didn't, man. She only opened the window and she wouldn't even come near it. She kept telling us we should leave the mountain," C.P. said, then added in a lower tone, "Now I know why."

Mattie knew that no matter what happened, William would beat her. There wasn't anything she could do to avoid that now. But if the others could get away she would be satisfied.

*Let them escape,* she thought. *If they escape they'll surely tell the police what they saw here, and then they'll come and take you from William.*

For a moment she faltered. William had always told her that no one would separate them, not even the police, so she shouldn't run away because they would just return her to him. Mattie belonged to William.

**He lied. Of course he lied. He wanted you to stay in the cabin, sweet and good and compliant.**

"You should leave," Mattie said to the three strangers. Griffin was struggling to his feet, swaying a little. "Just leave now, please. Get off the mountain."

"What about you?" Griffin said.

"She's my wife," William snarled. "She's no concern of yours."

"It is if you're going to beat her to death with that shovel!" Griffin said, starting toward William. C.P. grabbed the cloth of Griffin's jacket and pulled him back.

"Please," Mattie said. "Why won't you listen to me? Please leave before something terrible happens."

"Shut your mouth, Martha. You go back to the cabin and wait for me like you're supposed to. I'll deal with you after them."

Something snapped inside her, a strand of buried anger that she'd been barely aware existed.

"I'm not Martha. That's the name you called me, but it isn't who I am."

William stilled, the muscles in his face rippling under the skin. "Your name is Martha."

"Samantha," Griffin said. "Samantha. That's it!"

Everyone turned to look at him, his shout of realization completely out of place.

"Samantha! Samantha Hunter! I saw a picture of you on the news, one of those aged-up things they do in the computer, because it was the twelfth anniversary of . . ."

He faltered, a new realization in his eyes as he looked at William.

"Hey, that's right!" C.P. said, peering at Mattie. "Now I remember, too. They said you were . . . Oh, shit."

"What did they say?" Mattie asked.

"Don't say another word, boy," William said. His fingers were white on the handle of the shovel. "Don't say another word."

"What did they say?" Mattie asked again. "What did they say about me?"

"If you speak I will kill you," William said. "I will kill you where you stand."

Griffin pressed his lips together. Mattie sensed that he wasn't restraining himself because of William's threat, but because he was trying to be sensitive to her.

William shifted his weight, and Mattie glanced at him. Something had changed in his eyes. She saw realization, then calculation.

*He's going to kill them anyway.*

These people knew William had done something wrong. He couldn't have them going away and reporting that they'd found him.

*That's why he didn't want anyone on the mountain looking for the creature. That's why he never let me talk to anyone.*

But something puzzled her. If he was in danger of being arrested for a crime, how could he walk into town like anyone else? How could he shop and speak to people?

**They don't know he did anything wrong. You're the evidence. And if no one ever sees you then they won't know what he is.**

Griffin and C.P. and their thus-far-silent friend Jen knew. They could put William and Mattie together. And they could lead the police right to their door.

The three strangers were in more danger than they knew.

"Run, now," she said. "Run away. He's going to kill you. He can't have anyone know what he's done."

"I'm not leaving you here with him," Griffin said.

Mattie wanted to scream to the heavens. Griffin Banerjee was a very kind man, she could see that, but he needed to learn to listen when she spoke.

William moved then, like the sudden strike of a snake. Mattie saw the tensing of his muscles, knew exactly what was going to happen, and she darted in between him and the three strangers.

The shovel had been raised to strike a taller person than Mattie, so the edge of it only glanced off the side of her skull. It was enough to cut through her woolen hat and send her reeling, though. Blood poured down the side of her face, over her ear and down her neck. She heard Griffin and Jen and C.P. all shouting, their words a jumbled-up mess of noise.

"You goddamned little bitch!" William shouted. He was positively incandescent now, his fury brighter than she'd ever seen it. "How dare you stand in my way! How dare you defy me! YOU ARE MY WIFE! You are to obey me in all things!"

He threw the shovel to the ground and reached for her, his fingers closing around her neck.

*I knew it would come to this. I always knew I'd never be able to get away from him. It was only a dream, a silly girl's dream.*

His giant's hands squeezed her throat, his thumbs pressed against her windpipe, making her choke. She scrabbled at his arms with her hands, her small useless hands, her hands that had never been able to defend her from him.

"I should have killed you, too, long ago," he said as his hands stole her breath. "Useless little bitch. Couldn't even give me sons. I should have killed you after you lost the first one and got me a new wife, a better one, but I'd put so many years into you, training you in obedience, and I didn't want to waste my work. I should have killed you then like I killed your mother."

Her fingers stopped their fluttering movements as she stared into his ice-chip eyes.

*Killed your mother.*

*I killed your mother.*

William had killed her mother. Killed her mother and . . . stole her? Stole her away in the night?

*What about Heather? What happened to Heather?*

But she could hardly think now, because black spots were blooming before her eyes, black spots covered William's face and his ice-chip eyes and the truth that she'd forgotten. Forgotten because he'd made certain that she'd forget.

Then she saw Griffin standing behind William, saw the upraised shovel, saw it coming down on William's head. William's hands relaxed and she stumbled away, coughing.

If Griffin thought that one blow would take William down, he was soon proved wrong, for William turned on the younger man, growling like an animal. William punched Griffin in the stomach before Griffin could hit him again with the shovel. Mattie thought that William would wrench the weapon from Griffin, but just then, Jen stepped into the fray. She held a large rock in her right hand and she slammed it into the side of William's head with so much force that he staggered.

"Come on!" C.P. said, suddenly at Mattie's side, wrapping his arm under her shoulders to keep her upright.

It felt so alien to have a stranger touch her that she nearly jerked away, but she had barely enough energy to stand. Her body felt like a thing that wasn't attached to her head. She'd forgotten how to make all the parts move together. She slumped against C.P.'s side and he abruptly scooped her up into his arms.

"Jesus, there's nothing to you," C.P. muttered. He hurried away from William and Jen and Griffin, away from the direction of the cabin.

"Can't . . . leave . . ." Mattie said. "Can't . . . leave . . . them."

"I'm not," C.P. said, a little out of breath. He was carrying her as well as his gigantic pack, and even if she was small, it was still an extra burden on him. "They're coming right after us. Can't you hear them?"

Mattie tried to focus, to pick out some sound besides C.P.'s labored breathing and the rustle of his jacket. There. The sound of boots in the snow, and then Griffin saying to Jen, "I hope to God he stays down."

*William. They'd hit William and left him there in the snow.*

*William killed my mother.*

*Killed my mother.*

*I lived with him all these years and he'd killed my mother and I never knew.*

Tears flowed out of her eyes, running over her cheeks and mixing with blood on her face.

*I'll never see her again. I can't remember her face and now I'll never see her again.*

"I'm sorry, I have to put you down," C.P. said. "Do you think you can walk?"

She nodded, but he wasn't looking at her—he'd twisted his head around to see how close the others were following.

"Damn," he muttered, and released Mattie to the ground.

Her legs felt like water and she couldn't get them to prop her up. A second later she was folded up on the ground, her face in the snow.

"Ah, I'm sorry, I'm sorry," C.P. said.

His hands were at her shoulders, pulling her up, but she only managed to get to her knees. He noticed her tears then and she saw his look of alarm.

"Did I hurt you? I'm such a stupid klutz, I'm sorry. But you have to try to get up because that guy might come after us. I don't know how hard Jen hit him with the rock but he seemed like the Terminator type to me."

Mattie didn't understand what he was talking about with the Terminator, but she did understand that William would come after them. She'd run from him, so he would pursue. She understood this but she still couldn't make her body do what she wanted it to do. Every part of her wanted to curl up, to hide, to burrow beneath the snow so she could weep until she had no more tears.

"He . . . killed . . ." she said, and coughed. He'd bruised her throat again, and she'd hardly recovered from the last choking. She had no idea when she'd be able to speak again.

C.P. opened his mouth but whatever he was about to say was lost as Griffin and Jen finally caught up with them. Jen was half-dragging Griffin, her arm holding him up. The blow from the shovel looked much worse than the one that Mattie had taken. Griffin's face was drawn and he seemed to be barely holding on to consciousness.

"He can't walk," Jen said. "I think he might have a concussion."

"Her, too," C.P. said. "Every time she tries to walk she collapses."

"That motherfucker," Jen said, and the vulgarity was shocking to Mattie, who'd hardly ever heard William even say "damn." "I'd like to go back and hit him with his own shovel a few times."

"Was he down when you left?" C.P. asked.

"I didn't stop to look," she said. "I hit him twice in the side of the head with the rock, Griffin kicked him in the balls and then we started running. Well, running as much as we could with these packs on. Then Griffin started stumbling around like he was drunk. We can't stop here, though. We haven't gone very far, and once that guy gets up again, he'll follow us. We've left a pretty obvious trail."

She gestured behind her at the broken snow covered in their footprints.

"Go . . . down . . ." Mattie said, and coughed again.

"Why don't you give her some of your water, dummy?" Jen said to C.P.

"Oh, yeah," he said. "I forgot about water."

Jen rolled her eyes at Mattie, like they were sharing a joke. Mattie didn't really understand the joke but she felt a strange warmth in her chest, unwarranted by the small gesture. For a second it had been like having a sister again, having a person to share secret things.

C.P. fumbled a bottle off his pack and handed it to Mattie. She stared at it. It was bright red and had a black top and it looked so foreign after the metal cups she'd used in the cabin that for a moment she didn't know what to do with it.

"You unscrew this part," he said, taking it back from her and demonstrating.

"Thank . . ."

He waved his hands at her. "Don't try to talk. Just drink."

The water was very cold and it was hard to swallow, but she managed to force some down. She carefully screwed the top back on and handed it to him.

"I know you're in pain," Jen said, "but do you think you could walk a little if C.P. helps you?"

Mattie wondered why Jen thought she was in pain. Because her face was bloody? Then she realized she was still crying. The tears wouldn't stop. She swiped at her face with her mitten, but it didn't do any good.

"My . . . mother," she said, and gestured in the direction of William. "He . . . killed."

"You didn't know, did you?" C.P. asked.

Mattie shook her head, felt the grief swelling inside her, pushing against her skin, making her feel like she would burst. How could she live with this? How could she ever feel whole again?

*My mother is dead. What happened to Heather?*

What if William had killed her, too, killed her smiling sister who built fairy houses in the yard and danced with Mattie—not Mattie, Samantha—to loud music and built forts in the living room out of blankets and pillows? What would Mattie do then if there were no one to go home to?

*You're not going back to William no matter what.*

But she'd come away without the money she'd so carefully hidden, without any food or clothing.

"I'm really sorry," Jen said. She seemed to be feeling the effort of holding Griffin. Her face was tight and her voice strained. "About your mother, I mean. And I'm sorry it was such a crap way to find out about it. But we really have to run—or walk, or stumble, whatever. I've got a feeling that guy has a gun, and when he wakes up he's going to get it and then come after us."

Mattie nodded. "He . . . does. Gun."

C.P. gestured to Jen. "Let me take Griff. You take her."

"She has a name," Jen said. "Samantha."

It was strange to hear that name coming out of someone else's mouth, to hear someone else claim it on her behalf.

Jen passed Griffin to C.P. Griffin's eyes were rolling around in his head. He seemed to be barely conscious, and Mattie wondered how well he could walk even with assistance.

Jen held out a hand for Mattie to grasp. The other woman had a strong grip and she pulled Mattie up like Mattie was made of air. Mattie held tight to Jen's hand as her legs trembled. She wasn't sure if she could walk forward.

"You're just a little fairy thing, aren't you?" Jen said, scooping her arm around Mattie. Jen was much taller, almost as tall as William. The other woman smiled at Mattie to show that she didn't mean anything rude by her comment, and Mattie again felt that warmth bloom in her chest. She looked down at the ground, though. She didn't know if she ought to be so familiar with someone she'd just met.

**Someone who saved you. Someone who did what you should**

**have done to William years ago—hit him in the head with a rock until he stopped moving.**

Mattie would never forget how fierce Jen had looked, how she hadn't hesitated.

**You used to be like that. You were fearless until William beat it out of you. You need to stop thinking the way he taught you to think.**

They all shuffled along in the snow like weird three-legged animals, Griffin supported by C.P. and Mattie supported by Jen. Jen's long hair was loose under her cap and it kept tickling Mattie's face. Mattie was suddenly conscious of her homemade dress, her heavy coat and boots.

Jen wore trousers like the men—*jeans, they're called*—and a brightly colored jacket made of some soft material under a puffy vest. She seemed warm and comfortable and able to move easily, and Mattie was wearing clothes that trapped her, held her in place.

She was unable to stop herself from checking over her shoulder frequently for William. He'd never let Mattie go now, not when she knew his secret.

*I killed your mother.*

That was what he'd said. He'd killed her mother.

*I can't remember her face, and now I'll never see it again.*

"I gotta take a break," C.P. said.

They'd reached a place where there were several large boulders clumped up together. One of them had a low flat top, perfect for sitting. C.P. carefully lowered Griffin to the boulder and sat down beside his friend. Griffin slumped backward immediately, his body propped at a strange angle by his large pack.

"Get his pack off him," Jen said.

C.P. helped Griffin out of his pack and propped it under Griffin's head. Griffin closed his eyes.

"Don't go to sleep," Jen warned. "That guy could pop out of the woods at any minute."

She turned to Mattie. "You should probably sit down, too, and let me take a look at your head."

Mattie perched on the edge of the rock near Griffin. Jen took Mattie's hat off and Mattie saw the other woman flinch when she looked at the wound.

"It doesn't look too good," Jen said, wrinkling her nose. "It's clotting, but it's pretty long. You're lucky it's shallow, though."

"Lucky," Mattie said. Her voice was still small and strained.

"I bet it doesn't feel too lucky, though," Jen said with a little laugh.

Mattie gave her a half-smile back and shook her head. "Where . . . are . . . we . . . going?"

"Dunno," C.P. said. "I just wanted to get away from that nutjob."

Mattie said, "Down . . . the . . . mountain. Away."

"It takes about a day or so to get back to the base when we're all in good shape and moving along, and there's no snow to slow us down. With you and Griffin like this, it will take a lot longer, and I don't think either of you are in any condition to do a lot of walking. We need to find someplace to hole up for a day or so and rest before we try."

"A . . . day?" Mattie shook her head. "William . . . goes . . . to . . . town . . . and back. Same day."

"Well, I don't know how he does that unless he's got a vehicle, like an ATV or something. You just can't do the hike that quickly no matter what kind of shape you're in," Jen said.

"ATV?" Mattie asked.

"All-terrain vehicle. Like a little car, but with big wheels so it can go over rough ground. Does he have something like that?" C.P. asked.

"No," she said. "I've . . . never . . . seen."

Though now that she considered it, of course it made sense that William might have some kind of vehicle stashed away somewhere. How else could he have brought up all the heavy gear he'd bought the other day? Did she really believe that William had dragged it all up the mountain on a sled?

If he did have a vehicle he'd made certain that she didn't know of its existence, and the key would certainly be on his key ring. Which was on his person, and they'd never get it off him as long as he lived.

Not that it would do her any good if she found a vehicle, in any case. She didn't have the least idea of how to operate one.

Mattie shivered. She'd been sweaty from the exertion of the fight and the fast pace, but now that they were sitting still her body was cooling. Jen noticed and sat down next to her, so that all four of them were crammed on the flat lip of the boulder. Jen put her arm around Mattie's shoulder and pulled her close.

"You're not dressed for this weather," she said, rubbing her hand up and down Mattie's arm. "And it will be dark in a few hours. We need to find a safe place to pitch the tents and start a fire."

"We should go up to those caves," C.P. said. "You know, the ones where we saw the tracks."

Mattie stiffened. "You . . . went . . . to . . . the . . . caves?"

"Yeah," C.P. said, his eyes alight with enthusiasm. "We saw that weird cave with all the bones and stuff that you told us about, too. I've got some amazing pictures on my phone, and Griffin has even better ones on the camera."

"No," Mattie said. Her throat hurt so much. Every time she spoke she saw William's mad face above her, felt his hands on her throat again. But she needed to tell them, to warn them again. "No . . . no. Creature . . . warned . . . us. Can't . . . go . . . there."

The idiots. The absolute idiots. She'd told them not to follow the creature, not to play in things they didn't understand. They hadn't listened.

There came an unearthly roar, almost as if the creature had heard what they were saying, or had caught their scent. It wasn't too close, but it wasn't far enough away for Mattie to feel safe, either.

"What was that?" Jen asked. She didn't look scared, though. She looked curious, and a little excited—just like C.P.

"Creature," Mattie said. She stood up so quickly that her head spun. "Hide."

"Creature? You mean the thing that made the tracks on the mountain? I want to see it," C.P. said.

"No . . . no," Mattie said. She wanted to shake him. What kind of person saw a room of bones and organs and thought, *I really want to meet the animal that mutilated all these other animals?* "You . . . don't. Will . . . kill . . . you."

"It didn't kill you, right? You said you saw it. It came right up to your house."

The creature roared again, and this time it sounded different.

It sounded louder—and angrier. The roar echoed all around them, all through the forest—bouncing off the trees, filling up the air, echoing inside Mattie's ears so that she had to cover them with her mittened hands or else that sound would seep inside her head and stay there.

She hunched over, closing her eyes, vaguely aware of the cries of the other three people—their surprise, their fascination. After several moments the sound faded away, though something seemed to still linger in the air—an undefined malice that made Mattie want to hide away forever so that she might never cross the creature's path.

"That was awesome!" C.P. said.

Jen was smiling, and even Griffin had sat up and was staring around with an excited light in his eyes.

C.P. held some kind of device up in the air. It was flat and black and completely foreign to her. Mattie saw him draw it close to his face and tap on it. A moment later the creature's sound emitted from the device again.

"Stop," she said. She wanted to shout it but the small amount of talking she'd already done had strained her voice close to the breaking point. She flapped her arms so he would get the picture.

"Why? It's amazing! I didn't think we'd be able to capture a cry like that. We might even be able to get some video," C.P. said.

How could she explain? How could she make them understand? She could hardly talk and they didn't want to listen anyway. William was after them, and now the creature would be, too. There wasn't anywhere on the mountain where they would be safe.

# CHAPTER TEN

Jen noticed Mattie's distress and grabbed Mattie's wrists to stop the flapping.

"I know you're trying to tell us something, but I don't think you should try to talk right now. It's hurting me just listening to you. Do you think you could write it out?"

Mattie shook her head. "Can't . . . write."

Though that wasn't exactly true, she realized. She used to be able to write—or rather, Samantha could write. She had a vague memory of Samantha practicing her letters at the kitchen table—but she hadn't done it in so long that she didn't think she'd be able to write out anything legible.

"Creature . . . is . . . angry," she said. Her throat was at a breaking point, but they needed to hear her. "Don't . . . approach. Will . . . hunt . . . us . . . because . . . caves."

She hated the way she sounded, like a child who didn't know

how to talk. But she needed to make them understand the important thing—stay away from the creature.

"I don't understand what you mean, 'because caves,'" Jen said. "Are you saying that the cryptid is going to come after us because we went into its bone cave?"

Mattie nodded.

"But that's ridiculous. It's not human. It doesn't think like a human."

Mattie wanted to scream. Even Jen, who Mattie was certain would be sensible, didn't believe. They were all willing to believe in the existence of an animal they'd never seen before but they weren't willing to believe it could think and reason.

"Not . . . like . . . human. But . . . not . . . like . . . animal . . . either. Warned . . . us."

Griffin, who seemed to be barely following the thread of the conversation up to that point, spoke up. "You said that the marks near your cabin were a warning because you went into the caves."

Mattie nodded again, though she was worried about Griffin. His words were slurred together, and he seemed to have trouble focusing his eyes anywhere.

"So you're saying that because we—me and Jen and C.P.—went into the caves after the cryptid warned you to stay away, that it will come after us, all of us?"

Mattie nodded once more. She thought her head would fall off if she kept shaking it around like that. Anyway, at least one of them understood, or seemed to. She hated the way they kept using that word, "cryptid," though. It implied something benign, and the creature was not benign.

"So the wackaloon with the shovel is after us, and the cryptid is after us, too?" C.P. said. "Just what are we supposed to do here? There's no cell service, you and Griffin are on the injured list, and all we have to keep us safe are our tiny nylon tents."

Mattie had been thinking about this ever since she heard the creature's roar. The important thing was that at least one of them got off the mountain to get help—or better yet, all three of them.

"You . . . take . . . Griffin. Go . . . down . . . the . . . mountain. William . . . will . . . follow . . . me."

If Mattie stayed behind then the three of them would be safe from William. He'd only be interested in getting his wife back. The creature would probably follow her and William, as well, because it knew the scent of them and even where they lived. The three strangers would be able to escape, and Mattie would only have to worry about keeping out of William's grasp until they returned with the police.

"No way," Jen said. "Forget it. We're not leaving you up here with your kidnapper."

Kidnapper. That was the word for what William was. Of course William had kidnapped her, though she couldn't seem to remember that part. She only remembered William coming in the window—her bedroom window. It was the first time anyone had said "kidnapper" out loud, though, the first time it was explicitly acknowledged.

"You . . . get . . . police," Mattie said. "They . . . arrest . . . William."

"By the time we get down the mountain and then back to you he'll have chopped you up with an axe," Jen said. "We already know he's a murderer."

She covered her mouth with her hand then, her eyes appalled.

"I'm sorry," Jen said. "I'm sorry I'm so stupid. It was like I didn't remember who I was talking to for a second. I guess I'm more stressed out than I thought."

"Gee, I wonder what's stressing you out?" C.P. said. "Could it be that we're all going to die?"

"We're not going to die," Griffin said. He sounded worse every time he spoke. "But I do need to take a nap before we run anywhere."

"You can't take a nap here. It's too exposed," Jen said. She turned to Mattie. "You said we shouldn't go back to those caves up by that meadow. Are there other caves, maybe nearby, that we could use?"

They all looked at her expectantly. Mattie acutely felt the limitations of her life in the cabin then, her lack of knowledge about the environment in which she'd lived for more than a decade.

"Don't . . . know. William . . . not . . . allow . . . me . . ."

She trailed off. It would take too many words to explain that there were very few places she was allowed to go without William.

Jen watched Mattie closely, and Mattie felt a sudden flush of shame. How could Mattie explain to this woman, this woman so free and easy and independent, how one man had kept Mattie locked in a cabin for so many years? How could she explain that after a time she'd *allowed* him to do that? Mattie should have fought. She should have run. She should have tried harder, instead of just accepting her fate.

Jen's hand was taking Mattie's then, gripping it tight. "Whatever happened wasn't your fault. You were only a child when he took you."

"Eight years old, right?" C.P. said. "That's what it said on the news."

Mattie wanted to ask what else they knew, what else had been said on the news, if they knew anything about Heather, but Jen gave C.P. a quelling look and he went back to tapping his flat black box.

A third roar sounded through the woods, this one longer and fiercer than the last two. Mattie covered her ears again, and this time the other three did as well. As she hunched over, trying to block out the sound that leaked through, she had a strange thought. The creature sounded slightly different. It wasn't the triumphant cry it had made when it found its prey in the woods, not the cry of anger and warning it had given when it had stalked Mattie through the woods to the cabin. This call was still angry, but there was something else underneath it. What was it?

*Hurt. It's hurt, and it's . . . scared?*

"Trap," she said, and she didn't realize she'd said it out loud until the other three looked at her. "William's . . . trap. Bear . . . trap. For . . . creature."

Mattie had thought that the creature would be too smart to be caught, or that the trap wouldn't be large enough for the enormous thing, but maybe it had stepped inside the trap just so.

"That guy put out a bear trap for the cryptid?" C.P. sounded outraged. "Sure, the scientific find of the century and he's going to catch it in a trap and put its head on his wall."

"You think it got caught in the trap?" Jen asked. "Or fell into a pit?"

"If it did then that's good for us," Griffin said. His words came out of his mouth at half-speed, and he was clearly working hard to hold on to consciousness. "We can find a place to pitch our tents for the night and we won't have to worry about it finding us."

"Yeah, but we don't know for sure," Jen said. "Where did he— William—put the bear trap?"

"Path . . . to . . . stream. From . . . our . . . cabin," Mattie said. She pointed in the direction from which they had come.

"So the opposite direction from here," Jen said, and sighed. "I'd like to verify that the animal was caught, but I don't think it's smart to go back in the direction of the angry man with the shovel."

"And . . . gun," Mattie said.

*And knives, and grenades, and all sorts of other weapons you haven't even thought of yet.*

When Mattie considered it, she realized that William didn't even have to stalk them through the woods. He could follow them from a distance and shoot them with his rifle, or find a high ridge to perch on and then drop grenades on their heads.

"Must . . . go," she said, standing up. "Off . . . mountain."

C.P. had put away the strange black device and pulled something else out of his pocket—a compass. He peered at it closely. "Trouble is, we're going in the wrong direction to get back to the base of the mountain. The top of the mountain is west, and the base is east. We've been moving west."

"And east is where William is," Griffin said.

"We'll just have to find a way to circle around him," Jen said.

"How? You can see every step we take in the snow," C.P. said, gesturing at the path they'd taken. The ground-up evidence of their passage was clear for anyone to see.

Mattie looked up at the sky hopefully. If another squall moved in then it would cover their tracks, but there wasn't a sign of clouds.

"Have . . . to . . . try," she said. "Can't . . . stay."

"Samantha is right," Jen said, and Mattie felt that same startled shock as before, hearing the name she'd only just rediscovered. "We have to try. And anyway, we might get lucky. William might be too incapacitated to do anything."

"You don't think we killed him, do you?" Griffin asked. His voice was so low that Mattie barely made out his words.

"If we did, I don't think it's any loss to the world," Jen said. Her tone was light, but Mattie noticed the flicker of unease in her eyes. "And if he isn't dead, I don't think he's going to report us to the authorities."

"No, he'll just kill us," C.P. said.

He was clearly joking, or trying to, but Mattie nodded.

"Yes. Kill us," she said, and she looked at each one to make sure they understood. Once more she pushed through the pain, the reminder of the last time William had touched her. "You . . . took . . . me. I . . . am his wife. So you will . . . be . . . punished."

She needed them to understand this, even though they ignored her warnings about the creature in the woods. If William hadn't been knocked out by the blow Jen had given him with the rock, then he would follow them. He would follow them and take whatever justice he deemed necessary. He didn't feel himself bound to the same rules as other people. He didn't consider himself a part of society. These strangers were on *his* mountain, he would think, and on his mountain, his word was law.

"He can't just kill people who do things he doesn't like," Jen said.

"Yes," Mattie said.

Jen stared at Mattie.

"All the more reason to move as fast as we can," C.P. said, checking the compass again. "I'll keep checking for a cell signal.

Maybe we can get a rescue team up here so we don't have to walk the whole way. Hell, if they know you're up here, Samantha, there will probably be news helicopters and everything else. In the meantime, we have to move east. Maybe slightly southeast, to see if we can angle away from the cabin."

He scooped Griffin under the shoulders again. Griffin seemed to be trying hard to stay awake, but Mattie saw his head lolling and his eyes rolling back and forth. They didn't need to walk. They needed to find someplace safe for Griffin to sleep.

The sound of crackling branches came from the forest behind them, filling the air. *Crack, crack, crack. Crack, crack, crack.* Mattie froze, her heart pounding so loudly she was certain the creature could hear it.

"What is it?" Jen asked.

"Creature," she said.

"The cryptid?" C.P. asked, swinging around with Griffin to peer into the woods they'd just passed through. "Damn, I can't get my phone out to take a picture. Jen, you get yours."

"No," Mattie said, giving him a little push. "Go."

"But I want . . ."

"Go," she said, and wished she could put more force in her tone.

The crackling of the branches seemed to draw closer and closer, but Mattie couldn't be certain. Sound echoed strangely on the mountain, and everything was so still that every noise was amplified.

Another cry rent the air, a cry that made Mattie take an involuntary step forward. It wasn't the creature this time. It was a human cry, a cry of agony so terrible that it curdled the blood. Mattie felt bumps rise up all over her skin.

It sounded like William. It sounded like he was dying.

So the creature was not in the trap then, or it had managed to free itself very quickly. If that was the case then it was unlikely to be seriously injured, and there would be nothing to stop it from pursuing them.

"That sounded like . . ." Jen began, then trailed off.

Everyone already knew who it was, and what it sounded like. There was no need to speak of it. The knowledge was there on their faces.

"What should we do?" C.P. said. "It sounded like he was attacked or something."

For the first time he didn't sound excited by the prospect of encountering his unknown animal. He sounded shaken.

"Should we help?" Jen asked.

*Help*, Mattie thought. *Should we help the man who kidnapped me, who killed my mother, who beat me for years, who attacked these people for no reason?*

"Fuck that guy," Griffin said, his words slurred but clear enough to be understood.

They all looked at Mattie, who understood that the final decision was hers to make.

"Go," she said.

She couldn't be certain, but she thought they all seemed relieved. Relieved not to encounter William again, or relieved not to face the creature that suddenly seemed dangerous in their eyes?

They began their slow progress again. As they walked, Mattie felt unease bubbling inside her throat. She kept glancing over her shoulder.

"Won't we hear it coming?" Jen asked when Mattie did this for the fourth time.

Mattie shook her head. "Only . . . if . . . it . . . wants."

Jen looked skeptical. "Whatever made that noise we heard, that roar—that sounded like something pretty big. I don't know how it could sneak up on us."

Mattie thought of her terrible night in the woods alone, how she hadn't known the creature was there until it was almost too late.

"It . . . can," she said.

Jen gave Mattie a curious look. "It sounds like you know."

Mattie nodded, but didn't try to explain any more. It was too difficult to talk at the moment. She saw C.P. checking the compass he held in his left hand. His right arm was around Griffin, who was barely upright. Suddenly they stopped. Mattie and Jen walked a few feet behind them, and Mattie was too short to see what made them halt.

"Fuck," C.P. said.

"What?" Mattie said.

He pointed ahead, and Mattie and Jen moved up beside them to see.

There were still several feet of path ahead, but then it ended abruptly in a drop-off.

"That's the *exact* direction we need to go," C.P. said. He gently let Griffin off his shoulder, and the other man slumped in a sitting position on the ground. "Southeast. But unless you've got rappelling gear in your pocket, we've got to turn around and find another way down."

"Maybe we can follow the cliff for a while?" Jen asked.

"The face of the cliff is running east-west," he said. "So either we go directly east, which is really the way we need to go anyway but there's a supposedly huge killer monster in that direction eating up the guy who tried to beat us with a shovel. Or we go the other way and end up on the top of the mountain where the monster lives, which also happens to *not* be in the direction of home and/or the police."

"No need to be an ass," Jen said. "I only asked a question."

"A dumb question," C.P. said.

"Fuck off," she said, her face flushing. "What do you want to do, C.P.? We obviously can't jump off the mountain and land at the bottom, so we've got to go in one direction or the other."

"Why did I get picked to be the captain?" C.P. said, then pointed at Mattie. "Why doesn't she tell us the best way to go? She's the one who's lived here forever."

Mattie started. She'd felt herself shrinking backward, shrinking inwards while they argued. Shouting meant hitting. Hitting meant pain.

"Don't try to drag her into your stupidity," Jen said. "She already said that asshole never let her leave the cabin. She's a *kidnap victim*. How's she supposed to know the best way to go?"

C.P.'s face flushed the same angry red as Jen's.

*Warning. It's a warning. Don't argue with him. Don't contradict. Don't.*

"Don't," she said to Jen, tugging at her sleeve, trying to pull her backward.

Mattie stumbled, her heels catching in a protruding root buried in the snow. She fell onto her bottom, and everything spun and ached but she kicked at the snow with her boots, trying to find purchase, trying to move away, away from the shouting and the noise and the place where she would be punished for not knowing where to go and what to do.

"Hey," C.P. said, his face changing. "Hey, what's the matter?"

"You were shouting, you idiot," Jen said, but her own voice was much softer now, her tone gently chiding instead of angry. "And I was, too. I'm sorry. I'm sorry we scared you."

Jen crouched down in the snow, her hand out, like she was trying to lure a small frightened animal to her palm. "It's okay now. It's okay."

"Hit . . . you," Mattie said, looking from Jen to C.P. and back again. "Punish."

C.P. looked outraged. "I would never hit a girl! Or a woman, for that matter. What kind of man do you think I am?"

"I think," Jen said, very softly, "it's more the kind of man that *he* was."

Mattie's heart was still rabbiting away in her chest, but the sense of panic receded. She looked at Jen, and saw something that made Mattie turn her head away in shame.

Pity.

The other woman pitied her.

That pity made everything she'd endured somehow worse than before, made all the years of hurt and fear bloom afresh.

"Sorry," Mattie said. "I . . . didn't . . ."

"It's okay," Jen said again. "It's okay."

"We've gotta find somewhere to rest," C.P. said. "We're all half out of our minds. I can't remember the last time I ate, and Samantha and Griffin are dead on their feet."

"Not . . . cave," Mattie said. She might not be certain how to get off the mountain, but she was absolutely certain that they should not go in the direction of the caves.

"I don't really know that the wacko with the shovel is a better option," C.P. said.

"We've got to go in one direction or another," Jen said. "We might as well try to make some progress going down."

They both glanced at Griffin, looking for his opinion, but his eyes were closed.

"Griffin?" Jen said, kneeling in front of him and tapping the side of his face. "Griffin, come on."

Griffin's eyes cracked open, but it was clearly a struggle. "Want to sleep."

"You can't sleep yet," Jen said. "Come on, you have to wake up. It's not safe here."

*It's not safe anywhere,* Mattie thought, but as she watched Jen and C.P. try to bully Griffin into waking and standing, she realized they had no choice but to find a place to stop and rest.

*But not here. It's too exposed here. We're too close to William.*

Of course, William might be dead already, killed by a creature that he'd angered with his trap. And even if he wasn't dead then surely he was seriously injured. He wouldn't be able to chase after them—at least not right away.

The back of Mattie's neck itched. She was still sitting in the snow, and she pulled herself up, using a tree trunk as a prop. She clung to the tree, her eyes darting all around.

*Something's near.*

*Something's watching.*

The woods had gone silent, the way they always did when the creature was close.

Jen and C.P. were loudly cajoling Griffin to wake up, to stand up.

"Shhhhhh," Mattie said.

She stared up into the heavy canopy of the pines and realized then what good cover it was for the creature—a permanent camouflage, never lost in the winter.

The other three didn't seem to have heard her.

"Qu-quiet," she said, much louder than she'd intended.

They stopped their fussing then, and Jen said, "What is it?"

"It's . . . near," Mattie whispered.

"The cryptid?" C.P. said.

Mattie put her finger to her lips, then signed that they should both help Griffin up. She didn't know why she was bothering to be quiet—surely the creature could sniff them out—but her instinct, when faced with danger, was to make herself as small and unnoticeable as possible.

Jen moved toward Mattie, to help her, but Mattie shook her head. She still felt wobbly but she thought she could walk—or at least hurl herself from tree to tree as she'd done when William abandoned her in the woods. Griffin, on the other hand, seemed to be unconscious, and C.P. would not be able to carry Griffin on his own.

*If I can only let them get ahead of me, they'll be safe. The creature wants me, me and William. We're the ones it warned.*

*(But how do you know it only wants you? The other three went into its cave, too.)*

Mattie's teeth chattered. Her tongue felt heavy and numb inside her mouth. She didn't know the right thing to do. She didn't know how to save all of them, or even herself.

She pointed in the direction of the cliff, then east, the way that C.P. said they needed to go. If they followed the cliff for a while they'd surely find a place where they could turn south again. Maybe they could even find the stream. She knew for certain that the stream ran into the river, and the river would take them down the mountain. Plus, if they reached the stream from here, Mattie knew that they would avoid the cabin and William.

C.P. started dragging Griffin, but Jen didn't move. She stared at Mattie.

"What are you doing?" she whispered.

Mattie waved her hand, indicating that they should go.

"No," Jen said. Her voice was low but she sounded furious. "Don't get any funny ideas about distracting it, or sacrificing yourself to save us. You go with us or none of us do."

Mattie's fists clenched. Why would these strangers never listen to her? Why wouldn't they let her help? They had helped her. They'd saved her from William. Now she wanted to return the favor and they were balking.

"Go," Mattie whispered.

Jen shook her head, and C.P. said, "No way."

Mattie clamped her lips together in frustration. Her teeth clacked against one another inside her closed mouth. The creature was very close. She could feel it. Her eyes searched the pines, looking for some sign.

The creature's eyes stared down at her.

Mattie gasped and stumbled back, away from the tree she'd clung to. It was directly above them.

She didn't know how it managed to heave its enormous bulk up so high, but somehow it did. She didn't know how it had gotten so close without making a sound, either. They'd heard the branches breaking earlier.

*It can move silently when it wants to. It followed you through the woods and you almost didn't realize at all. You only hear it approaching if it chooses.*

She couldn't see any of it except its eyes, and even that wasn't exactly right—she couldn't make out their color or their shape, only the matched gleam of them so far above.

"What is it?" Jen hissed.

"Go," Mattie said, backing into the three of them, never taking her eyes from the creature's eyes. "Go, go, go."

C.P. looked up, squinting into the trees. "Is it there?"

Mattie almost moaned in frustration. *They have no sense of self-preservation. When I say "go," it doesn't mean "stay and attract the monster's attention."*

Jen finally caught Mattie's mood and indicated to C.P. that they should go. The two of them limped ahead, dragging Griffin between them, and Mattie backed away slowly, her eyes on the creature.

*We don't mean you any harm,* she thought. *Please, leave us alone.*

The creature didn't move. Mattie kept her eyes locked on its eyes until she had to turn or risk falling off the cliff.

Just as she turned she realized something, and the realization made her lungs constrict.

There wasn't one set of eyes watching them.

There were two.

# CHAPTER ELEVEN

Mattie stumbled along in the wake of the other three. They were moving along the cliffside, and they could see the cliff continuing ahead for quite some time.

*Why didn't they attack us back there? We were vulnerable, injured—surely an animal smart enough to stalk us through the forest would be smart enough to see that.*

She didn't have any answers. She only knew that it *had* let them go. She couldn't shake the feeling, though, that it was somehow worse that it had—that there was something more terrible waiting in store for them.

"It's getting dark," C.P. said. His breath was ragged. "I don't want to pitch the tents by moonlight."

It *was* getting dark. Mattie hadn't even noticed the sun going down. Her mind was full of what she'd seen, or thought she'd seen.

*Two* creatures? How?

And where had they come from in the first place? Mattie and William had lived on this mountain for years and never seen any sign of such things. How could two such enormous animals suddenly appear out of nowhere?

*You know what William would say. They are demons, sent to test you.*

But Mattie didn't believe in demons.

A rifle shot pierced the air.

The four of them stopped dead simultaneously, as if given an order—or rather, three of them stopped and Griffin lolled in between Jen and C.P. Mattie spun around, certain William would be right behind them.

There was nothing and no one, only the broken trail of snow and the cliff and the trees that never seemed to end.

"I don't think it was nearby," Jen said, and pointed. "It sounded like it came from that way."

If William was strong enough to go back to the cabin for his rifle, then the creature must not have harmed him as much as Mattie had thought—or hoped.

**(Die why couldn't you just die you killed my mother and you stole me away I wanted you to die)**

"Hurry," she said. If they got a little farther then maybe the dark would cover their tracks, make it harder for William to follow them.

"We really can't hurry," C.P. said. "In case you hadn't noticed, our friend has a head injury and can't walk."

"Stop being such a sarcastic jerk," Jen said. "She's only worried."

"And I'm not?" C.P. grumbled. "We came up here to do some

research and now we're in a horror movie with a monster and an unkillable redneck with a gun."

Jen retorted something but Mattie wasn't really listening. She couldn't stop herself from checking behind them frequently, looking for William's silhouette on the trail.

The air was getting colder as it grew darker, but Mattie still didn't see any sign of clouds. The only way they could hide their trail from William was if snow fell in the night. Without the cover of a fresh layer, then all he'd have to do is follow their tracks.

*And the creature can probably track us by sound or smell, so there's nothing we can do to keep it from us.*

Her stomach churned. The thought of William or the creature catching up to them made her want to throw up. She didn't know which of them frightened her more.

*William. If William catches up to you, it's a lifetime of hell for you. The creature can kill you in an instant.*

*Or creatures. If there actually are two and it wasn't a figment of your imagination.*

Mattie didn't have any idea how far they'd gone from the site where William had attacked. She knew they'd walked in a circle, or something like it, as they'd hurried away from William in the direction of the caves and now they were going back toward the cabin. Maybe they'd already gone past it.

"That's it," C.P. said, stopping so suddenly that Jen only kept Griffin from tipping forward just in time. "I can't walk anymore."

"We can't stop here," Jen said before Mattie could protest. "We're out in the open."

They were directly in the center of a trail, but there was another clump of large boulders to their left, on the forest side, and the trees rose up over them. The cliffside hadn't changed—it was still a steep drop-off to a ground that was far below. Mattie wondered when they would encounter the stream that was close to the cabin. It seemed they'd gone a long way from the place where she'd lived.

"It's not that exposed," C.P. said.

Mattie could see his point. The boulders seemed to provide a kind of cover, something sturdy to lean against. But the four of them were still easy to see, easy to find, especially since they had just stopped a few inches away from their snow trail.

"We can't keep going like this. Even with two of us we can't carry Griffin fast enough to get away from that guy if he's got a gun."

"So, what, we're just going to lay down here and let him find us and shoot us in our sleep?" Jen said.

"We have to pitch the tents now. The light is going to be gone very soon."

"We can't pitch the tents. Are you crazy? We have to get Griffin out of here and into cell phone range as soon as possible. He's been out cold for the last half hour. He's going to need a helicopter."

"Jen, we can't just keep trudging forward until we all collapse."

*Why not?* Mattie wanted to ask. That's exactly what she had done the day William abandoned her in the woods. And if C.P. truly understood the danger they were in, he wouldn't suggest stopping.

Mattie recognized that all of them were hungry and exhausted, including herself, but she couldn't imagine feeling safe inside a tent.

Her memory of tents was limited to a play tent that she and

Heather had pitched in the yard, a small pink-and-purple cabin for small children to run in and out of. Even if the tents that the others carried were sturdier than her play tent, they were still only cloth, and cloth was easily torn by claws or broken by bullets.

"Look, I've gotta eat something or I'm going to pass out, too," C.P. said. "Let go of him."

"We can't just drop his unconscious body in the snow," Jen said, clinging to Griffin's shoulder even as C.P. released him. "He's going to get hypothermia."

"Wait," C.P. said, slinging his large pack off his back and rummaging around in it. He removed a small object that Mattie couldn't quite make out in the gloom and waved it at Jen. "Wrap him in this. I keep them for emergencies."

"Good idea," Jen said.

"She actually said I had a good idea," C.P. said to Mattie. "I should mark this day on the calendar."

"Unwrap it for me, dummy," Jen said, handing the item back to C.P.

"Aaand everything's back to normal," he said, pulling off the wrapping and unfolding the object.

It was a large silver blanket, very shiny even in the deepening gloom.

"It's a space blanket," C.P. said in response to Mattie's questioning look. "They don't look like much but they really do keep you warm, and they don't take up a lot of room in your pack."

Jen and C.P. carefully wrapped Griffin in the blanket and lowered him down to the snow, propping him against one of the boulders. Griffin didn't move or protest. His eyes were closed and he appeared completely unconscious.

Mattie shivered. Now that they'd stopped moving and the sun was gone, she realized how cold it was and how unprepared she was—for the second time in just a few days—to be out in it.

**(Think how disappointed William would be if you died of the cold instead of at his hand)**

*I'm not going to die. I'm going to get off this mountain. I'm going to tell people what he did, what he did to me and my mother.*

C.P. and Jen were both rooting around in their packs. C.P. threw several items out in the snow.

"Take something," he said to Mattie. "You have to be starving."

She stared at the variety of wrapped objects. It was packaged food, something she hadn't seen in a very long time, and most of it was unrecognizable except for one item.

Even in the deepening gloom she could see the word on the package clearly, white letters against a dark background.

HERSHEY'S

"Can . . . I . . . have . . . that?" she asked, pointing at the chocolate bar.

"Have whatever you want," C.P. said. He picked up a bag, tore it open noisily, and began stuffing something crunchy into his mouth.

"Do you have to eat like a cow chewing cud?" Jen said. "Close your mouth, for god's sake."

Mattie tentatively picked up the chocolate bar. She felt the ridges of the bar through the wrapper and suddenly remembered breaking up a large bar into the smaller squares, lining up all the tiny Hershey's bars on a napkin at the table and eating them one by one. She could almost taste the chocolate on her tongue, feel the creaminess melting inside her cheek. She drew the bar near her face and sniffed at it. The faint sweet aroma permeated the wrapping.

She had to take off her mittens to open it, and almost immediately her hands started shaking. It was too cold to have bare fingers, but she wanted the chocolate. Mattie couldn't remember the last time she'd wanted something so badly.

After a few minutes of struggling she managed to tear the packaging enough to expose the top of the bar. The scent of chocolate wafted out, and with it, a rush of memories that she'd forgotten, an avalanche of the past that threatened to bury her completely.

*Standing in the hallway wearing a* Sleeping Beauty *costume, a pink ribbon in her hair. She held a plastic pail shaped like a pumpkin and so did Heather. Heather was Belle from* Beauty and the Beast *and Mom was holding up a camera that kept flashing in their faces as she said, "Just one more, one more, say 'cheese.'"*

*Saving her allowance so she could buy her own candy from the grocery store. She always selected a Hershey's bar, even though Heather said she was boring for picking plain chocolate when there were Reese's cups and Milky Way bars in the world.*

*Carefully placing half a chocolate bar on a graham cracker and smashing down with a scorched marshmallow on top before adding another graham cracker and stuffing the whole thing in her mouth. It was sweet and dry and sticky at the same time and also tasted of the campfire.*

Mattie carefully broke off a piece of the chocolate with her teeth and let it float onto her tongue, just resting there. She'd forgotten what sweet things really tasted like. The memory was nothing compared to the reality.

Jen put her hand on Mattie's shoulder. "Are you all right? Are you in pain?"

Mattie stared at Jen in confusion. Then she noticed that she was weeping, hot tears warming her cold cheeks.

"It's . . . been . . . so . . . long," she said. "Chocolate. I . . . forgot."

She wished she could explain properly but her throat still hurt. She hated that she couldn't speak to them, hated that her first moments with people other than William were limited by this. And deep down she was afraid they would think she was simple, or broken, because she couldn't make complete sentences without choking.

"How long has it been since you had chocolate?" C.P. asked.

"Since . . . before," Mattie said. "Before . . . William."

"So, twelve years, right?" C.P. said. "That's what they said on the news."

Twelve years. Mattie knew a lot of time had passed, knew that she'd been with William on the top of that mountain since she was a child, but William didn't celebrate birthdays or keep track of the days so she'd never been completely sure how long it had been.

*I lost my childhood,* she thought. *I lost my mother and my sister and my childhood.*

Now that the subject of the news program had come up again, there was something she wanted to know.

"Heather," she said. "On . . . the . . . news?"

"Heather?" C.P. asked, and looked at Jen, who shook her head.

"Sister," Mattie said, tapping her chest. "My . . . sister."

"They didn't say anything about a sister," C.P. said. "Not that I remember."

Did that mean that Heather was still alive? Or did it mean that she was dead and C.P. just hadn't been paying attention during the broadcast?

"The only thing they talked about was your mom, how she was . . . well, you know. And about you and how nobody had any idea what had happened to you. The tone of it kind of made it sound like you were dead."

"You have zero tact," Jen said.

"I'm just repeating what I heard!"

"Zero."

It happened then, so fast that Mattie wasn't sure what she'd seen.

An enormous shadow loomed out of the trees. Shiny claws gleamed in the darkness. A paw swooped down from the top of the boulders, curled around Griffin's shoulder and yanked him up, over the boulders, into the trees.

A second later Griffin was gone, nothing left of him except his scream that lingered in the air.

All three stood still for a moment. Then Mattie backed away a few steps from the boulder, her eyes searching for any sign of the creature. Would it return? Was it just stashing Griffin somewhere so it could come back for one of them? Would they all end up as part of its collection?

Mattie remembered the animals hanging from the trees, imagined Griffin's body dangling from one of the branches.

The old familiar panic bubbled up—the longing to hide, to make herself small, to go away someplace where there was no pain and no fear.

*Don't let it come for me don't let it take me don't I can't I just got away from William and now there's this what did I do why does this keep happening to me why was I not allowed to be happy and free.*

"Griffin!" Jen shouted, standing up and staring into the space where he'd disappeared. "Griff, answer me!"

Jen's voice made Mattie start. *What is she doing? Is she trying to bring the creature down on us again? We have to leave. We have to escape before it comes back for us.*

Mattie grabbed Jen's shoulder so the other woman would look at her. "He's . . . gone. The . . . creature . . . took . . . him."

"What do you mean, gone? What's it going to do to him?"

Mattie didn't know for certain but she had a pretty good idea. Jen and C.P. should have the same kind of idea. They'd seen the inside of the cave. They knew what the creature kept there.

"We . . . run," Mattie said. "Before . . . it . . . returns."

"What the hell are you talking about? We're not going to run. We have to go after him," C.P. said. "It's going to take him to the cave, right? So it can mutilate him?"

He didn't wait for an answer. "Look, let's leave the packs here and just take some food and water. We can tuck the bags into these boulders and come back for them. That way we can move faster."

"I don't know if Samantha can move that fast," Jen said.

"Then she can stay here with the packs. Or she can run away, if she wants," C.P. said. He said this last so dismissively that Mattie felt her terror covered over with shame.

*Is it so wrong to run? Is it wrong to want to avoid hurt?*

"Come on, if we hurry we can catch up to it before it carves Griff up into little pieces," C.P. said to Jen. It was clear that Mattie no longer mattered, in his opinion, if she didn't want to come along on his quest to retrieve Griffin.

Mattie did not want to say that she didn't want to be left alone in the woods, because she was certain C.P. would dismiss her as cowardly.

**You're not a coward. You lived with William all those years. You survived every day as William got crazier and crazier. C.P. doesn't know. He doesn't know what it was like.**

This sounded like what Mattie thought of as her Samantha voice, that strong and practical self that didn't seem quite merged with the Mattie she'd known for so long. Everything Samantha thought was true, though. Mattie wasn't a coward. She wasn't.

The truth that C.P. didn't want to face was that there wasn't much they could do about Griffin. How would they get him back from an animal that was so large, so fierce, so silent? All three of them had seen the size of the silhouette, the length of its claws. And nobody had heard it. They hadn't even known it was stalking them.

*You only hear the creature when it wants you to hear it.*

There had been no breaking branches to warn them, no grunt of its breath, no roar echoing through the forest. It had watched them and waited and then it had taken the most vulnerable person, the one who clearly wouldn't fight back. Griffin.

*There's always a chance Griffin might survive, or that the creature might not harm him. There's a chance.*

She thought this, but she didn't really believe it. It was more like a hope, or a wish—a little-girl wish. Mattie wasn't a little girl anymore, and she knew that stories didn't have happy endings.

Mattie felt a little pang at the thought of the kind-eyed Griffin, the man who'd been so concerned for her to get to a doctor, the stranger who'd attacked William so she could escape.

"What . . . will . . . you . . . do?" Mattie asked C.P., who was busily stuffing things from his pack in his jacket pockets.

"I don't know. Get Griffin back, I guess, and then figure it out from there."

"How?" she persisted. "Do . . . you . . . have . . . a . . . weapon?"

"No, I don't have a weapon," he said. "I didn't think I was going to have to battle a gigantic . . ."

He faltered, his voice trailing off. He looked at Jen.

"It wasn't what we expected. Not at all," Jen said. She hadn't moved a muscle since she'd stopped yelling for Griffin.

"I thought it would be more like a Sasquatch, or just a really big bear," C.P. said. He sounded thoughtful, though there was just a tremor of fear underneath. "But that wasn't a bear, unless bears are the size of elephants now."

"I don't understand how it could sneak up on us like that," Jen said. "And if it was so big, how can it have been in the trees?"

"Maybe we'll get a good look at it when we get Griff back," C.P. said.

"I don't know if I want to get a good look at it," Jen said. Her eyes were wide and shiny in the moonlight.

Moonlight. Full dark had come while Mattie had fallen away into a flood of memories set off by a chocolate bar. The nighttime was the creature's time. And William's.

"Jen, come on," C.P. said, grabbing her arm and shaking her. "This isn't like you. Yes, that was terrifying. Yes, I think I actually peed in my pants when I saw its claws. But if that happened to one of us, Griffin wouldn't just leave us out there. He'd come after us. You know he would."

William knew these woods, knew how to hunt. He could stalk Mattie through the forest just as silently as the monster who'd snatched Griffin away.

"I know," Jen said. "I know. It's just . . . what can we really do? We don't have guns or knives or anything."

Danger was all around her, in every twitching branch and every shifting shadow. She couldn't stay here alone. But it was utter foolishness to chase after the creature, to go back in the direction of William's cabin, to put herself in harm's way.

"We don't have to fight it," C.P. said. "I'm not going to have a boss battle on the top of a mountain, and neither are you. We can, I don't know, sneak up on it or something."

She should continue down the mountain. She could find the stream, the way she'd originally planned. She could get police, people who could help, and they would come back and rescue Jen and C.P.

*If they're still alive.*

"Don't you think it will be able to smell us coming? Or hear us? Whatever it is, it's some kind of animal and its senses are probably a hell of a lot sharper than ours," Jen said. Her voice was rising in pitch with every word.

Yes, the best plan, the most practical plan, was for one of them (*me, it should be me*) to keep going, to get others to come to the mountain. The rescuers could swarm the mountain and they could catch William in their net and then Mattie wouldn't have to look over her shoulder for the rest of her life, waiting for him to appear and snatch her away again.

"We'll just figure something out," C.P. said. "I mean, first we have to find out if Griff is even still . . ."

*William didn't snatch you away, though. You opened the window for him. You trusted him. Why did you trust him?*

"What if the monster eats Griffin?" Jen said. Instead of getting louder this time, her tone had dropped practically to a whisper, like she was saying something she shouldn't say, or didn't want to believe in.

*It's your own fault he took you. It's your own fault that your mother is dead.*

"No." Mattie shook her head from side to side. "No. No."

"I know, I don't want to think about it either," Jen said. "It's too horrible."

Jen thought Mattie was distressed over the thought of Griffin being eaten. And of course it was a terrible idea, that kind man torn to pieces like the fox Mattie saw in the snow. But that wasn't what made her shake her head and mutter "no." It was the seed that had planted itself in her mind that she could not dig out.

*It's your fault.*

*It's your fault that your mother is dead.*

*William knocked on the window in the middle of the night and you should have known better, you shouldn't have opened the window.*

"It might not eat him," C.P. said. "It might not kill him at all. But every second we stand here arguing is another second that we're not helping Griffin."

What would Mattie tell the police when she got to them? That she was a kidnapping victim? Was she still a victim if she opened the window for him, if she didn't try harder to run away from him?

What if the police sneered at her, said that she should have done more, should have fought back, should have let him kill her too rather than stay and submit?

"I know," Jen said. "I know. I just don't know what we can do."

**You used to fight back. You used to try to run. That was why William put you in the Box. And after a while you forgot about Mom and Heather and about your life before, and it was easier to do what he wanted than be hit all the time.**

"Hey, I bet you have stuff at that cabin," C.P. said to Mattie. "We can go there and take things, useful things to help us, I don't know, defend ourselves. I remember seeing an axe by a stack of firewood."

"No," Mattie said, her hands held out in front of her as if to ward off an attack. He wanted her to go back to the cabin? Back to where William was? She backed away from C.P. "Not . . . there. William."

"Are you crazy?" Jen said. "She's finally gotten away from her kidnapper and you want her to go right back to him?"

"He might not be there. We'll be able to tell from the outside," C.P. said, though he sounded a little ashamed. "It's just a dinky little place. If he isn't there we can take some stuff. A guy like that is sure to have all kinds of weapons, guns and knives and whatever. And if we come across him again and he's got a gun, then at least we won't be helpless."

*Oh, he has guns and knives and whatever,* Mattie thought. *He's got an arsenal to defeat a demon.*

"Do you really think you could shoot another human being?" Jen asked quietly. "Because I don't think I could."

If William wasn't at the cabin, if he was out in the woods searching for Mattie, then they could gather up some of the things he'd brought back, weapons they could use to defend themselves from the creature *and* William. Mattie didn't know how to use any of it, didn't know how to shoot a gun because William had always made certain she couldn't, but maybe one of the others could.

And there was the trunk. William's mysterious trunk. Mattie was sure there were items in that trunk that would help them, items that would help her remember where she came from. Maybe even items that would tell her what happened to Heather. She could break the trunk open now, no need to wait for William's key, no fear about leaving traces behind that would get her punished.

"I get the feeling that either we shoot him or he shoots us," C.P. said.

*He's hiding secrets in that trunk, secrets about me, secrets about my life before. I need to know.*

"We're not going back to that cabin with Samantha," Jen said.

"Yes," Mattie said, her voice still a strained frog's croak. "We are."

# CHAPTER TWELVE

t took them less time than Mattie expected to find the stream. The stream was her only geographical anchor—if she found the stream she could find the rabbit traps, and if she found the traps, she'd find the trail that led back to the cabin.

C.P. suggested that they just walk straight north, away from the cliff. Jen and C.P. shed their heavy packs and tucked the packs into the boulders so that they were well hidden from animals. Then they clambered over the boulders until they reached the cover of the trees.

At least, C.P. and Jen clambered—lightly, like goats darting from ledge to ledge—and Mattie struggled up behind them, hampered by her heavy, handmade skirts and her general lack of outdoor fitness. She did a lot of hard, heavy work in the cabin but none of it involved climbing, or walking for hours. The chocolate bar, while delicious, had also not been enough to satisfy the deep gnawing in her stomach. On top of everything, she was tired and heartsore and felt sick every time she thought of William, Heather, her mother.

What she really wanted was to lie down and sleep for several hours, and hope that when she woke her voice would be normal and her mind clearer. Everything had happened so fast. Was it only that morning when she'd woken to find an unnaturally cheery William ready to hunt the creature? Was it only a few short hours ago that she left the cabin and found William in the woods confronting the strangers?

Jen and C.P. reached down to help pull Mattie up the last few feet over the top of the boulder. Once she was on level ground again she hunched over, taking deep breaths. Climbing that short distance had been more difficult than it should have been. She felt ashamed of the sweat on her temples, the harsh breath that emitted from her mouth. She felt that she was an awkward appendage, something that was preventing the smooth and unimpeded motion of the other two.

*If I wasn't here they could have run right after their friend. I'm making things worse for them, slowing them down, making everything more dangerous.*

Mattie was about to open her mouth, to tell them these things, when Jen patted her shoulder and said, "Take your time and calm down. It can't be easy to climb in that outfit. Did you make it yourself? It looks handmade."

"Y-yes," Mattie said.

Something rustled, and a moment later a light clicked on. *A flashlight,* Mattie thought. It had been years since she thought about a flashlight.

It was C.P.'s, of course. He had the light pointed at the ground and he was moving it around.

"What are you doing?" Jen asked.

"Looking for tracks," he said. "That cryptid didn't fall out of the sky, grab Griffin and fly away."

"How do you know?" Jen asked. "We didn't get a proper look at it."

"We're not looking for the Mothman, Jennifer," C.P. said, his tone mocking when he said "mothman." "We're looking for a large, bearlike cryptid. That's what all the reports said."

Mattie wondered again about these "reports," but didn't feel it was the right time to ask.

"You know, you're amazingly close-minded for someone who claims to be the opposite," Jen said. "How do you know it's not the Mothman?"

"Please," C.P. said. "We've talked about this before. It's physically impossible for a creature like that to exist. You're not doing our field any favors by believing in stupid urban legends."

Mattie tugged on Jen's arm before she could argue more. "Griffin," Mattie said.

Mattie could just make out Jen's silhouette in the dark, see the other woman nod her head.

"You're right. This is not the time to engage with a person who claims to be a cryptozoologist but who actually doesn't believe in the vast majority of the historical evidence of cryptids."

"It's too easy to disprove most of the claims. That's why we're here. To gather actual evidence," C.P. said, still moving the flashlight over the ground. "Where the hell did that thing come from? The snow is totally untouched here."

"Trees," Mattie said.

C.P. pointed the flashlight up, but the light seemed frail and useless in that direction, swallowed up by the pine boughs.

"How can something that big—and that's the only sense I had of it, that it was big—move from tree to tree without breaking them? How did it carry Griffin?"

"Griffin," Mattie said again, to get them moving.

What had happened to their sense of urgency? C.P. seemed lost in thought, trying to solve the problem of the creature. She glanced nervously at the trees above them. There was a chance the animal was still up there, watching them, waiting for its chance to take the rest of them.

"She's right. Come on, C.P.," Jen said, grabbing his arm and pulling him along.

Mattie couldn't help wincing, bracing for C.P.'s response to this. If Mattie had done such a thing to William, he would have told her they would leave when he was ready and not a moment before, and there would have been a slap in it for her. But C.P. meekly turned the flashlight in front of them and let Jen pull him along.

The light made the pools of darkness outside its reach behave strangely. More than once Mattie was certain she saw a shape moving on one side of them and then the other, but when she stopped to peer into the shadows, C.P. would also tilt the flashlight in that direction, and there was never anything except the trees.

It seemed they'd been walking a very long time when Mattie heard the trickle of the stream. Her feet felt frozen, and the tips of her fingers had gone numb despite her mittens. She longed for the warmth of the cabin—the fire, a blanket, a hot cup of tea.

**And a monster waiting in your bedroom? The cabin isn't a safe haven for you.**

Mattie shook her head from side to side, trying to dislodge any thoughts of William. She wasn't going to enter the cabin if he was there. And if he wasn't around she was going to lock the door against him and leave him out in the night, just like he'd done to her.

*Maybe the creature will take him then. Maybe it will swoop down from the trees and take him away like it did with Griffin.*

Mattie knew that the banks of the stream were bare of trees, and that the three of them would be exposed once they exited the cover of the woods.

"W-wait," she said.

C.P. swung around to face her and the flashlight beam went right into her eyes. She covered her eyes with her hand and turned away, but her vision was temporarily ruined and all she could see were black spots on an orange background.

"Sorry, sorry," he said. "I thought I had the beam low enough but you're a lot shorter than me."

"Give me that," Jen said, snatching the light out of his hand. "You can't be trusted."

"That's not fair," he protested.

They were going to argue again. Mattie never knew that people could enjoy arguing, but these two seemed to do just that.

*They might enjoy it, but it's making me crazy. Why can't they just be quiet? Don't they understand that every time they make noise they're bringing danger nearer to us?*

"Q-quiet," Mattie said with as much authority as she could

muster. It wasn't a lot, especially given that her voice still resembled something like a mouse squeak, but she'd had enough and she thought they could tell.

She felt their gazes upon her, even though she couldn't make out their expressions in the dark.

"The . . . creature. William. In the woods," she said. "Quiet."

It was so frustrating not to be able to talk like a normal person, trying to cut her conversation down to only the necessary words and hope they would understand.

"Right," Jen said in an apologetic whisper. "We're making too much noise. Sorry."

"Sorry," C.P. repeated, and he grabbed the flashlight out of Jen's hand again and started toward the stream.

"Wait," Mattie said again.

"She wanted to tell us something in the first place, dummy," Jen said.

C.P. halted and spun around. Mattie heard the quick indrawn breath that meant he was preparing his retort.

"No . . . fighting," Mattie said. "Listen."

All three listened to the woods around them—the running of the stream over rocks, the sound of night birds fluttering in their nests, the sway of branches in the wind.

She carefully stepped closer to the other two, trying not to make too much noise as her boots crunched in the snow. She pitched her voice low as they leaned in.

"Stream . . . is . . . in . . . a . . . clearing. No . . . trees."

"I get it," C.P. said. "We'll be exposed. I should shut off the flashlight."

Mattie thought they ought to keep the flashlight off anyway. If they just let their eyes adapt to the night they'd be able to see more than just the pool of light illuminated by the beam. But this was too much to explain with her throat damaged.

*What if it's permanently damaged? What if William broke you forever?*

She couldn't let herself think like that. She would get better. Her voice would return. It had to. She had to be allowed to have a normal life, a life without hurt, a life without William in it.

Mattie couldn't let him break her forever, not in any way.

C.P. clicked the flashlight off and the three of them crept to the edge of the woods. Mattie peered out at the clearing, trying to force her night vision along though she knew it took several moments for her eyes to adjust.

"Do you see anything?" Jen whispered, her mouth close to Mattie's ear.

Mattie started, and Jen patted her arm, whispering, "Sorry, I didn't mean to scare you."

It wasn't that the other woman had scared her, exactly. It was more the way she was so familiar with Mattie—the way she patted Mattie's arm or her shoulder, the way she came up close and invaded Mattie's space. The only person who'd come near Mattie for twelve years was William, and it was unnerving to have a stranger treating her in such an intimate way, like they'd known each other all their lives, like they were sisters.

*Sisters. Heather.*

Mattie wished she knew what had happened to Heather.

"I don't see anything," C.P. said.

"Quiet," Mattie said again. "Listen."

She wanted to explain that if William or the creature were hiding in the woods on the other side of the stream they might hear. William could be standing there with his rifle, waiting for Mattie or just waiting for the creature so he could take down his demon. If he was, he might shift his weight and they would hear the rustle of his clothes or the slide of his boot soles in the snow. There would be something, some slight noise out of place.

And Mattie knew the sound of William, knew how to gauge his mood by the rhythm of his breath or the way he strode across the cabin floor or even the way he swung the axe when he chopped the firewood. She knew him. She would hear him if he was hiding in the woods. She was certain of it.

Mattie closed her eyes so she wouldn't be distracted by the shadows she thought she saw around the stream. She listened hard, tuning out the sound of C.P. and Jen breathing, the scrape of their sleeves against their jackets. She felt like she was stretching out her hearing, extending it over the stream and into the woods beyond, like she was a sensing bat.

Mattie opened her eyes. There was nothing. No William.

Was the creature there? She couldn't hear it, hadn't seen anything like its gigantic shadow. That didn't mean anything, though. It could hide in the trees. It could make itself soundless and invisible if it wanted.

*It's not natural,* Mattie thought, and she wondered, just for a moment, if William was right and it actually was a demon.

*William isn't right about anything,* she told herself. *Not a single thing.*

"So do you think it's okay to cross or what?" C.P. whispered. He and Jen had ranged themselves on either side of Mattie, and she felt like a very small book between two oversized bookends.

Mattie's eyes had finally adjusted to the shadows, and there was a pale cast of moonlight over the clearing. She realized then that they were standing in roughly the same place from which the creature had emerged a couple of nights before, when Mattie was curled up on the bank of the stream. That meant that they were very close to the traps and the path back to the cabin.

*We didn't get very far at all,* she thought. *I thought we were so far away from William, from the cabin, from the life I wanted to run from.*

It had seemed like they'd walked and walked, but Mattie supposed that it had only seemed like that because their progress was so slow. They'd been dragging Griffin along at the end.

*Griffin.* It already seemed like days since the creature snatched him away and disappeared.

"Carefully," Mattie whispered. "Follow me."

She stepped out of the trees and immediately wished she hadn't. She imagined this was how a chipmunk felt, dashing from the cover of one bush to another, always hoping not to catch the eye of a hawk or an owl.

*Except the hawk that would catch you has claws the size of your face.*

Mattie couldn't even dash—she was far too weak to run. Her body protested every step, all the bruises that William had inflicted over the past days crying out. She was tired and hungry and none of it mattered because they had to survive. If she was uncomfortable, if she was in pain, then what did it matter? It meant that she wasn't dead.

Jen and C.P. huddled close to her on either side. She heard C.P.'s breath coming in harsh pants, and Jen gripped Mattie's arm.

*They're relying on me,* she thought in wonder. *They think I can keep them safe, that I know what I'm doing.*

The idea made her want to shrink away. She couldn't be responsible for their lives. She didn't know what she was doing or how they would find Griffin or how they would escape the creature when they did. She wasn't even sure if they should go back to the cabin. William could be waiting there, secretly, waiting for her to walk through the door so he could grab her and put her in the Box.

She thought of the money she'd hidden under the couch. If she had that money, if she could get off the mountain, then she could use it to buy something like freedom. But it wasn't worth it to risk the cabin just for that. It was the weapons, and maybe the knowledge she could gain once she opened the trunk.

Maybe inside the trunk there was information about Heather.

Mattie needed to know if her sister was still alive, if Heather was somewhere waiting for her. She needed to know if she had a home to go home to.

They reached the stream, and Mattie pointed out the place where there were some rocks to cross and indicated they should follow her.

"C-cold," she said. "Don't . . . fall . . . in."

"Yeah, because I'm really worried about hypothermia or frostbite at the moment," C.P. said as he followed behind Mattie.

"You should be," Jen said, the last one to cross. "It's not a joke."

"I know it's not, but hypothermia is kind of low on my list of things that could kill me. A gunshot wound seems more likely."

C.P. was the one who'd suggested going to the cabin but he

seemed reluctant now. Mattie didn't have time to soothe him, to make him feel better about his choice. She walked along the bank of the stream until she found the place where they kept the snares. No one had checked them in the last couple of days, and there were two dead rabbits in the traps. One of them had tried to gnaw its foot off but bled out before it finished. A dark stain of blood was visible against the snow.

She indicated that the other two should follow her. "Stay . . . close. No . . . light."

The deer path was obvious to Mattie, who'd walked it so many times, but she knew it wouldn't look like much to those unfamiliar with it. She didn't want to lose one of them in the dark.

Jen followed Mattie, and C.P. behind. The path was wide enough to admit two side-by-side but Mattie stayed close to the edge of it, hugging close to the trees. She had a vague idea that this made her less obvious, that anyone (*anything*) watching the forest would have trouble deciding if it was her or a tree they'd seen.

It was hard not to remember the last time she'd walked this trail in the dark, how the creature had moved in time with her, how it had stalked her so silently.

*It's not there now,* she told herself. *You would know. You would feel it.*

But she couldn't be certain. Jen and C.P. both wore clothes that made a lot of noise—the slick surfaces of their jackets, the rough cloth of their pants. They both walked heavily, too, and their boots squeaked in the snow with every step. She couldn't detect the presence of the creature—or of anything else that might be nearby—with all the racket. Mattie felt like they were announcing their presence to William, who'd hear them coming even with all the cabin windows closed. She tried not to be irritated, because she knew they couldn't help it. They didn't know how to be quiet because they'd never really needed to be. They didn't have to hide from monsters that might hurt them.

The tip of Mattie's boot touched something hard in the dark—*a rock*, she thought—and she automatically moved right, skirting around it. The last thing she needed was to trip and fall. The other two were following so close behind that they would probably fall on top of her.

Then there was a sound of metal, a hideous snapping, and Jen was screaming.

*The trap. William's bear trap.* She'd forgotten all about it. He'd gone out that morning to set it, to catch his demon.

"Jen! Jen!" C.P. said. Mattie saw his silhouette against the trail, standing stock-still.

"Flashlight!" Mattie said to C.P. Maybe Jen wasn't hurt too badly. Maybe they would be able to get her out of the trap.

He clicked the light on and Mattie heard him say, "Oh, god."

The trap had imbedded itself in Jen's leg, below her knee. Blood poured from the wound, rolling down her pants, making a stain in the snow.

*Just like the rabbit*, Mattie thought.

She twisted and writhed on the ground, screaming, "Get it off, get it off, get it off me, oh my god, get it off!"

"Hold still," C.P. said, but Jen was thrashing around, the part of her body not caught in the trap trying to escape. "Hold still!"

*William will come*, Mattie thought. They were too close to the cabin. He would hear Jen screaming and C.P. shouting and he would come and finish off the other two and drag Mattie away.

"Shh," Mattie said, falling to her knees next to Jen. She grabbed the other woman's flailing hands and squeezed them tight. "Shh."

"It hurts," Jen whimpered. Mattie saw the gleam of tears on her cheeks. "It hurts."

Mattie squeezed her hands tighter, trying to comfort. *This is my fault. I should have remembered the trap.*

C.P.'s flashlight bobbed around as he knelt down to inspect the trap. "I have to loosen the springs. When I do, you pull your leg out as fast as you can. Don't move around until I loosen it, OK?"

He put the flashlight on the ground close to the trap.

"Do you know what you're doing?" Jen asked. Her voice was strained. Mattie could tell that she was making an enormous effort not to cry out.

"I saw this in a movie once," he said.

"Oh, great."

He ignored her comment. "You press down on the springs on either side and it loosens the jaws, but you have to get your leg out fast because I don't know how much pressure the springs need or how long I'll be able to hold it."

Mattie looked at C.P. It was hard to tell with the puffy jacket but he didn't seem muscle-bound. She didn't think he'd have enough arm strength to open the springs, and it seemed to her that faster was better. They needed to get Jen out of the trap quickly.

"Stand," she said.

"What?" he said.

Mattie pointed at the springs. "Stand . . . on . . . it."

"She's saying to step on the springs instead of trying to do it with your hands, dope," Jen said. She sounded stronger, like the act of potentially arguing with C.P. gave her energy.

"Oh. Good idea," C.P. said.

He stood up and positioned himself in front of the trap.

"Don't move around," he said. "I don't want to make this worse."

C.P. raised up the toes of his boots in front of each spring and then pushed down on the metal on either side of the jaws.

The teeth loosened so suddenly that Mattie wasn't ready for it. She'd had an idea that it would be a slow process, but once C.P.'s weight was on the springs, the jaws popped open.

"Pull your leg out!" he cried, but Jen didn't need telling. She was already freeing herself, pulling away with another cry of pain.

As soon as Jen was loose, C.P. stepped off the trap, which snapped shut again with a clang that seemed to echo all through the woods.

"Oh god," Jen said. "Oh god, it hurts like hell."

Then she turned her head away from Mattie and threw up.

"Did that guy put this trap out here?" C.P. asked Mattie.

She noticed how C.P. never called him "William"—always "that guy" or "that nut" or some equivalent. It wasn't really the right time to ask about this quirk, though.

"Yes," Mattie said. She wanted to explain that William thought the creature was a demon, and that killing it was a trial sent by God in William's eyes, but her limited ability to talk made it impossible. Perhaps she could tell them tomorrow.

*If we live until tomorrow.*

She realized she didn't feel very certain about this. Griffin had been taken by the monster, and now Jen had been caught in the trap. Jen wouldn't be able to run or climb or even walk very well with that leg—what Mattie saw of it did not look good.

Mattie herself was hardly at her physical peak—she still bore the bruises and pains from William's beating and choking her.

*One missing and two wounded. Only C.P. is still standing. How are we ever going to get off the mountain like this?*

C.P. held his hand out to help Jen stand. She did, whimpering and crying, and leaned heavily on his shoulder. Mattie picked up the flashlight and turned it out again. No point in broadcasting their location any more than they already had.

"Do you think you can walk?" C.P. asked.

"I can't stay here," Jen said.

"I think you're going to need a tetanus shot," C.P. said.

"I think I'm going to need stitches."

Jen took a few tentative steps forward with C.P.'s assistance. Mattie didn't need the flashlight to tell that the result was not good. She heard Jen's labored breath, the little cry of pain when Jen tried to put weight on her injured leg.

"What about Griffin?" Jen said, and Mattie heard the tears in her voice. "I can't go after him like this."

"I'll go myself," C.P. said. "Don't worry about Griffin."

"You can't drag him on your own. And the animal might have hurt him."

"Samantha will help me. Won't you, Samantha?"

Every time one of them said that name, *Samantha*, Mattie had to stop herself from correcting them, from saying, "No, my name is Mattie." Mattie wasn't her name. Mattie was the name William had forced on her so that she would forget herself.

She realized that they were waiting for her answer. Did she really want to go to the creature's cave again to find a man that she was fairly certain was already dead? No, she did not. She thought their hope was foolish.

*But as long as there's a chance . . .*

And these people had been good to her. They'd helped her. What kind of person would she be if she didn't help them?

*I don't know what kind of person I am. William took that from me.*

"Yes. I'll . . . go . . . with . . . you," she said.

"See?" C.P. said to Jen. "We'll find a good place for you to wait and we'll find Griffin and come back for you."

Mattie heard Jen's indrawn breath, thought that the other woman was about to argue with C.P. as usual. Then another sound intruded.

The crunch of a boot and then a slide through the snow—the unmistakable sound of a person limping.

*Thunk-drag-thunk-drag-thunk-drag.*

It was coming from the direction of the stream.

Mattie whispered, "William."

# CHAPTER THIRTEEN

The only reason William would be coming from that direction was because he'd been following their tracks. Mattie couldn't tell how far away he was but the noise made it clear that he moved steadily, if slowly, in their direction.

"Cabin," she said, pushing Jen and C.P. along the trail. "Hurry."

Mattie wanted to run, wanted to sprint for the safety of the cabin, wanted to lock the door and pull the curtains shut and huddle under the bed. She realized then that she was more scared of facing William again than the creature in the woods. William was the boogeyman, the monster in her nightmares. William could hurt her far more than the creature ever could.

*Thunk-drag-thunk-drag-thunk-drag.*

The creature must have hurt William's leg and that was why he was walking that way. It explained the horrible scream they'd heard earlier, when she thought (**hoped, you hoped with all of your heart**) that William was dying.

They hurried as best they could, Jen stumbling frequently, C.P. dragging her along when he had to. Mattie darted ahead and then back again, biting her lip, her throat burning with sick acid bubbling up from her churning stomach.

*Hurry, hurry,* she thought.

For no matter how fast they moved, she heard the inexorable *thunk-drag-thunk-drag-thunk-drag* behind them.

They weren't even trying to be silent now. All three of them knew that William was following their tracks in the snow, and the only thing that mattered was reaching the cabin before he did, so that they could bolt the door against him.

*Hurry, hurry, hurry.*

Mattie thought she heard William approaching faster, thought she felt his hands reaching out to grab her braid, pull her down into the snow, his fists pounding into her body, his lips saying, *A man's got to have sons, Martha, and you're the one to give them to me.*

But no, he wasn't there, he wasn't dragging her away, he was still behind them, not close enough to see and they could still escape, they could still reach the cabin before he did.

*Thunk-drag-thunk-drag-thunk-drag-thunk-drag.*

Where was the cabin? She didn't think they were that far away from it. For a moment Mattie worried that she'd gotten turned around in the dark, that they weren't on the path to the cabin at all.

Then the clearing was before them, and the little cluster of buildings that had been her home for the last twelve years.

*No,* she thought as she ran for the cabin door. *It has never been a home. A home is a place where there is warmth and love and safety, and I have never had those things here.*

Mattie heard Jen and C.P. limping along several feet behind her, and beyond them the sound of William approaching.

*Thunk-drag-thunk-drag-thunk-drag.*

The cabin could only be locked from inside, not without, so Mattie knew that William could not bar it against her if he wasn't home. Her boots clattered over the porch and she threw the cabin door open.

Inside it was cold and dark, the fire that she'd carefully tended earlier down to only a few embers.

"Hurry," she croaked at Jen and C.P. as she stood at the door, ready to slam it shut the moment they were inside. All the world seemed to be inside the frame of the door—the bit of clearing, Jen and C.P. seeming to grow larger and larger as they approached, the watchful trees beyond.

*Thunk-drag-thunk-drag-thunk-drag.*

He was closer. He would be upon them in a moment.

Jen banged her leg into the bottom step that led up to the platform of the porch and cried out. C.P. half-lifted Jen over the wooden lip of the porch and shoved her in the direction of the door. Jen stumbled through, past Mattie, and collapsed on the floor just as C.P. hurried in behind.

Mattie slammed the door shut and threw the bolt home. Her heart was hammering so hard that she felt sick.

*I did it. I beat him. I locked him out in the night just like he did to me.*

Her hands shook and her teeth chattered and part of her brain was in panicked overdrive, shouting at her, *Open the door you're not supposed to do that he's going to hurt you so much when he gets inside you need to make him happy or he'll hurt you more oh god what have you done?*

Even through the locked door she heard him coming for her.

*Thunk-drag-thunk-drag-thunk-drag.*

The windows. Could he get through the windows? No, William was a big man and the windows were small. They should try to block them, though. They shouldn't give him any path inside.

"Windows," Mattie said through her chattering teeth. "We . . . need . . . to . . . block . . . them."

"With what?" C.P. said. "I can't see anything in here."

Mattie pulled the flashlight out of her pocket. She didn't know how to turn it on. It had been years since she'd touched a flashlight and all she could think about was William: William following their trail through the snow, William stalking through the clearing, William's footsteps going *thunk-drag-thunk-drag-thunk-drag* across the porch, William's fists pounding on the door.

Mattie's mittened hands slid over the plastic light, panicked and unsure, but somehow she accidentally managed to click it on. Jen and C.P. appeared in the pool of light. Jen lay on her back, out of breath, her eyes streaming. C.P. knelt on the floor beside her, his head bowed, his hand held up to block the light.

"Turn it away!" he said. "If you want stuff to block the windows then point it at that stuff."

The trouble was that Mattie couldn't think of what they might use. All the chairs were heavy, handmade by William and difficult to move. They'd have to stack the chairs to get high enough to cover the glass. What they really needed were boards or something like them, but there was nothing like that in the cabin.

Mattie darted the flashlight all around the cabin—at the table where she'd eaten her cheese and bread earlier in the day, at the couch that hid the roll of money she'd stolen from William, at the leftover pile of supplies he'd purchased for "fighting a demon."

*Thunk-drag-thunk-drag-thunk-drag.*

Even through the walls of the cabin she heard the inexorable steps, the sound that meant William was nearly there.

"At least let's block the door," C.P. said. He grabbed one of the heavy chairs away from the table and dragged it toward the front door, forcing Jen to roll away or else she'd be run over by the chair and his tramping feet.

Mattie followed his progress with the flashlight, watched him push the back of the chair up against the door and then sit in it, adding his weight to block the door. Sweat glistened on his cheeks and forehead.

"There," C.P. said. "He can't possibly get through this."

*Thunk-drag-thunk-drag-thunk-drag* came William's boots across the porch.

Mattie's hand shook as she pointed the flashlight at the door. "He's . . . coming."

She wanted to dive under the bed, or dive through the window at the back of the cabin. She wanted to crawl up the chimney and perch at the top, far out of William's reach. Why had they come back to the cabin? Why had they done such a foolish thing? She'd escaped her prison. She should never have returned, not for anything in the world.

The footsteps paused at the door. The flashlight showed the doorknob turn slowly, then the door shifted slightly in its frame as William pushed against it. Mattie saw C.P. press his feet into the ground and his back against the chair. His face was just out of the pool of light but she saw the cords of his neck straining.

"Martha, you open this door now," William said, and there was no hot anger in his voice, only the ice of winter, and Mattie knew what that meant.

She shook her head from side to side *no no no no no no* but she didn't know if she was saying no to opening the door or no to the inevitable punishment she'd receive for defying him.

Mattie heard Jen shifting on the floor, heard the slide of her pants against the wood. *Don't make a sound,* she wanted to shout. *Don't let him hear you. He's going to get you. He's going to hurt you.*

"Martha!" William barked. "You do what I say now, girl, or it will be the worse for you later."

"Don't answer him," Jen whispered.

"I know you're in there fornicating with those men. You're a sinner, Martha, and it is the duty of a husband to discipline his wife and save her soul for heaven," William said.

Mattie would have laughed if she hadn't been so terrified. William still thought she was having affairs with strange men? When was she supposed to be doing that—before or after she'd trekked through the woods in the night, certain that at any moment the creature would appear out of the trees and snatch her away like it did Griffin?

"You can't hide forever. When you open that door, I'll be here, Martha. I'll be waiting for you."

She heard the rustling of clothes, saw the door shift again. William must have sat down on the porch in front of the door.

"No," she moaned. What were they going to do now? They

couldn't escape with William right there. There was hardly any food in the cabin because William hid it all from her in the storehouse. And Jen could barely walk, so even if they managed to get past William, they would be unable to run if he chased them.

Why had she thought she could get away from him? She should just give herself up now, hope that she could bargain for Jen and C.P.'s safety. Surely William would let the other two go as long as he had her. Surely they would be safe.

**Don't be stupid. He can't let them go. They know what he did to you. They know he kidnapped you. They heard him say he killed your mother. He can't risk them leaving, telling the police, bringing them back here to arrest him.**

This was Samantha again, bossy Samantha who always made Mattie feel slightly stupid.

*Then what am I to do?* She heard the plaintiveness in her own thoughts, could feel defeat slumping her shoulders, rounding her back.

**Stop letting him grind you up under his heel,** Samantha said. **There has to be a way if you'd only think.**

Mattie felt the wall of the cabin press against her back. She'd retreated from the door as she thought (*no, you weren't thinking, you were panicking*), her body moving as far from William as possible.

"Now what?" C.P. whispered.

He couldn't sit there by the door. Anything could happen to him there. Mattie felt sure that William would find some way to reach through the door and hurt him—break it down with the axe, or shoot him right through the wood.

"Come . . . here," she said, beckoning him toward her.

He carefully levered his body out of the chair, trying to make as little noise as possible, and started toward Mattie.

Jen had stopped moving around on the floor. Mattie turned the flashlight toward her and saw she was completely still, her eyes closed.

"Shit," C.P. said. "I think she's passed out."

He knelt beside her and felt for her pulse, then put his hand on her forehead.

"She's still alive, but she feels like ice. She's probably in shock or something. Let's put a blanket on her."

Mattie dragged one of the handmade blankets off the couch and covered Jen with it. Jen was so still and cold that Mattie felt certain they were covering a corpse.

"Probably we should disinfect her cuts," C.P. said. "But we can't clean them unless we cut her pant leg off, and I don't want to move her around now. So, what are we going to do?"

He was staring at her so expectantly. He seemed to think she had answers. Did he know that she didn't know anything, that she was hoping *he* would have ideas? Didn't he know that her whole world had been in this room for twelve years?

**Stop. Panicking. Stop right now.**

It was so easy to say this but so hard to do. She'd spent more of her life afraid than not.

Mattie swallowed hard, because it was still difficult for her to talk. "Can't . . . leave . . . with . . . William . . ."

"With that guy out there. Yeah, I figured that much out." He spoke in a low whisper, his shoulders rounded and his head bent so the words stayed in the space between the two of them. It felt uncomfortably intimate, but since Mattie was already pressed up against the wall there was nowhere she could go to make space for herself. "So what are we going to do about it? Is there a gun in here that we can use?"

William had two rifles—the deer rifle and the large one he'd just acquired to kill the giant creature in the woods. It was probable that the deer rifle was still in the cabin, leaning next to the wall on William's side of the bed. It was so much a part of the furniture that Mattie never really thought about it. And she only remembered seeing him take the larger rifle that morning, though she supposed he might have returned to the cabin for more firepower after the events of the day.

"Maybe," Mattie said, and started toward the bedroom. Her boot heels rang out on the floor even though she was trying to be quiet.

Mattie paused. She didn't want William to know what she was doing, or where she was moving to in the cabin. She was certain he was listening hard at the door for any sounds that might indicate what they were doing, and that he was calculating how he might take advantage.

She handed the flashlight back to C.P. and crouched down to take her boots off.

"You're worried about the floors?" C.P. said. "I don't think the finish is a priority, you know."

Mattie frowned up at him. "Noisy."

"Right," he said. "Sorry. I'm just really wound up, I guess. First Griffin is taken and then Jen got caught in the trap and now we're stuck in this place with a psycho outside. I don't know how we're going to get to Griffin or what kind of state he'll be in when we find him."

Mattie didn't say anything. She was certain that Griffin was dead now, or would be soon, and that as soon as they broke out of the cabin they should head down the mountain with all possible speed. But she didn't want to explain this to C.P. while her bruised throat made it difficult to talk. He seemed to be depending on the idea that they would find Griffin alive.

*He's like a child,* Mattie thought as she slid out of her boots and moved silently toward the bedroom. *He thinks there should be a happy ending just because he believes in one.*

Mattie didn't believe in happy endings. She didn't even believe in happy middles. It was only at that beginning part of the story, when you were young and didn't know any better, that you could be happy and carefree. Once life piled up on you, happiness was impossible.

If she managed to escape William, she didn't think all her problems would magically be solved. His shadow would chase her for the rest of her life, and she hated him for that, hated that her mind would never be completely easy, that she'd always be looking over her shoulder for a monster.

Mattie paused in the doorway between the bedroom and the main room of the cabin. The window curtains were open here, allowing the moonlight in. The bed loomed in the middle of the room, a haunted place made of her pain.

*A man's got to have sons, Mattie.*

She shook her head from side to side, shook away the ghosts that circled there. They needed the rifle, William's rifle, and it was right where he'd left it, leaning against the wall on his side of the bed.

C.P. directed the flashlight over Mattie's shoulder and it caught the gleam of the rifle barrel. "Score!"

She scurried into the room, her heart galloping. She hadn't realized he was standing so close. He needed to stop standing so close to her. Every time C.P. came near she thought of William, thought of William's hands closing around her neck, William's fists breaking her flesh, William's body pressing down into hers.

*He's not William,* she told herself. *He won't hurt you.*

She needed to close the curtains. She needed to do that in case William snuck around the outside of the cabin and tried to peer inside. But if she closed the curtains then she would be alone in this room, in the dark, with a strange man.

**He won't hurt you. Stop being such a little mouse.** Samantha again. Mattie wanted to tell Samantha that if she had so much to say then maybe she should drive instead of leaving all the work up to Mattie.

Mattie forced herself to go to the window and close the curtains. The moonlight disappeared but it didn't really matter because C.P. had the flashlight, and of course he wasn't waiting to menace her. He was picking up the rifle and examining it with the light.

"It's loaded," he said. "Where's the extra ammo?"

Mattie went to the top drawer of William's dresser. This was a small piece, only three drawers, and she was never allowed to open the top. She was, however, supposed to place his clean and mended clothes neatly in the other two drawers. He liked his shirts folded a particular way. It had taken Mattie a long time to learn how to do it right.

C.P. followed her, the flashlight beam bouncing, and Mattie pulled open the top drawer. There were boxes of ammunition there, and several hunting knives of various sizes, and the extra grenades that William hadn't put in his pack that morning.

"Holy hell," C.P. said. "Grenades? What is he going to use them for?"

"The . . . creature," Mattie said. "He . . . thinks . . . it's . . . a . . . demon."

"For real? Like he really thinks that thing is an actual demon in the woods?"

Mattie nodded. Their faces were just barely illuminated by the circle of light from the flashlight.

"And he's what, exactly? Some kind of holy warrior out to smite it?"

"Yes," Mattie said.

"This is getting more fucked up by the second," he said. He grabbed several boxes of ammunition and stuffed them in his jacket pockets.

"Do . . . you . . . know . . . how?" Mattie asked, indicating the rifle.

"Yeah, I've been target shooting since I was pretty young. My dad loves it so he taught me."

Now they had a gun, and someone who knew how to use it. But Mattie still wasn't sure how they were going to get out of the cabin. William had positioned himself right by the door. If they opened it he could just pick them off one by one as they went through. Even if he didn't manage to hit any of them—an unlikely prospect, given that William was a seasoned marksman—then he would just follow after them.

And they had Jen, who was now unconscious. Griffin had also been unconscious, and C.P. and Jen had barely managed to drag him along. Mattie was much shorter than Jen. She couldn't imagine supporting the taller woman, even with C.P.'s help. And William would easily catch up to them.

*Unless we kill him. The only way to make him stop coming after us is to kill him.*

But she wouldn't be the one to do that. She didn't know how to use the rifle. C.P. would have to kill him. Could she ask this stranger to take on that burden?

Mattie rubbed her head. Every decision seemed so full of consequences that would lead to more troubles. She felt a sudden surge of anger at Griffin and C.P. Why hadn't they left the mountain when she told them to? Why hadn't they listened? If they had listened then none of this would have happened. She wouldn't be burdened with the responsibility of their lives as well as her own.

*I can barely take care of myself. How can I save them, too?*

She swayed on her feet, suddenly lightheaded. She needed to rest. Her body was shutting down, defending itself.

"Hey," C.P. said, putting his hand on her shoulder so she wouldn't tip over.

Mattie knew he was only trying to help. She knew it, but she couldn't help wriggling away when he touched her. She couldn't help thinking of William, who would pretend to be kind and then hurt her in the next moment.

"I was just trying to help. You looked like a bowling pin about to fall," C.P. said, and his irritation was clear in his voice.

Mattie shifted a few extra inches away from him. She didn't

want to be within arm's reach, although she didn't know where she could run to inside the cabin. He had the gun, too.

*What have I done? William is outside with a gun and the only other man is inside with a gun and I have nothing, nothing to keep them from me if they want to hurt me.*

She took a deep breath, because panic was bubbling up again and there was no value to it. C.P. wouldn't hurt her, wouldn't hit her. He had no reason to. They were in this together. They had to find a way to get past William, and safely get all three of them down to the village.

*Four. He'll never leave without Griffin.*

"I'm going to check on Jen," C.P. said when Mattie didn't respond. He left the bedroom in a huff, taking the flashlight with him, leaving her standing in the darkness.

There was a tap at the bedroom window.

Mattie spun around, staring at the curtains she'd pulled closed. William was there. William was on the other side of the glass. If she opened the curtains he would be there, waving at her, asking her to open the window.

*Just like he did before.*

William waved at her and she got out of bed and pulled open the glass even though it was the middle of the night. She had to stand on her desk chair to push the window up because she was so small.

He told her to stay in the bedroom, that he had a surprise for Mom. So she'd gotten back into bed because her feet were cold and she'd pulled up the covers to her chin and waited to hear her *mother's cries of happiness when she saw whatever surprise William had for her, but then she was curious about the surprise.*

*"I want to see," she said and hopped out of bed and put on her slippers and tiptoed toward her mother's room. The light was off but her eyes were adjusted to the dark and she could see that the door was partway open.*

*She didn't hear any voices but she did hear strange sounds, grunts and harsh breaths and then a wet squelchy noise. The last sound made her feel funny in her stomach, sort of sick and scared, and she wanted her mom then, wanted to run and jump into Mom's bed and feel her mother's arms around her.*

*She pushed the door open and the first thing she saw was William silhouetted against the faint light coming in through the window, and there was something in his hand, something that looked like a knife but it couldn't be a knife, why would he have a knife?*

*Then the smell hit her and she gagged. It smelled like the bathroom, like poop and pee and also something else, something metallic that left a faint film of sick on her tongue.*

*"Sam," William said, and his voice was very steady and very cold, like a frozen river in winter. She'd never heard his voice like that before. "Go back to your room. I'll be there in a minute."*

*"Mom?" Samantha said. "Mom, can I come in bed with you? I'm scared."*

*"You can't get in bed with her right now," William said. "Go back to your room."*

*"Mom?" Samantha said, and she went toward the bed even though she was sick and terrified, even though William had told her twice to leave.*

*She saw her mother's profile just for a moment, very still, then*

*William came around the bed in a few strides, tucking away the thing he could not possibly have into his belt. He scooped Samantha up into his arms. She'd always liked to be held by William, because he was big and tall and she was so small, but now he didn't feel safe and she tried to wriggle away. His arms were hard as iron and his voice was the same way when he said, "Stop trying to get away, Samantha," but she couldn't stop because Mom was so still and she hadn't answered when Samantha called and Mom always answered, she'd never ignore Samantha when she was scared.*

*"I said stop," he said again. "You will listen and do as I say from now on. You belong to me now."*

*"No," she said. "I want Mom."*

*He put his hand over her mouth and there was something sticky on his fingers, something that smelled like metal. "Your mother has decided that I'm to take care of you now. We're going away. You will listen to me and obey and if you do that you'll be the happiest little girl in the world. If you don't then . . ."*

*He trailed off. Samantha didn't know what might happen to her if she didn't listen to William, couldn't begin to imagine it. She only knew that she didn't want to go with him. She wanted to stay with Mom and Heather. She squirmed again, trying to escape his grip, and he sighed.*

The tapping sounded at the window again, firm, insistent. She wasn't there, on the stairs with William. She was in the cabin, and William wanted Mattie to open the window.

He wanted her to open the window like she had before and he was sure, he was certain that she would because Mattie always listened to him, Mattie always obeyed. She'd opened the window for him in the first place.

The bedroom window was the only one large enough for William to fit through, she realized. The two windows in the main room were small, too small for his shoulders, but the bedroom window was larger. He could climb through there. He could reach her again, punch her in the face, throw her to the floor, remind her that her duty was to make sons for him.

*Tap tap tap*

He was so sure, so certain.

Mattie's feet moved toward the window.

The creature roared out in the night, so close that it could have been in the cabin with them.

Then the screaming started.

# CHAPTER FOURTEEN

Griffin," C.P. said from the other room.

Mattie heard him run across the wood floor, heard the front curtains swish open. She hurried into the main room and nearly tripped over Jen, who was lying in the middle of the floor, still as death.

"Get . . . away . . . from . . . window," Mattie wheezed out.

The creature roared again, and the person outside was screaming, screaming long horrible cries of pain that seemed to push inside her ears and press against her eyeballs and stop up her throat.

"That's Griffin out there," C.P. said. "We have to go out and help him. We have to do something. He sounds like he's dying."

"We . . . can't. Creature. William," Mattie said, and rushed toward the door. She sat down in the chair that C.P. had placed there earlier, determined not to let him outside.

She wished she could speak properly, or that Jen was awake to help talk some sense into C.P. How could he consider going outside? If the creature didn't get him then William would, and once the door was open, William would come inside.

"I don't care what you say, I'm going out there! Griffin would have done the same for you. We're only in this mess because of you anyway. He couldn't stop talking about you, kept saying we had to help because you were being abused by your asshole husband. We only came back in this direction because he wanted to do something about it and now you're going to sit there like a cowardly little bitch and let him die outside your door?"

Mattie stared at C.P., stricken by the sudden change in him, the snarl in his voice, the contempt she felt radiating from him. Griffin's screams filled up the empty space between them.

*Cowardly little bitch.* Was that what she was? Was this true? Had the three strangers only been put in harm's way because they wanted to help her?

A rifle sounded outside, a huge booming rifle that made a noise like Mattie had never heard before.

"Demon! Go back to hell!"

William. William was shooting the creature.

C.P. moved from the window to stand in front of Mattie, who pressed herself back in the chair that blocked the front door. The flashlight was in one of his hands and the rifle in the other. He trained the flashlight on her.

"Get out of the way or I'll throw you out of the way," C.P. said. "I'm going out there to get my friend."

Griffin's screams faded out then, overwhelmed by the angry roars of the creature, William's screams, the report of the rifle.

If C.P. went out there, he would only get caught in the crossfire—shot by William, or snatched up by the creature like his friend. She couldn't let him leave.

**And if he leaves you'll be all alone with an unconscious woman and who will protect you then? Isn't that right?**

Mattie wanted to shout at that voice, that smug little Samantha, the one who knew that Mattie was helpless, nothing unless she had a man to protect her.

*I'm not helpless,* she thought. She curled her fingers around the seat of the chair. He'd have to pry her off if he wanted her to move.

"Can't . . . let . . . you," Mattie said. "You'll . . . get . . . hurt."

"Do you really think that matters? Griffin's my best friend and I can't leave him out there. Move."

Mattie shook her head, half-blind from the glare of the flashlight. He was nothing but a silhouette to her, a silhouette of an angry man looming.

*He's going to hurt me he's going to hurt me he's going to hit me and throw me on the floor and throw the chair after me like I'm nothing but garbage and maybe I am because I don't want to go outside and help the screaming man but there's nothing we can do there isn't anything the creature is too big William is too dangerous the world is too big and dangerous altogether it's safer just to stay right here with the door closed.*

The creature stopped roaring. William stopped firing the rifle. There was a strangled cry, and everything was silent.

Mattie's fingers squeezed against the wood of the chair. What was happening now? Had William killed the creature? Was he even now stalking back to the cabin, triumphant in his defeat of the demon?

She listened. She didn't hear anything, not the *thunk-drag* of William's walk, not Griffin's screams, not the flurry of breaking branches that meant the creature was moving through the trees.

But Mattie knew the creature could be silent when it wanted to be.

A second later, the front window shattered.

There was another huge roar, loud and close. Mattie covered her ears, curled up on the chair with her legs tight against her chest, trying to make herself as small as possible. The cold night air rushed in behind the open window.

C.P. turned the flashlight toward the window, and for a moment Mattie saw claws shining in the beam of light, thought she smelled the sticky metallic sweetness of blood, and then it was gone.

Neither of them moved. Mattie realized she was holding her breath and it was making her lightheaded. She exhaled but her whole body trembled.

"Was that its *paw*?" C.P. said. He sounded scared but fascinated at the same time.

Mattie hadn't seen anything like a paw. She'd only noticed the claws—long, almost impossibly long things the color of night and sharper than any falcon's, not the claws of a bear at all. Those were claws to rend and tear, claws to peel open flesh.

Her teeth were chattering again. The freezing air poured through the broken glass and the fire wasn't lit.

*And I'm scared. I'm more scared than I've ever been before. If the creature grabbed me with those claws there's nothing I could do. It would tear me open like all those little animals it hung up in the forest and I would scream and scream but I couldn't stop it.*

"Do you think it's still out there?" C.P. said.

"Yes," Mattie said. She felt it, felt its malevolence, felt its eyes watching her even through the door of the cabin.

"Do you think it got that guy?"

For a moment she didn't know who C.P. was talking about.

"William."

"Yeah, do you think it got him or that he just dropped the gun or ran away or what?"

Any of those options were plausible. The creature could have injured William—injured him for a second time, if Mattie's assumptions about why William was limping were true. He also could have dropped the gun, or had it swiped out of his hands by an animal furious at being shot. Or he may have just decided to cut his losses, to run into the woods.

That last seemed unlikely. The cabin was William's and he would have run toward it if he could, not away from it. He would have banged on the door and demanded they let him in.

*If he could. But if he's been injured again, he might not have been able to do that. Or the creature might have blocked his way.*

"We gotta cover this window," C.P. said. "You don't have any wood or anything? Tools?"

There were tools, but those tools were in the storehouse along with the food. William never left anything lying about that might tempt Mattie.

*He never left anything I could use as a weapon. No matter how he crushed me, he was always afraid that I might show some spirit, so he never left a hammer within reach of my hand.*

And there wasn't any wood to cover the window. It was the

same problem she'd encountered earlier when she thought about covering them up.

"No," she said. "Tools . . . are . . . outside."

"Well, we've got to put a quilt over it or something," he said. "Jen's going to freeze to death if we don't, and so will we."

Jen hadn't moved an inch, not while all the screaming and shooting had happened outside, not even when the creature broke the window. Mattie didn't think that was a good sign.

"We . . . should . . . put . . . her . . . in . . . the . . . bed," Mattie said. "Get . . . warm."

"Right. If she was awake she would say I was a dummy, wouldn't she?" He choked on the last couple of words and Mattie realized he was crying. "Griffin's probably dead and Jen's probably dying and there isn't a damned thing I can do about it. I'm not even smart enough to cover up a sick woman with a blanket. I'm useless."

He was crumpling up before Mattie's eyes, the terror of it all finally punching through his shell.

"Not . . . useless," she said, pushing away from the chair and standing on unsteady legs. "You . . . and . . . me. We'll . . . take . . . care . . . of . . . her."

C.P. wiped his eyes. "Right. We'll take care of her. We'll take care of her and we'll get out of this. You were right. It was stupid of me to want to charge outside. What good will it do if all of us are injured? You take her feet and I'll take her shoulders."

Mattie quickly untied Jen's heavy leather boots and pushed them aside. Then she grabbed Jen's ankles as C.P. lifted her shoulders and the two of them carefully walked into the bedroom, C.P. bumping into the doorway and then the dresser, cursing both times.

"We need some light in here. This is ridiculous. How do you live without electricity?"

They heaved Jen onto the bed. C.P. unzipped her puffy jacket and then maneuvered her under the blankets. Mattie collected some extra quilts from the closet, finding them in the dark by feel. They piled the extra layers on top of Jen.

"Her breath is so quiet," C.P. said. "Should it be so quiet like that?"

Mattie didn't know. She didn't know anything except basic first aid, things that William had taught her when he'd been hurt or sick and needed help.

"I . . . don't . . . know," she said. "Sorry."

"She needs a doctor. I don't think this should happen—her being asleep like this—just because she got her leg caught in a trap. She didn't bleed *that* much. And it's clotted by now, or it should be. Do you think we should check? Try to cut off the bottom of her pant leg and clean the wound and wrap it?"

Mattie considered. There was always a risk of infection, and the metal teeth had bitten deep into Jen's leg. However, the other woman was plainly unconscious and Mattie worried that it was dangerous to try to wake her.

"No," she said. "Let . . . her . . . rest. Check . . . on . . . her . . . later."

He stood there, a darker shadow against a dark room. Mattie didn't need to see his face to know that he was looking at his friend and worrying.

"OK," he said. "She'll kill me if I cut those pants off anyway—those are her favorite hiking pants."

Mattie didn't point out that the pants were already ruined by the trap. He was clearly miserable and trying to make the best of it.

They filed out of the bedroom and Mattie pulled the door shut so Jen would be warmer. Even without the fire, the smaller room could feel quite snug, and cold air was still gusting through the broken front window.

"Anyway," C.P. said, and it was clear that he was trying to push away his worry about Jen and focus on something else. "I don't think we should try to go outside again until morning, so let's cover up the window and at least get the fire going. I wish there was some kind of cell reception up here. I'd call the nearest rescue copter to come and get us ASAP."

"Cell?" Mattie asked.

"Yeah, you know, for cell phones? There's no signal here."

Mattie remembered a phone in her mother's house, a black wireless handset standing in a big black charger, but she didn't think this was what C.P. meant.

She had a flash of someone in the grocery store—a man. He took something out of his pocket that was making noise, something silver with an antenna sticking off it, and flipped it open and put it up to his ear.

*Cellular phone. Right. Mom never had one. She couldn't afford it, and she said she didn't need it anyway. She wasn't some important business person. She was just a waitress at an all-night diner, although she tried not to take those late shifts because she had to find someone to watch me and Heather.*

Mattie stilled. Her mother was—had been—a waitress at an all-night diner. This was the first time she remembered something concrete about her mom. Her mother felt less vague suddenly, more like she was coming into focus.

*I don't want her murder to be the only thing I remember about her.*

C.P. seemed to be waiting for Mattie to respond, to commiserate with him over the lack of a signal, whatever that meant.

"You . . . have . . . one? A . . . cellular . . . phone?"

"Yeah, everyone has one." He paused. "Well, I'm guessing you don't."

"No . . . phone. No . . . electricity."

"Well, let's get some light in here. You have candles or whatever? Torches for the wall? We've got to get that window covered up and then figure out our next move."

Mattie could find the candles and matches in the dark. She didn't want C.P. crowding her into the corner so she said, "Stay . . . here."

The candles were in a basket near the window that the creature had broken. As she approached it she felt the rush of winter air through the shattered panes, felt the glass grinding into the floor under her boots. She had a sudden, irrational fear that the creature was outside waiting for one of them to approach the window. As soon as she was within reach, its giant paw would emerge again, grab her like it had Griffin, pull her through the window and out into the night.

She hesitated, listening. Could she hear its breath outside, the rustle of its fur, the scrape of its claws against the snow?

*Stop being a fool, Mattie. It's not waiting for you.*

But Mattie wasn't so sure about that. This creature, it didn't act like an ordinary animal. It had shown terrifying cunning more than once already. And it was angry with them—with her and William and Griffin and C.P. and Jen. The creature had left the warning in the snow, told them to stay away. Then the three strangers had gone into its cave even after Mattie told them not to do so. It might be waiting, there by the window, just out of sight.

"What's the matter?" C.P. said. "Do you need the flashlight?"

"No," Mattie said.

She was acting foolish, the way William always said she did. They needed candles and they needed to block the cold air from coming in and they needed to light the fire. The monsters were out in the night—William and the creature—and Mattie and C.P. and Jen were inside the cabin, tucked away where it was safe. She stepped in front of the window, feeling her way around the table for the candle basket.

Her hand touched something wet and sticky.

Mattie let out a startled cry. C.P. clicked on the flashlight again and pointed it toward her.

"What is it?" he said.

The flashlight beam bobbed around her head and shoulders. She pointed at the table. "Something. There."

C.P. approached the table, angling the light down. Mattie screamed again and stumbled backward, banging into one of the dining table chairs.

The creature had left something for them when it crashed through the window.

"That's a heart," C.P. said. He sounded sick. "A human heart?"

Neither of them said what they both were thinking. There were only two people the heart could belong to—Griffin or William.

And Griffin had been screaming, screaming in agony, until he'd suddenly stopped.

*But I won't stop hoping that it was William,* Mattie thought. *It could be him. It might be. He's not standing outside the window demanding that I open up the door so maybe the creature cut his heart out with those razor claws and oh I hope it's him I really do.*

"Why would it do that?" C.P. said. "Why? It doesn't make any damned sense."

"It's . . . a . . . warning," Mattie said. "Another . . . one."

"Animals don't act like this," C.P. said. "They eat what they kill. They don't take their kills apart and sort them into component pieces."

The flashlight beam was steady on the heart, like C.P. couldn't stop looking at it.

"I thought it was weird when we were in the cave. Weird, but fascinating. I guess it's only fascinating when you're not the one being sorted into those component pieces."

His voice sounded strange and distant, like he was drifting away from everything—Mattie, the cabin, the heart.

Mattie didn't think. She grabbed the heart and threw it out the window. They heard a wet *splat* against the snow.

For a moment Mattie thought there would be a response from outside—that the creature would rush to the window again, or that William would emerge from the woods. But there was nothing—only the sway of the trees and the cold wind and the press of night all around.

"What did you do that for?" C.P. said.

He was angry, swinging the flashlight toward Mattie's face, but for the first time she felt relieved to hear his anger. It meant he was himself again. She'd been frightened by the distance in his voice, the feeling that he was floating away and leaving her behind. She couldn't do everything on her own. She needed him.

"We . . . don't . . . need . . . that," she said.

She wanted to explain more—explain that it wouldn't help him or Griffin to keep the heart, that it would only frighten and upset them more to have it in the room with them—but her voice wouldn't let her say the words. Her throat hurt terribly now, almost worse than it had when William was strangling her.

C.P. didn't respond, only stood there, and she didn't know what he was thinking. This was, in some ways, more disconcerting than his anger. In the brief period she'd known him, C.P. had always made his feelings clear from moment to moment.

Mattie found the matches for the candles. There were several in metal stands on the mantel over the fire, and she lit these first. C.P. stayed where he was, not watching her, not appearing to see anything at all. After his initial burst of anger he seemed to have faded out again, his mind gone someplace where he didn't have to think about his friend having his heart removed by a monster.

*He's gone away to a place where he's safe, where he doesn't have to think about it. I recognize the signs.*

Mattie had used this tactic herself many times, so she wouldn't have to feel what William was doing to her. The trouble was that she couldn't stay where her mind brought her. She always had to come back to the present world and the pain William left behind. When C.P. came back, his friend would still be gone and they would still be trapped in the cabin and there would still be a monster outside the door.

There was no wood to cover the window so Mattie took one of her thick quilts and folded it up. She used a chair to climb onto the worktable, knelt in front of the window and then carefully tucked the quilt into the frame, wrapping part of the top edge around the curtain rod so it would stay in place. Some of the draft still leaked around the edges, but at least the cold wasn't pouring into the room. More importantly, the empty eye of the window was covered again. The monster (*monsters?*) couldn't see inside.

She climbed down from the table. There was still plenty of firewood in the cabin, because William had expected her to stay inside all day. Mattie assembled the firewood and lit the kindling, feeling terribly daring as she did. She was only allowed to start the fire if William was watching.

Her stomach rumbled. The bread and cheese and butter were still on the dining table, just as she'd left them, and there was enough water for tea.

Mattie bustled around, slicing the bread and cheese, tending the fire, preparing the kettle and putting it over the flame. She felt soothed by the normalcy of it, the routine of doing chores. She set out two plates, just like she always did, and two cups for the tea, and when the water boiled she poured it out.

She noticed then that C.P. wasn't in his fugue state any longer, but watching her with a curious expression on his face. Was it pity? Mattie felt herself flush. She didn't need his pity. She didn't deserve it, either.

"Sit . . . down . . . and . . . eat . . . something," she said. She felt ashamed of the meager offering, unable to explain that William kept all the food in the storehouse under lock and key. They only had this much because he'd been in a generous mood, thinking that once he killed the demon he'd return home, the triumphant hunter.

*And the triumphant hunter would then get sons on his little wife.*

She felt the gorge rise in her throat but she swallowed it down. She didn't need to submit to him anymore. Never again.

C.P. looked at the neat assembly of sliced bread and sliced cheese and the plate of butter Mattie had put out.

"We could make grilled cheese sandwiches with what you've got there. You have a pan, right?"

"Grilled cheese," Mattie said, and she had a sense memory so strong it made her sway on her feet. Crunchy bread that tasted of butter and a thick layer of melted yellow cheese, still hot from the pan, and next to it a bowl of soup and the noodles in the soup were shaped like letters.

"Hey, are you okay?" he asked, making a movement like he was going to help her stand.

Mattie waved him away, closing her eyes. She could almost still smell the soup, taste the bread on her tongue.

"We don't have to make it if you don't want to," C.P. said. "I just thought it might be better than cold bread."

"We . . . can," she said. "But . . . I . . . don't . . . know . . . how."

"Oh, well, I can do that. I can make four things in the kitchen without a microwave, and grilled cheese is one of them. Well, five things if you count cold cereal, but is it really *making* food if you just pour the cereal in a bowl and put milk on top? Sometimes I don't even put the milk in, either, just eat the cereal out of the bowl like chips. That's usually only if I have sugar cereal, though—you know, the stuff kids like to eat. Griff says it's gross, that I have the habits of a four-year-old."

He'd started buttering slices of bread while he talked, and at the mention of Griffin he faltered for a moment, his hands going slack. Then he started up again, with more energy.

"Can you put the pan over the fire, please? You're lucky I've cooked over a fire before when we've been camping, otherwise who knows how these would turn out."

Mattie didn't respond as he chattered away, but he didn't seem to need her to do so. He was filling the space with words so he wouldn't have to think. She knew that. She placed the heavy pan on the fire on the same grate that she used to fry eggs.

He carried one plate full of cheese slices and buttered bread over to the fire. Mattie watched as he put the bread into the pan. It sizzled immediately, filling the air with the scent of browning butter, and C.P. laid a slice of cheese on each slice of bread.

"Gotta keep a good eye on it with a cast iron pan like this," he said. "The bread could burn before the cheese melts. I need a spatula or something, and a clean plate for the sandwich."

Mattie handed him the turner she used for the eggs and after a very brief time he flipped the two bread slices together and then took the sandwich out and put it on a plate.

"Ta-da!" he said, and handed it to Mattie before repeating the process twice more.

"I always make two sandwiches," he said. "One isn't enough for me. It would be awesome if you had some bacon and tomato. That's the best way to make a grilled cheese—cheddar, bacon and tomato. Although sometimes I like to get really fancy and use mozzarella and prosciutto. Griff got this fig butter from Trader Joe's and I put it on a mozzarella and prosciutto sandwich and it came out *ah-may-zing.*"

Mattie wasn't really listening. She was staring at the sandwich he'd made for her—at the browned edges, the caramel-colored crumb, the ooze of yellow cheese over the side.

"Eat it before it gets too cold. Grilled cheese is one of man's greatest inventions but it is not delicious when it's cold."

Mattie placed the sandwich on the table and sat down in her accustomed chair. She lifted the sandwich to her mouth, bit down, chewed slowly.

A moment later C.P. sat down across from her with his own plate. "How is it? Hey, are you crying? Is it that bad?"

Mattie shook her head, wiped her streaming eyes. "Been . . . so . . . long . . ."

"So long since you had a grilled cheese sandwich?"

"No. Yes," she said. She wished she could explain. "So . . . long . . . since . . . sandwich. But . . . also . . . since . . . someone . . . made . . . for . . . me."

Mattie was always the one who did the cooking. It was expected of her, even if she was sick or injured. William didn't do women's work.

But she remembered her mother standing at the stove, stirring a pot of soup, flipping sandwiches together just like C.P. had done, and when Mom put the meal in front of her it wasn't just food to fill her up. It was love, love that made her mom buy the soup with the letters in it in the first place, love that had her standing at the stove cooking sandwiches when she was so tired all she wanted to do was shove two slices of cheese between bread and hand it to her daughter cold.

Mattie didn't know how to explain to C.P. that she was crying because the sandwich reminded her of her mother, and of home, and William had made certain she would never have her mother or her home again.

# CHAPTER FIFTEEN

t was strange having another man in the cabin. C.P. talked continuously, about everything, about things Mattie didn't even understand. He talked about television programs she'd never seen on channels that she didn't know existed, about countries he traveled to, about the things he studied at school, stores he liked to shop at, board games he liked to play, foods he liked to eat.

"A lot of Asians are lactose intolerant, they can't even eat a grilled cheese or ice cream or whatever without getting a stomachache, but my grandfather—my mom's dad—is actually French so I guess I got the French cheese-eating gene. Lucky for me. I went to France a couple of years ago, just backpacked around during the summer school break, and all I ate was cheese and pastries for two months. And wine, of course."

Mattie had never had wine. She only had the vaguest idea of France, of where it was, of what its people were like.

The more C.P. ate, the more he talked. It was like filling his stomach released some kind of block in his brain, and he talked and talked and talked.

William never talked like this. He told Mattie what she needed to do, and sometimes what he planned to do for the day, or he gave her a list of chores they'd need to complete to get ready for the next season. He never chattered idly or talked about his likes and dislikes.

Mattie didn't know what William would list as a like or dislike, in any case. He didn't seem to like anything, not even the girl he wanted to own so much he'd taken her from her family in the dead of night.

The fire warmed the room and the food warmed their bellies and the terrors of the night seemed far away. They were safe inside four walls that kept the monsters at bay.

Mattie felt her head falling forward, her eyelids drifting at half-mast. She sat up with a start.

"Hey, you're dead on your feet," C.P. said. "I am, too, I guess. Why don't you go get in the bed with Jen and I'll sleep out here on this couch thing?"

Mattie hesitated. She didn't know if she wanted to get into bed with a stranger. She also might disturb Jen if she got in the bed with her. And was it really safe to go to sleep? She didn't know if they should let down their guard so completely. Anything might happen while they slept.

*Anything might happen, but anything might happen even if you're awake. He's right—you're dead on your feet and the only way you're going to get off this mountain is if you rest. You don't have the energy to walk three feet right now, much less a day or more.*

"Jen won't care, if that's what you're worried about," C.P. said, waving his hand. "You'll probably help keep her warm, to be honest. Let's check and see how she's doing, anyway."

Mattie opened the door to the bedroom. The room seemed very chilly compared to the main room where the fire burned.

"Maybe we should leave this door open now that the front window is covered, huh?" C.P. said. "It's freezing in here."

The light from the main room cast just enough illumination for her to see the lump that was Jen on the bed. She didn't seem to have moved at all. Her face seemed unnaturally still to Mattie.

*What if she died? What if she died right there in bed while we ate grilled cheese sandwiches on the other side of the door?*

C.P. entered behind her, crowding her as always, and Mattie moved to one side. He crossed to the bed and put his hand on Jen's forehead.

"She's not quite as cold as she was, and she doesn't seem to have a fever. I wish I knew what was wrong with her." He reached under the blanket and pulled out Jen's arm so he could feel her wrist. "Her pulse is slow. Like, super-slow. She is a running nut so maybe it's just that her resting heart rate is low but I don't know. What if she had a heart attack or a stroke or something? That's crazy, right? More likely she's just in shock and she just shut down. I mean, between that guy chasing us with the gun and the cryptid and Griffin and everything . . . it's a lot. Plus her leg got caught in the trap. Her brain might have just been on overload."

Mattie felt a surge of resentment. She, too, had been terrorized by the monster and she'd been strangled by her husband and she'd been chased through the woods. And it wasn't even the first time these things had happened to her. Why didn't she get to faint and let someone else cope with all the horrors? Why did she have to keep pulling herself up and pushing on?

The resentment was almost immediately crushed beneath the weight of shame—shame that she would feel that way, shame that she would blame Jen for something she couldn't help.

But Mattie was worried about what they would do in the morning if Jen still wasn't moving and functioning. They didn't know if William was still alive, but if he was, he would certainly chase them. And the creature would, too. They would never escape if they tried to drag Jen between them, and Mattie didn't think C.P. would be willing to leave herself and Jen behind in the cabin while he went for help.

*He might leave you behind. You're nobody to him, and he made it clear that the only reason he helped was because of Griffin. He wouldn't leave Jen, even if it's more practical for him to go for help and return later.*

What would happen in the morning would happen. Mattie needed to stop worrying about it and sleep. Maybe Jen would wake up, refreshed and ready to run. Maybe William would be dead, and Mattie would have one less fear.

"Well," C.P. said. He said this often, Mattie noticed. He filled in empty spaces with words that had no purpose. "I guess I'll go pitch my tent by the fire. Seems kind of unfair. It's so much warmer out there. But you guys will be more comfortable in the bed, right? If you'd rather sleep by the fire I could climb in with Jen."

Mattie must have looked as appalled as she felt, because C.P. laughed.

"I bet your religion says men shouldn't sleep with women who aren't their wives or something, right? It's not like that. We're just friends. We've slept in the same tent more times than I can count."

It did seem strange to Mattie, very strange, but she pushed back against the strangeness because she knew this was something that William had taught her and everything William taught her was a lie.

"I . . . think . . . it . . . would . . . be . . . better . . . if . . . you . . ." Mattie gestured toward the bed.

"Are you sure?" C.P. asked. "I'm not going to lie, the couch didn't look long enough for my legs, even if the fire is out there."

Mattie nodded. This was preferable. C.P. said Jen wouldn't mind but Mattie had a lot of trouble reconciling herself to the idea of sleeping next to a stranger. And this way C.P. could monitor his friend. Mattie suspected that if he slept in the main room he would be in and out of the bedroom several times, checking on Jen.

C.P. started pulling off his coat and boots and Mattie left the room quickly. She didn't know if he would strip down to his underwear or not and she wasn't comfortable staying in the same room if he did.

"Leave the door open," he called after her

She wanted to take off her own heavy skirts and petticoats and change into a nightgown, but she heard the rustle of C.P. settling into the bed and decided not to go back in to get her night things. She hadn't taken off her coat since they'd entered the cabin, though, so she put it away and then crouched in front of the couch, fairly certain that nobody would be able to see her from the bedroom. She slid her petticoats off so she just wore a wool skirt and stockings and her heavy sweater. Then she stoked the fire, adding wood so that it would burn well into the night.

Mattie climbed onto the couch and covered herself with a knitted blanket. It was warm and comfortable by the fire, and she was exhausted and her belly was full. She listened to the sounds of C.P. rolling around in the bed, clearly trying to get comfortable in a strange place. She wondered if she would be able to sleep with two strangers in the cabin.

*William carried her down the stairs, away from Mom, away from her mother's strange stillness and the sticky-sweet smell. Sam wasn't wearing anything except pajamas, not even socks on her feet, and she knew that something was very wrong no matter what William said because Mom loved her and she would never let someone else take her away, not even William.*

*William was only Mom's boyfriend. Sam had always liked him, because he played with her and Heather and sometimes he carried Sam on his shoulders when they were out. Sometimes she felt like he was a dad. She didn't remember their real dad, who went away a long time ago.*

*But now William was acting weird and Mom didn't answer when Sam called and she didn't want to leave with William. He wasn't her real dad. He couldn't take her away. And Heather wasn't home, Heather was at a sleepover party with a bunch of girls from her class and if Sam left now she wouldn't even have a chance to say goodbye to her own sister.*

*"I don't want to go!" she said. "Let me go!"*

*"Samantha," William said. "I told you once that you are to listen to me and obey. I will not tell you again."*

*Sam squirmed and wriggled but his arms were so strong. William's arms were much stronger than her little self, and instead of making her feel safe and happy they felt like a prison. She never felt* so small as she did at that moment, when William changed from Mom's silly boyfriend to a giant from a fairy tale, a giant with blood in his teeth.

"I didn't want to do this," he said, and his hand covered her nose as well as her mouth and she couldn't breathe and then there was no more Mom, no more William, no more strange smells or the shadows of her bedroom at night.

When she opened her eyes she was in a vehicle and it was moving fast. She heard the rumble of the tires on the road and the whooshing sound of the wind outside. She was buckled into a seat belt that seemed too big for her—she was so small that her mother insisted she still use a booster seat in the car even though all of her friends were out of them. There was no booster seat now, and her feet were very far from the floor, and she could see the dashboard. That wasn't right. She wasn't supposed to sit in the front of the car—only in the back. Grownups sat in the front.

She wasn't in a car. She was in a truck. Sam peered out the window and saw trees going by very fast. She sat up a little straighter and saw an empty highway ahead.

There was a jacket draped over her but it wasn't her jacket. It was a leather jacket with a quilted lining and it was William's. She recognized it right away. Her feet were cold even though the heater was blowing.

Then she remembered—William at the window, Mom lying so still in the bed, William covering her mouth with her hand.

"Awake, sleepyhead?" William said. "How's my pretty girl?"

Sam sat up straighter and looked over at the driver. William was smiling at her as he drove. She didn't smile back.

"Where's Mom?" she said.

"I told you before, your mother wants me to take care of you for a while. It's very difficult for her, you know. She's all by herself with two little girls. You want to help your mother, don't you? You want to make things easier for her?"

This didn't make any sense to Sam at all, and she said so.

"If you want it to be easier then you should come and live with us and we can all take care of each other. That's what Mom always says—that we take care of each other. She wouldn't send me away with you." She wanted to get out of the truck. She wanted to go back home. She was cold and hungry and scared and she didn't understand any of this.

William's smile faded, and when he spoke his voice had the frozen-river quality she'd heard earlier, the one that made her feel cold deep in the pit of her stomach.

"Now listen to me. From now on you will do as I say and when I say it. You will not argue or talk back. You will not speak of your mother or your sister anymore. You are to forget about them."

"I can't forget about Mom and Heather! They're my family! You're not my family! I don't belong with you!"

Sam started to unbuckle her seat belt even though the truck was on a highway and she should never unbuckle her seat belt while the truck was moving. She didn't even know where she would go. If she jumped out she'd probably die.

"Do not unbuckle your seat belt," William said in that dead-of-winter voice.

Sam didn't care what he said. He wasn't her father. He wasn't in charge of her. She was going to unbuckle her belt and as soon as she saw another car she was going to roll down the window and shout for help.

*She never saw it coming. One moment she was pressing on the red seat belt release and the next moment there were stars in her eyes and her mouth tasted like blood.*

*"I didn't want to do that," William said. "But I will, if you don't listen to me, Samantha. You'd better start listening right now. Do not unbuckle your seat belt."*

*He hit me, she thought in a daze. No one had ever hit her before, not for any reason. Her mother didn't believe in spanking, and Sam wasn't the sort of child who got in fistfights on the playground.*

*"You can't hit me," she said. "My mom doesn't even hit me."*

*She was just as unprepared for the second blow as the first.*

*"I told you not to speak of your mother again," William said. "As far as you are concerned, your mother no longer exists."*

*Sam wanted to shout again, wanted to scream that he couldn't take her mother away from her, couldn't do what he was doing. But her head hurt and her cheek hurt and her mouth hurt and she was really scared now, scared of what he would do if she didn't do what he said.*

But he can't make me forget Mom and Heather, *she thought.* He can't see what's going on inside my head. I can remember them all I want. And as soon as I have a chance I'm going to run away from him and go back to them. I just have to pretend to be good, to think and pay attention.

*"Where are we?" she asked.*

*William flashed a smile at her again. His smile used to seem so happy but now it made her feel sick.*

*"We're on our way to a special place, my pretty girl. A special place just for you and me." He frowned then, looking at her bare feet. "We'll have to stop somewhere and get you some shoes,*

*though. And warm clothes. It's cold where we're going, even in the summer."*

*If they stopped for clothes then she could run away from him in the store, could shout and scream until someone came to help her. There were usually security guards in big stores and security guards were almost like police, right? Some of them carried guns.*

*She'd seen security guards with guns at the mall where Mom took her and Heather shopping sometimes. They couldn't afford new things very often but they all liked to go and window shop, and imagine how they might look in new jeans or a new blouse. They'd go into the department stores and spray all the perfume samples, and sometimes ladies would try to put makeup on Mom but she always said no. Mom didn't really wear a lot of makeup, just lip gloss or mascara sometimes, and Sam knew that even though the ladies were acting like trying on makeup was free, they really would want Mom to buy some of it after.*

*After they sprayed lots of different perfumes on themselves Mom would take them to get ice cream cones from the McDonald's in the food court. It was fun when they did that, and Sam didn't even feel so bad that they didn't have the money for new clothes or shoes. She didn't mind just looking as long as she got to go somewhere with Mom and Heather.*

*Sam looked at William out of the corners of her eyes. She didn't think shopping with William would be like shopping with Mom. She remembered how hard his arms had been wrapped around her on the stairs. She'd have to pay attention for her chance and run so fast when it was time, or else he'd just grab her and cover her mouth again and she'd never get away.*

*She must have fallen asleep again because the next thing she* knew the truck had stopped and William was opening the passenger door and lifting her out.

"Come on, my sweet girl. Rest stop."

She wished he'd stop calling her that. He used to say things like that at home, when Mom and Heather were there, call her "sweet girl" or "pretty girl," but he'd say them to Mom and Heather, too, and it didn't seem so weird. Now it felt strange and it made her belly feel sick.

They'd stopped at a small brick building next to a long parking lot. There was no one else in the lot and it was so cold. Her bare feet felt like bricks of ice. William held her very close as they went inside.

"Hey, this is the boys' room!" she said as he took her into the restroom with him. "I can't go in the boys' room!"

"You have to stay with me," William said, and she knew better than to say anything else because his eyes were like chips of ice and she sensed danger.

He set her down in front of a stall. The tile floor was freezing and dirty, and the bathroom smelled of disinfectant and pee. "Go do your business."

Sam didn't want to walk on the tile, and she especially didn't want to go into the toilet stall in her bare feet, but she did because William was looking at her in a way that told her she'd better.

There was grit and dust and hair on the floor, and Sam tried very hard not to think about what she was stepping on. The toilet was very high and she was so small for her age that she had trouble sitting on it to pee. Her feet dangled off the ground while water came out of her in a tiny trickle. She always had trouble peeing when she was nervous, would hold on to it compulsively until she *was able to relax again and then she'd have to sprint to the bathroom before she wet her pants.*

*After a minute William said, "Hurry up," and he had that tone in his voice again, the one that said she had to listen. Sam wiped herself and hopped off the toilet. William picked her up again as soon as she came out of the stall. He seemed like he was in a big hurry all of a sudden.*

*"I have to wash my hands," she said. She really wanted to, for a change, wanted to wash them properly (that was what Mom always said, that she didn't wash them properly) because the toilet had been so gross and she wanted to scrub her hands really well.*

*William hesitated, then said, "You're right. You should always wash your hands after you've dirtied them because cleanliness is next to godliness."*

*Sam thought this was a very strange thing for him to say but she didn't care as long as she got to wash her hands. He wouldn't set her down in front of the sink, though. He kept hold of her while she wet her hands and rubbed soap all over them. A second later there was some noise outside in the entryway, the sound of voices, and a young man entered the bathroom.*

*Now Sam knew why William had seemed like he was in a hurry. He'd heard the other car outside and he didn't want to run into anyone. This was her chance.*

*Sam saw his face in the mirror—he wasn't too much younger than William, actually—and her heart leapt. All she needed to do was say something and the strange man would help her. But it was like William read her mind, could see inside her eyes, because he squeezed her very hard and she felt the warning and instead rinsed the soap off her hands and dried with the scratchy paper towel that*

*William handed her. The young man went about his business, didn't even seem to notice Sam and William there.*

*She felt her chance at freedom slipping away. She had to open her mouth and say "Help me" before William took her out of the bathroom and put her back in the car and took her away forever.*

*Just then William leaned his mouth very close to her ear and said, "If you say one word to anyone I will kill them. I have a knife on my belt and I will slash their throats open with that knife and it will be your fault. Do not speak."*

*Sam began to tremble, because the young man looked nice and he probably had a family and if she said one word, said anything at all, then William would kill him and there would be blood all over the bathroom.*

Just like Mom.

Just like what William did to Mom.

*But the idea that her mother had been slashed to ribbons by this man was so terrible that her mind turned away from it.*

No. Mom's not dead. She can't be. She has to be alive so that she can come for me. She wouldn't leave me with William. She wouldn't.

*William carried her out of the bathroom. There was a young woman, about the same age as the young man Sam had seen in the mirror, idly flipping through the tourist pamphlets and maps. She turned when she heard the door, clearly expecting the young man. She had long brown hair and a purple knitted hat with a pompom on top. She waved when she saw Sam.*

*"Your daughter is so cute," she said to William. "How old is she?"*

I'm not his daughter! *Sam wanted to cry.* Help me. Help me. He's stealing me.

"She's five," William lied.

Sam wanted to cry out in outrage, I'm not five, I'm eight, I'm just small. She knew it was a trick, though, a trick that William had done to see if she would talk, but Sam wouldn't be the one who let William kill this pretty lady with her long brown hair.

"Sooo gorgeous with that blond hair and brown eyes. You don't really see that combination, huh? Her mom must have brown eyes," the lady said. She'd gotten closer as she talked.

William laughed. Sam was amazed that he could laugh and sound normal when he did it, like he wasn't doing anything wrong at all. That was the first time she realized what a good liar he was, that he could lie about anything, that his face would say one thing while in his heart he was thinking something completely different.

"Yeah, she didn't get my eyes, that's for sure. My pretty brown-eyed girl," he said.

"Just like the song," the young woman said, and she was clearly delighted. "I'm ready for a little girl of my own. I hope she looks just like you!"

Sam felt William's muscles tighten, felt the warning there, so she didn't say anything but gave the young woman a little smile. She hoped the smile would alert the lady that something was wrong, that the lady would see that Sam wasn't smiling the way a real person smiles, but then William made sure the young woman wouldn't think anything of it.

"She's really shy," William said. "She doesn't usually talk to strangers."

"I guess that's a good habit to have, huh, cutie? So many scary people in the world."

He's a scary person, you're talking to a scary person right now, oh please help, please help me get away.

*A moment later the young man came out of the bathroom and the young woman joined him.*

*"Have a good trip!" the young woman said, and the two of them exited the rest stop.*

*William picked up one of the pamphlets and glanced at it like he was interested.*

*"That was very good, Samantha. You did exactly as I told you to do. My good little girl."*

I'm not yours I'm not your little girl I want to go home I want to go back home right now

*Sam heard the sound of the car engine outside, heard the people who could have saved her driving away.*

*William carried her outside again, looking left and right and all around to make sure there was no one else in the rest area. Then he went around to the back of the truck and lowered the gate with one arm while keeping a tight grip on Sam.*

*There was a long wooden trunk in the back of the truck, like old-fashioned luggage. It had a brass-colored lock on it and William opened it with a key. Inside it was lined with a blanket, and there was a pillow on top of this and another blanket. It looked like a nest.*

*William looked left and right again, and before Sam knew it, he had dropped her inside the trunk and shut the top.*

*"No!" she screamed, and pounded on the sides of the trunk. It was dark and it was small, so small, and she couldn't breathe in there. She would die. "Let me out, let me out, let me out!"*

*She heard the lock clicking, then William's voice, very close and clear.*

"*Stop that yelling right now. There are three holes drilled in the side so that you can breathe. I'm talking through them. Now I know you were good in the rest area but we're going to a shopping center now to get you some clothes and some other things and I can't take a chance that you'll run away on me. You just stay in there until I'm done and then I'll let you sit in the front seat again.*"

"*No,*" Sam sobbed. "*Let me out. Let me out. I'll be a good girl.*"

"*I know you will be,*" William said. "*You'll be my good girl forever.*"

# CHAPTER SIXTEEN

M attie woke with a start, sitting straight up on the couch, her heart pounding. She'd forgotten the trunk. She'd forgotten so many things.

*That trunk, that's the same one that William keeps at the foot of the bed. He locked me inside it like I was a bad dog and left me there.*

The fire had burned down but wasn't completely out. The room was cold again, and Mattie rose slowly to put firewood on. The draft leaking in from the broken window seemed worse and she noticed that the bottom part of the quilt had come free from the window frame and was flapping in the breeze. It was no longer night outside.

She shuffled to the table where she kept the jug of water and poured some out for herself. It had little chunks of ice in it and hurt going down but she swallowed it all. She felt sick to her stomach, the lost memory lingering.

*How could he have done that to me? How could I have forgotten it all?*

She glanced at the bedroom. Through the open door she saw the piles of blankets and the unmoving lumps underneath them that told her C.P. and Jen were still asleep.

*Today we leave,* Mattie thought. *I don't care how hard it is, or what objections they raise. We have to get off this mountain, away from all the monsters.*

Despite the cold and her fear she felt better than she had the previous day. Her throat didn't feel as tender, and all her aches and pains had receded to dull throbs instead of sharp klaxons. Food and sleep were like magic.

**That's why William was always starving you, always working you when you were exhausted. Without food and sleep you couldn't think, couldn't fight him.**

There was no food left in the cabin. Mattie wondered if the storehouse was unlocked as she'd suspected it was the day before.

She also wondered if it was safe to go outside.

No noise of any kind had disturbed her sleep the previous night. After the screaming, the roaring, the firing of William's weapon there had been nothing. Mattie hoped that meant that both William and the creature were gone.

*If we can only get a head start,* she thought. The creature had to sleep sometime, and if they were lucky it had dragged William away somewhere.

The memory that had emerged while she slept prompted a

fierce and burning hope that William had been ripped to shreds by the creature.

Mattie pulled on her coat and boots and went to the front door. She put her ear against it, listening for the sound of William leaning against the door. No matter how still he was he would make some noise, even if it was just the scrape of his jacket against the wood.

For a moment she thought she heard him breathing, heard the sound of his heart pulsing

*(pulsing like the heart the creature gave us last night when I touched that thing it was still warm and I'll never tell anyone that never)*

but then she realized it was her own heartbeat thrumming against the wood. He wasn't out there. He couldn't be. If he was then he would be knocking on the door, demanding that Mattie open up and make his breakfast.

Her stomach rumbled. She was used to going without food, used to waiting for William to decide what they would eat and how much she should get. But the sandwich she'd eaten the night before—that decadent, buttered thing—had somehow made her hungrier than she'd ever been. She'd been full when she went to sleep, a feeling that she could not remember ever having since she came to live with William. And having felt full it seemed that she was greedy for that feeling again, the feeling of having eaten all she wanted and not needing any more.

"Are you going out?" C.P. asked.

Mattie started. She hadn't heard him rise from the bed. She'd been listening through the door and then she'd gotten distracted, drifted away in her mind the way William always told her not to do.

*William doesn't have any say any longer. You don't belong to him. You never did.*

C.P. stood in the doorway to the bedroom, wearing his pants and shirt and socks. His very black hair was rumpled from sleep and he yawned.

"I was going to go out to the storehouse," Mattie said, answering his question. She was very happy to hear that her voice was practically back to normal. It only sounded a little strained, and it didn't hurt to talk—at least, it didn't hurt as much as it had the day before. "There's no food left here."

"Do you think it's safe to go out? Not to be crude or anything, but my back teeth are floating."

Mattie tilted her head at him, confused. What did his teeth have to do with anything?

"I have to take a piss," C.P. said.

"Oh," Mattie said, and flushed. "Of course. The outhouse is behind the cabin."

"Yeah, we saw it the other day," he said. "Me and Griffin. I can't believe you lived here for twelve years without a flush toilet."

Mattie thought of telling him that the outhouse was hardly the worst indignity she'd suffered, but decided it wasn't worth it. He only looked half-awake anyway. She wasn't sure he'd understand anything she said.

"Look, I'll get my jacket and the rifle," he said. "And then we can go out and get some food from the storehouse and I can, erm . . ."

"Yes," she said quickly, and turned away to get her own coat and boots.

A moment later C.P. emerged from the bedroom dressed for the cold and carrying the rifle. He stopped to check the ammunition before they went out.

"I'd feel like an ass if it wasn't loaded," he said. "Now, you get behind the door and open it slowly. If there's anything outside I want to take care of it right away and I don't want to shoot you by accident."

Mattie positioned herself against the door while C.P. stood facing it, the rifle at his shoulder. She pulled the door open, using it as a shield, all the while thinking, *He's taking all the risk on himself. I shouldn't let him do that. I should be ready to defend us, too.*

But she didn't know what she would defend herself with, or even how.

She felt an unbearable pitch of suspense in her throat, expected William to charge through the open doorway, expected C.P. to fire the rifle. Instead C.P. huffed out a long, relieved breath.

"Nothing there," he said. "Let's go out. You stay behind me."

He didn't lower the rifle, but stayed ready to fire. He stepped out onto the porch, Mattie close behind him.

The clearing was empty. There were tracks everywhere in the snow. She picked out the prints of her own small feet, and the close three-legged prints of Jen and C.P., Jen's bad leg dragging.

She saw William's tracks, too—the large print of his right boot, and the sweep of his left leg. It hadn't been her imagination, that *thunk-drag*. William's leg was hurt, and he was limping.

There were also gigantic paw prints that led right up to the front window, and here and there streaks of blood. The paw prints returned to the trees in the same direction as the stream.

*What if the creature is waiting there for us? What if it knows the only way we can get down the mountain is by following the water?*

C.P. said, "Do you think it's still here?"

Mattie shook her head. "I can't feel it watching us."

This, she realized, was true. Whenever the creature was near before she'd always felt its presence, even if she wasn't entirely aware that she felt it.

"But," she said, looking around, "the heart is gone."

C.P. looked sick. "Do you think it came back for the heart? Or it was waiting for us to, I don't know, respond?"

"I don't know," she said. "It's not like a regular animal."

*It took the heart back for its collection,* she thought, but she wasn't going to remind C.P. of the cave.

"But you don't think it's here now?"

"No," she said, although she didn't feel as relieved about this as she ought to.

"I'll be right back," he said, lowering the rifle and heading around the side of the cabin.

Mattie stepped carefully off the porch, examining the snow. William's prints definitely went away from the cabin, toward the woods, and they didn't return.

*Maybe he's dead,* she thought, but she knew she wouldn't believe it unless she saw his body.

*It might be right there, just inside the trees. If you follow the trail into the woods then you'll find him, his heart torn out by the creature and his ice-chip eyes colder than they've ever been.*

She was halfway across the clearing before she realized what she was doing, the idea of a dead William calling her like the piper of Hamelin. She couldn't stop herself, and she couldn't stop because she wanted it so much to be true. She wanted him to be gone forever, this monster who'd taken her life from her.

"Hey, where are you going?"

She heard the alarm in C.P.'s voice, heard the rush of his boots crossing the clearing, but she couldn't stop, couldn't answer.

"Hey!" he said, and grabbed her shoulder, forcing her to look at him. "Are you nuts? Where are you going by yourself?"

"William," she said.

He frowned at her. "Don't tell me you're worried about that guy."

Mattie shook her head. "I want to know if he's still alive. He might not be. He was firing the rifle and then he stopped. I can't believe he would stop trying to kill the creature if he could."

Understanding crossed C.P.'s face, and a flicker of pity, too. Mattie didn't care about his pity. She needed to know if the monster was dead.

"Okay," he said. "We'll look around, just a little. But I don't want to go far. I don't want to leave Jen alone in the cabin."

Mattie had forgotten about Jen. "Is she better?"

C.P. shook his head. "She's still asleep, and she's not as cold as she was, but she didn't make a noise all night. It's like she's in a coma or something, but I can't figure out why."

"Maybe we shouldn't . . ." Mattie began.

"No, you're right. We should try to find out what happened last night, if we can. But we shouldn't stay out here too long."

They followed the tracks into the cover of the trees. C.P. spotted a couple of discarded rifle shells. There were splashes of blood and disturbed snow everywhere, and then suddenly there was nothing. All they saw before them was a smooth field of white, unbroken except for the tiny tracks of a rabbit.

"Where did they go?" C.P. asked. "Did they disappear into a portal or something? A door in a tree?"

It was exactly like when Mattie had encountered the dead fox. The prints in the snow had just disappeared, like the bear—or what they'd thought was a bear then—had taken flight. She looked up, expecting to see claw marks on the tree bark as she had then.

And screamed.

*I should have known I should have known I should have known this would happen because it happened before I saw it*

C.P. looked up too, and she heard him say, "Oh, Jesus. Oh, god-damn," and then he stumbled away from her, gagging.

Griffin was there, hanging from the tree by his own intestines. Mattie could see the gaping hole in his torso, the place where the creature had torn out all of his organs. The shredded remains of his shirt and jacket hung around him like a pathetic shroud.

*The creature hung him just like it did the animals by the cave, the ones that I saw, the ones that I tried to show William but William didn't want to see because he was so angry that I looked at Griffin and Griffin looked at me.*

Griffin's eyes were closed. Mattie was grateful for that. She didn't think she could bear to see him wide-eyed, accusing her of not doing more to save him.

*I couldn't have done more.*

**(you could have let C.P. go out when we heard the screaming)**

That was Samantha, Samantha who lectured and harangued, Samantha who would never let Mattie off the hook.

*No, then C.P. would be dead, too. I was right about that. There wasn't any way for us to help.*

(you just wanted to stay in the cabin because you were afraid
of William you're nothing but a little coward)

*I'm not. I'm not a coward. I just didn't want anyone else to die.*

(Coward)

C.P. stood up again, rubbing his mouth. "We have to get him
down from there."

Mattie gave him a helpless look. "How? It's too high for us to
climb."

"I don't know! But we can't leave him up there like that. We
can't." The last word came out as a choked sob. Tears streamed
over his cheeks. "He was my best friend and I can't leave him there.
What am I going to tell his mother? How can I explain this to
anyone? No one will even believe us if we say that there's a great
big monster on the mountain killing people. Our families already
think we're nuts for searching for cryptids in the first place. If I go
home and say Griffin was eviscerated by a . . . well, I don't even
know what it is, and that's 90 percent of the problem right there.
This is crazy. This never should have happened. Never."

Mattie knew she ought to comfort him, ought to put her arm
around him or say how sorry she was, but she didn't know how.
She didn't know how to behave around people, didn't know how to
act without William telling her what to do.

**Just be human,** a voice whispered in her head. Samantha again.

Mattie reached out a tentative hand, rubbed his arm. "I'm
sorry. I know he was your friend."

This seemed like very little to give, but her hesitant comfort
was enough to make him scrub his face with his hands and visibly
pull himself together.

"Let's go away from here," he said. "Back to the cabin. I can't be here with him like that. If we can't do anything about it then I don't want to be here, looking at him."

It wasn't very far back to the clearing. Griffin had been murdered and mutilated just inside the trees.

*Close enough to touch.*

**(Close enough to save)**

*Shut up, Samantha.*

"This was supposed to be a fun trip for the three of us. We all like winter hiking and camping, and this mountain isn't very far from our college—just a couple hours' drive. It seemed perfect. Plus, we wouldn't have to do any really technical climbing, although there are a few places where you have to scramble over boulders, but that's not a big deal. You can even avoid them if you want, take different paths or whatever. Griffin came up early because he finished his exams first and he was so excited about the reports he read online. And when he found those prints up by the cave—man, he was over the moon. I mean when I met up with him he was just bubbling, you know? About to overflow. That was all he could talk about. That, and you."

Mattie stared at the ground. She couldn't look C.P. in the eye. "I'm sorry."

He tugged at her sleeve so she would look up. "No, listen. I'm really sorry I said that last night. I really am. It was a jerk thing to say. If Jen had been awake she probably would have slapped me for saying it. It's ridiculous to blame you, and you were right. If I'd gone outside when Griffin started screaming, I would have ended up hanging from a tree, too. So thank you. For keeping me from doing something stupid. For saving my life."

This was giving her far too much credit. Mattie looked at the ground again, at the scuffed toes of her heavy leather boots. "I didn't save your life. I just didn't want you to die."

"That's saving my life, dope," he said, and gently tapped her shoulder.

*Dope*. It was a funny word, and it meant she was being stupid. But he'd said it in such a gentle, affectionate way—almost like the way Jen called him *dummy*. It made her feel strange, like she belonged to them somehow. Like she was part of them. A friend.

"Let's get some food," Mattie said, because she didn't know how to respond and she didn't know how to think about the idea that she might not have been a coward at all, but a savior.

They crossed the clearing to the storehouse. Mattie turned the knob, half-expecting it to be locked because she could hardly believe that William had made such a mistake in the first place. The knob turned easily and the door swung open.

"Whoa," C.P. said. "Look at all this stuff."

There were haunches of meat, hunted and dressed by William. There were cartons of eggs and milk and butter purchased from the town, and some loaves of bread and packages of cheese. Those things Mattie expected, because those were foods that William brought into the cabin for Mattie to eat.

But there was also an entire wall of shelves filled with packaged food—canned soups, pasta, sauce, bags of chips, cans of soda, candy bars, crackers, cookies, wrapped pastries. There were gaps in the items that made it clear William had been eating some of these things.

"He had all of this in here? And he never told me?" Mattie could hear the astonishment in her voice.

*And he never shared it with you, never brought you anything that might remind you of home or of the real world, but he kept it all for himself and had it in secret because he wasn't going to do without his comforts. That was your lot, not his.*

"Just looking at all of this is making me hungry," C.P. said. "Let's just grab armfuls and bring it inside, okay?"

"Wait," Mattie said, before C.P. started grabbing everything in sight. She didn't think there was any point in removing a lot of food when they were leaving as soon as possible. "Let's just take what we need for now, for breakfast."

"But Twinkies," C.P. said, pointing to a box of the cakes. "What about coffee cakes? Coffee cakes are basically a breakfast food."

Mattie couldn't remember what a coffee cake tasted like. She stared at the blue-and-white box, at the picture of the cake with crumb topping. She suddenly longed to know what it was, how the texture of the cake would feel on her tongue.

"Okay," she said. "The coffee cakes."

She collected a full carton of eggs—*I'm going to eat as many eggs as I want, William's not here to stop me*, she thought with a savage satisfaction—and a package of bacon and a loaf of bread. She noticed a small bin in the corner and found that it was filled with food wrappers. She realized then how careful William was to never let her see the packaging from the eggs or bacon or bread. He always carried everything inside in a basket or wrapped in a towel, so that she would never think about the modern world he'd dragged her from.

She turned away from the bin to find C.P. balancing a huge load of packages.

"I thought we were only taking coffee cakes," she said.

"Just in case we get stuck in the cabin. For whatever reason," he said. "I do want to get out of here as soon as possible. But there might be a siege, or whatever."

"A siege?"

"Yeah, you know. The monster might come back. Or that guy. We didn't see his body."

That was true. Mattie had forgotten she was looking for evidence of William. The sight of Griffin hanging from the tree pushed it out of her mind.

*Is William still alive? If he is, why hasn't he come back here for me? Maybe the creature took him away to the cave.*

She wished very much that this was so, that the monster was tearing William's organs out one by one and that he was screaming the whole time, screaming the way he used to make her scream in pain and misery.

Mattie led the way out of the storehouse and C.P. followed. "Make sure the door is pulled tight, otherwise bears can get in there."

"You don't think a bear is hanging around with that giant thing on the loose, do you?"

Mattie thought about it. It was true that she and William had noticed fewer animals about in the last month or so. She'd assumed, once she knew about the creature, that it was eating all the available meat. But perhaps it wasn't. Perhaps some animals had just moved on, ceding their territory to the new monster in their midst.

"Maybe," Mattie said. "You never know with bears. But it's true that I haven't seen much evidence of bear activity around, and neither has William. He does all the hunting, so he should know."

Mattie checked the fire and started preparing breakfast as she always did. It was so much a part of her that she did everything automatically.

"What can I do to help?" C.P. asked.

She was slicing the bread when he said this, and the question shocked her so much that she nearly sliced one of her fingers.

"Help?"

"Yeah, you know, I could set the table or toast the bread or whatever."

He wanted to help. William never helped. Kitchen work was for women. It was the responsibility of women to prepare the food that men had hunted.

*But he didn't hunt all of it, did he? He went to the supermarket and bought it and carried it home and forced you to feel grateful.*

"I can toast the bread on a fork," he said. "I'm really good at that. I do it around the campfire all the time."

Mattie never made toast. William didn't like it.

"Yes, that sounds like a good idea," she said. "Just leave me enough room to cook the bacon, please."

Soon they were sitting down to breakfast and again the cabin felt cozy and safe, filled with the smells of food and the wood burning in the fire. Mattie reflected that she'd never felt this way with William, even with the same fire burning and the same food on the table.

C.P. shoveled food into his mouth with abandon. "God, I'm so hungry. I shouldn't be this hungry, not with Griffin gone and Jen in the state she's in and who knows what waiting for us outside. But I am. I'm starving."

Mattie watched him dip his toast into his egg yolk. She'd never done that before. She copied him and took a bite and discovered she liked it.

*I feel like a baby animal, learning the world anew,* she thought. *William took so much from me.*

"So what are we going to do?" C.P. said. "We left the packs somewhere. I don't know what I was thinking, doing that. I don't even know how we'll find them again but we need that stuff, because we're going to have to spend at least one night outside. Jen can't walk, obviously, and we're going to have to fix up some way to drag her. Make a travois or whatever."

"Travois?"

"Like a sled, but with long poles to pull instead of a rope."

"The sled!" Mattie said. "I forgot about it. William bought a sled so he could carry the bear trap. I wonder where he put it. I saw it yesterday morning."

"It wasn't in the back," C.P. said. "I would have noticed."

"Maybe he put it behind the storehouse," she said.

"I'll look after I have some more magic bean water," he said.

"Magic bean water?"

"Coffee," he said.

"You say a lot of funny things," Mattie said, then covered her mouth with her hand, shocked that she'd said that out loud. "I'm sorry. That was rude."

"Nah," he said. "I bet a lot of things sound funny to you. You've been here for a long time, and I don't see a TV or a radio or anything. Or even books."

"I'm only allowed to read the Bible," she said, and she hated how she sounded when she said this, like a docile cow herded into a pen.

"Well, if we can fix up the sled for Jen then we can get out of here and try to find the packs again and then get off this mountain, or at least get to where there's a cell signal again. I had a spotty signal for a while, but it was closer to the base. If I can call 911 and give them our location then we'll be saved. Someone will come and get us with a helicopter or ATVs or whatever."

He used that word a lot, *whatever*. It was a strange word, vague but at the same time full of possibilities.

After eating the eggs and bacon, C.P. ripped open the box of coffee cakes and dumped the wrapped cakes on the table.

"Here, try one," he said. "They're not as good as a real home-baked coffee cake but they'll do in a pinch."

Mattie picked up a cake and started unwrapping it, then stopped.

"Where does he get all the money for these things?" she said.

"Does he have a job?"

"No," she said. "He's always here, unless he's hunting. And speaking of money . . ."

She dropped the cake on the table and went over to the couch, kneeling in front of it and reaching underneath for the roll of money she'd hid there yesterday. For a moment she thought William had found it but then her fingers brushed against paper and she grabbed it.

"What are you doing?" C.P. asked, his mouth full of coffee cake. Mattie had a sudden idea that he was eating to hide his grief—that if he kept eating, kept busy, then he wouldn't have to think about what happened to Griffin.

She held up the roll of bills. "William left this in his trousers the other day. I hid it, because I thought if I got away from him I would need money."

C.P. tilted his head to the side, studying her. "I didn't think you had the guts for something like that, to be honest. When we first met you, you were such a scared little mouse."

Mattie felt her cheeks reddening. "You were two strange men wandering around our property, and I hadn't seen anyone other than William in years. You can't blame me for being cautious."

"That wasn't caution. That was terror."

"Are you trying to make me angry?" she said, standing up. She felt something in her chest, something bubbling and boiling.

"I don't know. Can you even get angry?"

"I'm sure I can," Mattie said, stung by the way he dismissed her. "I think I am now."

He held up his hands. "I'm sorry, I'm sorry. I have to stop treating you like a regular person, I know. You haven't had the same life as everyone else. If Jen was awake she'd definitely be beating me about the head and shoulders right now."

*William grabbing her shoulders. William's fist in her face.*

"You shouldn't joke about things like that," she said. "I know that you're trying to be funny so that you don't think about your friend, but it's not funny at all."

C.P. rubbed his face with one hand. "Yeah, you're right. It's not funny. I'm sorry. For real. I'm sorry. It's not like I'm not sitting here looking at your black eye and the marks around your neck. They just kind of faded into the background, and I forgot who I was talking to. Let's see how much you've got there."

Mattie had forgotten about the money, even though she was holding it in her hand. She was still angry, still felt the bubbling and the boiling at the edge of her consciousness, but she recognized that he was sorry if he said so. He was foolish and awkward and often said the wrong thing, but he was sorry. She handed the money to C.P., who unrolled it.

"Holy crap!" he said. "These are mostly hundreds."

He started counting the bills, putting the different types into piles. When he was done he looked up at her, his expression dazed.

"There's $2,517 dollars here," C.P. said. "Where did he get all of this money? Is he rich?"

"I don't know," Mattie said. There was so much she didn't know about William. There was so much she still didn't know about herself, huge chunks of her life that were missing, puzzle pieces that had no connector.

"I could buy a train ticket with that, right? And pay for a place to stay?"

"You could buy a plane ticket with that, never mind a train," C.P. said.

"A plane," Mattie said. She'd never been on a plane, not even when she was a child. She remembered longing to fly, longing to be so high up in the sky that everyone below was smaller than an ant. "William could never find me if I was in a plane."

"Don't you worry," C.P. said. "That guy is going to be arrested once I can call the police. Your case is really famous, you know? It's probably not something you want to be famous for, I guess. But you went missing and your mother was killed in a really brutal way—not to be mean about it or anything, I know it's probably upsetting for you. There was a big search for you. It was on every TV station. And every year on the anniversary of your disappearance there are stories, you know, 'what happened to Samantha Hunter,' those kinds of things."

"Samantha Hunter," Mattie said. "I forgot that name for a long time. William told me my name was Martha, and he called me Mattie."

She paused, taking a deep breath before going on. "In all those times that you heard those stories—did they ever say anything about Heather? About my sister, Heather?"

C.P. frowned. "I don't remember anything about her. They always talk about you and your mom and they always show this same clip from around the time you were taken, of some guy, your mom's boyfriend talking about . . ."

Realization lit his face. "Your mom's boyfriend—it was that guy! The guy who kidnapped you! He was talking to reporters, acting like it was such a tragedy, and that he didn't have any idea what had happened. The police interviewed him, I remember now, and they searched his house and everything but they didn't find any sign of you and they had to eliminate him as a suspect. What did he do, stash you somewhere while he was off pretending to be worried about finding you?"

*"You have to stay here while I'm out," William said. "I can't trust you not to run away."*

Mattie looked at the floor, at the small multicolored rug that covered the area behind the couch. There wasn't a rug anywhere else in the cabin.

"He put me in the Box," she said.

"The Box?"

"The Box is for bad girls who try to run away," she said. Her voice sounded very distant to her own ears. "I was always trying to run away at first, and he had to put me in the Box so I would learn how to be good, to listen and to obey."

She walked toward the rug as if in a dream. C.P. pushed his

chair back and followed her. She sensed his uncertainty. He didn't know what to do or how to respond. Mattie pulled up the rug to reveal a trapdoor in the floor. She tugged the ring to open the door.

Underneath was a wooden, coffin-like structure, narrow and long. It hadn't been used in many years, and it was dusty inside. The corners had the remnants of spiderwebs and their prey, the shells of dead, desiccated insects.

"He put you inside here?" C.P. sounded like he was going to be sick again. "And left you here?"

"Yes. When I was bad."

"You weren't bad. You were a little girl, and you were scared, and you wanted to go home."

He sounded angry, but Mattie wasn't afraid of his anger the way she'd been before. It wasn't anger that could hurt her. She'd gone away again, away to a place where she was safe and she didn't have to think about the door closing over her head.

"Hey," he said, tapping her shoulder with one finger. "You weren't bad. You didn't deserve this. Nobody deserves this. Except maybe that sicko. I'd like to see how he'd like it if someone shoved him in a wooden box."

Something broke inside her then, some tide of fear and hurt that she'd been bottling up for longer than she could remember.

"I just wanted to go home. I just wanted to go home to Mom and Heather. William told me that Mom gave me to him to keep, that I belonged to him forever, but I didn't believe him and I just wanted to go home."

She wept then, wept like she never had before, wept like she would never stop, bent over her knees with her arms over her head and the musty smell of the Box inside her nose and the feeling of this stranger's eyes on her, helpless to stem the flood tide of her grief.

After a long while she felt dried up and exhausted, and she sat up. C.P. looked away from her, like he was embarrassed to have seen her outburst.

"Let's cover this up," he said. "Nobody needs to see this."

He closed the trapdoor to the Box and pushed the rug back over it while Mattie watched him, drained and dazed.

"We're leaving," he said. "We're getting off this goddamn mountain and never coming back. Come on, pull yourself together. We have to pack up some stuff and figure out how to get Jen out of here. I'm going out to see if that sled you talked about is somewhere around."

He stood, and held out his hand for Mattie to grasp. She hesitated, because there was a part of her that was still saying *William will be angry you're not supposed to talk to strange men* but she pushed that part of her down, down, down and away. That person didn't exist anymore, that little mouse Martha. But she wasn't quite Samantha yet, either. She was something in between.

She took C.P.'s hand, and stood on her own two feet.

# CHAPTER SEVENTEEN

Mattie went to check on Jen while C.P. was outside. Jen was still asleep, breathing lightly, but she didn't rouse at all when Mattie touched her forehead or shook her shoulder. There was certainly something more seriously wrong with Jen than just the wound from the trap, but Mattie was at a loss. She didn't have any real medical knowledge. If anything she was the one who'd needed medical care over the years, particularly after the losses of her children. William had always taken care of her then.

She went to the closet and took out her trousers and a heavy sweater and changed into them. At least she wouldn't slow everyone down by trying to walk in skirts and petticoats. Her hair was falling out of its braid—it had been more than a day since she'd combed and bound it—and it was in her way as she dressed.

She didn't have time to brush it all out—that was a very long task, one that required assistance. William usually brushed her hair for her. It was the only time he was anything like tender with her. He liked to sit by the fire with her sitting in front of him, and he would carefully brush the waist-length strands until they gleamed, and call her his little Rapunzel, his princess in a tower.

She felt a deep and sudden revulsion. William had liked her hair this way. William wanted her to have it long, long, long and never cut it because she was his doll to do with as he pleased, a doll he could play with if he wanted or break if he wanted, a doll that only moved and talked at his whim.

Mattie rushed out of the bedroom and to her worktable. There was a very sharp knife there that she used for slicing carrots and potatoes and deer meat, and she wondered that he let her have such a sharp object within reach. He must not have been afraid that she would try to kill him with it.

There were so many times she could have. He slept so heavily at night. She could have slit his throat and he wouldn't have been able to do a thing about it. He might have slept through the whole thing.

*Why didn't I? Why?*

**(Because he made you think you couldn't. He made you think that you belonged to him.)**

She picked up the knife, pulled her braid taut with her other hand, and sawed through the hair close to her nape.

The knife cut through the thick braid easily, and a moment later she held the long messy rope that used to be her hair. The braid had blood in it, and she felt the cut on her head where William had hit her with the shovel. It was clotted over now.

She swung her head from side to side. Her head felt so light. It almost didn't feel like her own head. She looked at the braid and a thought came, unbidden and unwanted.

*William will be so angry when he sees.*

No. She needed to stop worrying about William, what William wanted or didn't want, how William would feel about things. William didn't matter anymore.

C.P. opened the cabin door and stood on the porch for a moment, stamping the snow off his boots. Cold air swirled around her feet and she noticed then that she hadn't put any socks on.

"That sled is a little on the small side—Jen's pretty tall—but I think we can figure something out. It's wide so maybe we can lay her on her side and tuck her up so her head and legs don't hang off."

He shut the door, looked at her properly for the first time, and did an exaggerated double take.

"Time for a new look?"

She dropped the knife on the table, let the braid fall to her feet.

"William liked my hair long."

"Ah," he said. "I bet it got in your way."

"Yes," she said.

She felt like new, like an animal shedding its winter coat, fresh and ready for spring. She felt less like Mattie and more like Samantha.

"I found something out in the snow," he said, reaching into his pocket and pulling something out, something that jingled. He held it out to her. "Do these belong to that guy?"

"William's keys," she said, her heart leaping. "He always keeps them on him, or near him."

"They must have fallen out of his pocket last night. Maybe when he was chasing us. The thing is, there's a vehicle key on here. He's got a truck or a jeep or maybe an ATV stashed somewhere. You said he goes down to the town and comes back the same day, right? So wherever he had it hidden, it can't be too far away."

"But it has to be far enough that I won't find it by accident," Mattie said. "He never lets me go very far from the cabin by myself, but he's very cautious. I'm sure it's at least an hour's walk, maybe more."

"Still, an hour's walk, or even two—that's nothing. If we can find it then we're saved. We can load Jen up and just drive down the mountain. I wonder if there's an access road somewhere that he's using. We didn't see one when we were coming up, but then we followed marked trails from a parking area, and the marked trails pretty much stay away from this part of the mountain. Griffin only drifted in this direction by accident, and then he found the caves, and he was so excited . . ."

C.P. trailed off, and Mattie knew he was thinking about Griffin hanging from the tree, not so far from them. But she was thinking about something else, something she'd wanted to know about for a long time.

"May I have those keys, please?"

"Sure, they technically belong to you, I guess."

Mattie took the keys and went into the bedroom. C.P. followed her like a duckling. He did that, she'd noticed. Just sort of trailed along in her wake, almost like he hoped she wouldn't see him there.

She knelt before the trunk, staring at the batch of keys.

"It's probably that one," he said, reaching over her shoulder to tap at the smallest key. "The other ones look too big."

Mattie lifted the key to the lock, hands trembling. She'd been told so many times not to try to enter the bedroom when William opened the trunk. She was to never, ever look inside.

The lock clicked. She opened the trunk.

"Whoa," C.P. said.

Mattie didn't understand what she was looking at, and felt a little disappointed. There was a jumble of small packets filled with brown stuff on the top layer of the trunk.

"That's heroin," C.P. said. He sounded excited and scared at the same time. "That guy is a heroin dealer. That's how he has all that money."

"Heroin?"

"It's a drug, an illegal drug. But jeez, where is he getting it? He's not making it, not up here. I wonder if some big cartel does a drop from a plane, maybe, or brings it up on snowmobiles and then he takes the stuff into town and distributes it to dealers who take it elsewhere. Because that is a lot of shit, right there. Way more than he could sell in town, unless everyone in town is an addict. Although I guess it is possible, because there is a meth crisis and everything. There are some towns where like 90 percent of the population is addicted to meth."

Mattie didn't understand most of this. She sort of understood the concept of illegal drugs, because she remembered posters at school admonishing the students—"DON'T DO DRUGS"—but she'd been far too young to know what drugs really were, or what they did to people.

She remembered then that there were days when she heard a noise like an engine, coming near to the cabin, and whenever this happened she wasn't allowed to go outside for anything, not even to use the outhouse. But William would go out carrying his ruck-sack, and when he returned he would go into the bedroom and shut the door.

"William sells this?" she said. "And that's how he gets all of his money?"

"Yeah," C.P. said. "Move it around and see how much of it is in there. No, wait. Put on some gloves before you do that."

"Why?"

"Because when the cops come to arrest him, you don't want that guy to say you were his accomplice. You don't want your fin-gerprints on the packets. He might try to implicate you, even though you were his victim and everything."

"Fingerprints," she said. "Right."

She still didn't really understand, but she went to the closet and took out a pair of mittens.

"Don't you have anything with fingers?" he asked as he watched her pull them on.

"No, I only know how to knit mittens," she said. "Do you have gloves?"

"Not exactly," he said, and took his out of his pocket and put them on. They looked like mittens at first, and then he unbut-toned a button at the top of the palm and they were half-gloves underneath, leaving the tops of his fingers bare. "Not very good for hiding your fingerprints, although they are useful when you need more mobility with your hands than you can get from a mitten."

Mattie knelt in front of the trunk again and swept some of the packets to the side. Underneath there were several stacks of wrapped bills and a pile of newspaper clippings.

"There must be *thousands* of dollars," C.P. said. "If you took this you could buy an island in the middle of the ocean."

"An island," Mattie said. She'd never been to an island, although she had a sudden vision of sand and sun and a lone palm tree.

She picked up the pile of newspaper clippings. There was a black-and-white picture of a little girl with light hair and dark eyes smiling awkwardly from the first one, her head tilted just a little too far back so that she appeared off-center.

"That's you," he said. "Oh my god. I don't think you should look at those clippings."

"Me?" she said, staring at the little girl. "This is me?"

There were no mirrors in William's cabin. Mattie hadn't tracked the changes in her face and body as the years passed because it had been years since she'd seen herself. It had been such a long time that she'd forgotten the shape of her eyes and her nose and her mouth and her cheeks.

The little girl in Mattie's hand wavered, and she realized her hand was shaking.

"Here, give me those. You don't need to see those," C.P. said.

"No," she said, and forced herself to take deep breaths, to make her hand stop shaking. "I know you want to help. But I need to see. I need to know."

There was a headline above the picture of the awkwardly smiling girl. "TRAGEDY—8-year-old girl missing after mother found brutally murdered."

She placed the clipping to one side. The next clipping had the same picture of herself, this time below larger text that said: "MISSING—police seek information."

The third clipping made her breath stop.

The headline read: "MURDER AND KIDNAPPING IN A SMALL TOWN." And there was the picture of herself again, smiling her awkward smile. But Mattie didn't care about that picture. Next to it was a candid photo of a woman wearing a checked shirt, her smile a little too wide to be considered pretty, her right hand pushing her hair back from her face.

Her mother.

"Mom," she said. She felt the tears—they were blocking her throat and pushing against the backs of her eyes. But she didn't cry. She stroked the picture with her finger, because she had a face now for the person she'd once loved most in the world. "I forgot your face."

And even though Mattie stared down at her mother, she still couldn't dredge up a memory of her mom's face.

"Look, we should, um, stay on track," C.P. said. "I know this is important to you, and finding this stuff explains a lot, but we really need to get going. There are only so many hours of daylight."

"I know," Mattie said, and sighed. She folded up all of the newspaper clippings and put them in her pocket.

"I can't believe that sicko kept cuttings of his own crime," C.P. said. "You should take some of that money. I think you earned it."

Mattie hesitated. Now that she knew how William earned his keep, the money felt wrong, somehow dirty. She didn't know exactly what heroin was but C.P. said it was a drug and all she remembered from childhood was that drugs were bad, that they ruined lives. Should she take money earned on the back of someone's ruined life?

*He ruined your life, too. And principles won't feed you.*

She took two stacks of bills, which seemed like more money than she would ever need, and then closed the trunk and locked it again. She stood up, holding the keys in one hand and the money in the other. The money felt like it was burning her.

"You get all your cold weather gear on. Do you have a backpack or bag that we can use to carry some of that food in the storehouse?"

"William has a rucksack. He usually keeps it in the storehouse, but I don't know where. I've just seen him carrying it in and out."

"I'll go look while you put the rest of your things on. I'm really hoping that we can find whatever vehicle that key goes with," he said, pointing to the keys. "I think it would be smart to take provisions, though, just in case we don't find it. Without a car we'll be spending another night on the mountain for sure. Anyway, don't lose those keys. It would suck if we did find a car and didn't have any way to start it."

Mattie felt very nervous then, felt the sudden burden of not losing their way to escape. She went out in the main room, C.P. trailing her again, and rummaged in her work basket until she came up with a ball of wool. She cut off a long length of it, pulled the key ring over the string, made a second loop through the key ring just in case, then tied the double loop with the keys dangling from it around her neck. She tucked it all inside her sweater.

"OK, that works," he said. "You won't drop them by accident, I guess."

Mattie put on her socks and boots and coat while C.P. went out to the storehouse. She wrapped a long scarf around her throat, pulled a hat over her shorn hair, and carefully tucked the stacks of bills and the money she'd hidden under the couch inside her coat pocket. C.P. returned just as she was putting her mittens in the opposite pocket. He was carrying William's haversack. He held it out to her.

"Do you think you can carry this? I tried not to overfill it. We're going to need to get my pack, and maybe Jen's if we can manage it. The tents are with the packs, and if we have to sleep outside we're going to want tents. Though I have no idea how we'll even find the packs again. It's like we ran through a maze last night in the dark."

"It will be easy," Mattie said. "We came along the deer path from the stream. All we have to do when we get back to the stream is follow our footprints in the snow. It didn't snow overnight, so the trail will still be there."

C.P. frowned. "Yeah, OK. But then what? How do we get down the mountain from there?"

"William always said the stream fed into a river, and the river goes down the mountain. So we just follow the stream."

"Is that the way he goes when he leaves for town?"

Mattie nodded.

"Good, that means his vehicle is probably that way, too. We'll be back in civilization in a few hours."

Mattie noticed that they were both careful not to mention the creature, or the possibility that William was still out there some-where. The sun was shining and they were rested and fed and all those things made the terrors of the night recede. It didn't seem possible that bad things could happen to them in the day.

Mattie put the pack on her back, and then the two of them half-dragged, half-carried Jen out to the sled. She was so still and so pale that it was like carrying a corpse, but C.P. checked Jen's pulse and breathing once they had her loaded on.

"She's still alive," he said, giving Mattie a thumbs-up.

They'd had to put Jen on her side, pulling her legs into a fetal position. She wouldn't fit otherwise—she was far too tall for the sled platform. Mattie tucked a blanket around Jen. There were straps on either side and C.P. used these to buckle Jen into place.

"If she's not waking up after all this . . ." he said. "Jesus, what the hell can be wrong with her?"

He didn't seem to expect an answer, because he picked up the rope and started pulling. "This way, right?"

Mattie pulled the cabin door shut and trotted after him. She felt something huge swelling in her chest. She was leaving. She was really leaving. She was never going to live here again.

She felt an inward tug, something telling her she should look back, commemorate the moment properly.

**Don't look back. Don't ever look back. There's nothing for you there, nothing you want to remember. Don't give him another second of your attention.**

And then they were into the trees, and the moment passed, and Mattie knew if she looked back the cabin wouldn't be visible anymore.

C.P. was too busy pulling Jen to chatter as he usually did. Mattie listened to the sound of the woods—the wind rustling in the trees, the busy chirping of winter birds. As long as she heard those birds then they were safe from the creature.

*And even if William is alive he can't really be a threat any longer. He can't be. He could barely walk last night. He couldn't run after us.*

But Mattie listened hard for the *thunk-drag* of his walk all the same.

After a very brief time they came upon the trap. It had been reset.

"Did that guy actually stop to fix his trap last night?" C.P. said, sounding disgusted.

Nearby there was a dead squirrel in the snow. Mattie noticed a graze on its flank, like it had brushed against the teeth of the trap. But a little cut like that wouldn't kill a squirrel, unless . . .

Mattie remembered that amongst the pile of seemingly random things William had purchased to defeat the "demon" was a liquid in a small brown bottle. She hadn't looked closely at the bottle but she did recall that there was a skull and crossbones on the side of the label.

"Poison," Mattie said. "William put poison on the trap. He bought some. I saw it."

C.P. followed her eyes from the squirrel and back to the trap again. "That's why Jen's out cold? Because that son of a bitch put poison on the bear trap and now it's killing her?"

"I'm not certain," Mattie said. "But it makes sense, doesn't it? What else could have killed that squirrel?"

"What kind of poison is it?"

Mattie shook her head. "I didn't look at it very closely."

"We have to get her to a hospital. I was worried about an infection before, or stress or shock or whatever. But poison—I mean, it could be damaging her brain or her organs permanently right now while we're standing around talking." He grabbed the ropes and pulled at the sled with more energy than before. "That guy is a garbage person, you know that? A complete and total garbage person."

"I don't want to defend William," she said. "But I think if he put poison on the trap it was because he wanted to make sure he caught the creature."

"It doesn't matter what his reasons are," C.P. said. "He's still a garbage person. Leave aside what he did to Jen. Look what he did to you."

"I know what he did to me," Mattie said quietly.

"I know you know. And that's why you should agree with me when I say he is a garbage person."

"Yes," Mattie said. "He is. A garbage person."

She giggled, and it so surprised her that she covered her mouth with her mitten. She couldn't remember the last time she'd heard a noise like that come out of her own mouth.

C.P. noticed, and he laughed, too. "Total garbage. A wet bag filled with trash."

The laugh bubbled up again. "Yes. Nothing but trash."

Soon they were both laughing, laughing so hard that tears streamed out of their eyes.

"Garbage person, garbage person," Mattie said. She'd never heard such a phrase before and it was so funny, so funny because it was true and because she was scared and because she was running away from the man who'd kidnapped her for twelve years, that complete and total garbage person.

After a few minutes their laughter seemed to peter out, though they still grinned idiotically at one another.

And that was when Mattie noticed the woods had gone silent.

"What is it?" C.P. asked, halting.

"It's here," Mattie whispered.

The back of her neck prickled. She tilted her head back, trying to see the monster hiding up above. She knew it was there. It was always there, impossibly so. How could something so large hide in the shelter of pine boughs?

"How do you know?" he whispered back, his eyes scanning the trees as hers did.

"It's quiet," she said. "Go, go, as fast as you can but don't run."

"The rifle," he moaned. "I forgot the rifle. I was thinking about food and about Jen and about maybe getting to the vehicle, and then we found that trunk and everything was so weird and I left the rifle in the cabin."

"It's okay," Mattie said. She didn't think that rifle could do anything against the creature in any case.

She heard the harshness of her breath, the sound of their boots in the snow, the swish of the sled's runners, the rustle of their clothes. But she didn't hear the creature, though she knew it was keeping pace with them above.

*It can be silent when it wants to,* she thought, not for the first time.

And thus far it had always been silent when it didn't intend to attack. So maybe they were safe. Maybe it was just watching them, making certain that they didn't go anywhere near its lair.

Maybe it would let them go.

Maybe.

A branch cracked above them.

Mattie felt a rush of air, smelled rank and rotten meat, saw an impossibly huge paw tipped by shining claws. Then C.P. was screaming, and Jen was gone, and so was the creature.

"Jen!" he shouted. "Jen!"

There was nothing. All that was left was an empty sled, the

straps sliced in two, and the remains of the blanket that had fallen off Jen as the creature lifted her into the trees.

"Why?" C.P. shouted. "Why her? Why? Jen! Jen!"

Mattie grabbed his arm and pulled. "She can't hear you. Come on, come on, run now."

But he seemed in a daze, half-furious and half-baffled, and his legs moved in slow motion.

"Why did it take her? Why? She was unconscious. She wasn't any threat. Why didn't it take me instead? What am I going to do? How could they leave me here alone?"

"Run," Mattie said, tugging him along. "You're not alone. I'm here, too. Come on, run."

The creature watched them. Mattie felt its eyes on her. But it didn't follow. It had its prize and it didn't need to. She wasn't sure how she knew that but she was certain.

C.P. stumbled along beside her, mumbling about Jen, about Griffin, about their families and what he would say to them. Mattie didn't listen to the exact words. She just wanted to get to the stream, where they would be out in the open and the creature wouldn't be able to swoop down upon them. It would have to show itself.

They broke into the clearing, and Mattie kept pulling C.P. until they crossed the water and were safely on the other bank.

*There,* she thought. *It can't sneak up on us now. It's on the other side of the stream.*

C.P. bent over, holding his stomach with both arms. "I don't understand what's happening. I don't understand. Why would it take Jen? Why did it take Griffin in the first place? Why wouldn't it just kill all of us?"

Now that they weren't running for their lives Mattie wondered that, too. The creature was so much bigger than them. All of their strength combined couldn't have prevented the monster from killing them. So why had it taken Griffin away? Griffin had been unconscious at the time, and no threat at all. And it had been the same for Jen.

"Wait," Mattie said, trying to grab at the threads of an idea. "Wait. I think it took them *because* they were no threat."

"What? That doesn't make any sense."

"It does, if you think about animal behavior. Even animals that you think of as big and powerful will try to take down the sick and the weak in a herd. It's because predators don't want to risk being injured. They just want to get their meal without getting hurt."

"So, the giant monster that lives in the woods, the one that's five times the size of us—it took Griffin and Jen because it knew they wouldn't hurt it?"

"I know it sounds strange. But there were four of us. Five, if you count William. It had to have thought that its odds were better if it removed us one at a time."

"It doesn't make any sense," he said. "Why did we come here in the first place? Stupid, stupid, stupid. We didn't think we would really find anything, you know. We never do. Sometimes we find prints or fur or something like that, or we listen to people tell stories of their sightings, but we never actually expect to find a cryptid. At least, I don't. I like the idea that there's something unexplained out there but I don't think it actually exists, you know? But Griffin and Jen love this stuff and I just want to hang out with my friends. And now my friends are gone, taken by a monster that I still barely believe in, even though I've seen it with my own eyes."

"What did you see?" Mattie asked. "I only saw its arm, and the paw."

"That's all I saw, too. But it wasn't any bear paw, that's for sure. And it moved so fast—almost faster than I could see. Like an alien or something in a movie."

Mattie had very little memory of aliens, but the picture that immediately came to mind was of a little man-shaped being with a round head and large eyes.

"It's not an alien," she said.

"I didn't say it was. I just said it was superfast like an alien in a movie, like a computer-generated effect."

Mattie didn't know what a computer-generated effect was, but she didn't think they should stand around arguing about it any longer. C.P. seemed less dazed than he had a few moments before.

"We have to keep moving," she said. "It could come after us."

She said "could," but what she really meant was "it will." She didn't doubt that the creature would harry them until they died or were off the mountain.

"Right," C.P. said, rubbing his face. "Right. We have to get the packs. At least, we have to get mine. And Griffin's camera, too."

"I don't think we should waste time going back for things," Mattie said. "We're at the stream now, and we know that the stream leads to the river and the river will take us the way we need to go."

C.P. looked at the stream. "It goes more or less straight east right here, like the cliffs that were near the place we stashed the packs. That means the stream turns southeast at some point but right now its running parallel to the path we took yesterday. If we collect the packs and then keep going along the cliffside, we'll run into the stream again at some point."

"Maybe," Mattie said. She understood his reasoning, but she didn't want to risk being away from the only landmark they had.

"Look, I have the compass," he said. "If it seems like we're going off track for whatever reason, I'll get us back to the stream, OK? I've got to get Griffin's camera. It has evidence on it. I don't want him to have died for nothing. And my pack has a tent, food, warm clothes—things we might need if we have to stay out here tonight. It makes sense."

It made a kind of sense, but Mattie was starting to feel the press of urgency. The creature could return at any moment. And if they went back into the woods then they would be in its territory again. It could cross the stream behind them and hide in the trees. It could stalk them until night, and no tent or bedroll would be protection.

"I think we should just go," she said. "As fast as we can, and not worry about the things."

"Then go," he said. "I'll follow our footprints in the snow. They're here, just like you said. Maybe I'll catch up to you."

"No," Mattie said. "That's crazy. If we're alone then the creature could pick us off easily."

"I'm not leaving without Griffin's camera," he said, and started toward the woods.

This wasn't about an object, Mattie realized. This was about his friend, and his need to honor that friend. It was about trying to make sense of something senseless. She glanced back the way they came. The forest was silent there, no birds twittering. The creature was still there. It hadn't followed them yet.

She ran after C.P., her stomach churning with anxiety. "Fine, but let's hurry. Please."

*Hurry, hurry, the monster's in the woods and it's coming for you.*

Their tracks were clear and easy to follow. Mattie saw the cluster of their footprints—her own, C.P.'s, Jen's—and just beside them she recognized William's boots, one of them dragging in the snow.

They were at the cluster of boulders where they'd stashed the bags sooner than Mattie thought. The walk had seemed terribly long in the dark, all three of them afraid and huddled together.

"Awesome," C.P. said. "That only took like fifteen minutes. Just give me a few minutes to transfer some stuff from Griffin's bag and we can go."

They climbed down the boulders and stood in the same place where they'd stood the night before—a lifetime ago, Mattie thought, when they were four instead of two and she ate a Hershey's bar that had tasted like a miracle.

C.P. rummaged in Griffin's pack, digging out the camera and a notebook, then transferred the items to his own pack. He slung the bag on his back, adjusting the straps.

"Ugh, I forgot how heavy this thing is," he said. "Okay, let's go."

One moment he was smiling at her and the next moment he was on the ground, and only then did she register the sound of the rifle that had fired a moment before.

# CHAPTER EIGHTEEN

Thought you could get away, didn't you, you little slut?"

*Thunk-drag, thunk-drag, thunk-drag.*

Behind her. He was behind her and C.P. was on the ground. She didn't see blood but that didn't mean anything. C.P. could be bleeding to death while she stood there, paralyzed, unable to help him or to turn around, unable to face the specter that she'd called William.

"Found those bags last night. I knew you'd come back for them. I thought I'd catch up to you before that but I made a note. You can't outsmart me, Mattie girl."

**Think. Move. Run.**

*(No, don't run. If you run he'll shoot you.)*

**He's going to hurt you anyway. If you run he'll shoot and if you stay he'll use his fists and no matter what he'll find a way to**

drag you back to the cabin, to the place you thought you left forever.

She heard his footsteps coming closer and closer, *thunk-drag thunk-drag thunk-drag*, but she couldn't make her body obey the screaming in her brain that was telling her to move, to run, to get away before his hands were on her.

**Move, Samantha!**

*Yes, I am Samantha, I am brave and strong, I am not little Martha mouse and he's not going to take me back to that place, not again, not ever.*

She turned to face him, and gasped.

He was a few feet away from her, and she didn't know how he could be walking at all.

His right leg had been torn by claws, long deep gashes that swept from his hip down to his knee. The gashes were clotted over but his pant leg—or what was left of his pant leg—was coated in dried blood. There were tears in his coat, too, at the shoulder and over part of his chest, and Mattie could see the wounds underneath the ragged flaps of clothing.

*And skin*, she thought with a sickening realization. *Some of those flaps are his skin.*

But his body wasn't even the worst of it. The creature had swiped its needle-sharp claws over William's face, tearing the flesh from his hairline to his jaw on the right side. The eye was sealed shut by black clotted fluid.

He should have been dead, or at least immobile. His wounds would have stopped a normal man. But William was not a normal man.

And he would do anything, *anything*, to capture her again, including roam half-dead through the woods in the night. She knew that. In William's mind, she belonged to him, and he wasn't about to let his possession go.

"I'm quite a sight, aren't I, Mattie girl?" he said, and grinned. His grin was hideous, his teeth coated in blood, the claw marks contorting his face. "And you've led me on quite a chase. But you should have known better. God made you my wife, and a wife must submit to her husband and obey. You've defied the will of God and the will of your husband, but the Lord made certain I would find you again. He knows where you belong, even if you don't."

"I'm not your wife," she said, backing away as he approached her, her hands raised to ward off an attack.

Why hadn't she taken some weapon from the cabin—a knife, the axe, anything? Why had she let herself think that William might be gone forever? He would never be gone. He would always be there, following, if she tried to run.

"You are my wife. You have lived as my wife ever since you became a woman."

"No," Mattie said, and her voice was stronger than it had been a moment before. "You stole me. You killed my mother. You never married me. You only told me you did, told me I belonged to you, told me if I tried to leave someone would only return me to you. You beat me and starved me and made me think that everything I knew, all of my life before, was a dream, something that never happened."

"Anything I did was only for your own good, Martha," he said, and his voice was the frozen cold of winter.

That cold would have chilled her marrow even the day before, would have made her bend and submit. But now she saw that she was proof against it, that he only had power because she'd believed it.

"My name isn't Martha," she said.

His brows drew together and his left eye, the one that wasn't damaged, was a roiling storm of fury, but his voice was still frosted over, calm and cold.

"Your name is Martha and you are my wife," he said, like his saying it would make it true, would make her believe it again.

"My name isn't Martha," she said. "I don't belong to you."

She'd backed away from him, moving across the trail toward the cliffs. Now she realized how close she was to the edge, that if she took one step backward her foot would only find empty air.

*I could fly away,* she thought. *I could fly into the sky and William would never be able to capture me again. I'd be free, free as a hawk, and I'd never again be a scurrying mouse for him to snap in his trap.*

**(Don't be a little coward)**

Samantha again, Samantha always harrying her, always pushing her to be stronger, to try harder, to fight.

*I don't want to fight anymore. I'm tired. I tried to fight him, to get away, and look where I am now.*

**(Yes look where you are now)**

*I don't want to fight. I don't want to hurt anymore. I just want to be free.*

**(Look where you are now)**

*It's so hard.*

**(look)**

"Come away from there now, Martha," William said, and for the first time Mattie heard alarm in his voice. "You're too close to the edge."

He was closer to her now, less than three feet away. If he grabbed her, if he got hold of her with those powerful hands, then she would be lost. There would be nothing left of Samantha. She'd be crushed beneath William's fists..

**(Don't let him grab you)**

*I know,* she wanted to shout. *I know now what I'm supposed to do. I don't need a bossy little girl like you to tell me.*

**(Then do it)**

William was closer. She was just about in his arm's reach. His right eye was horrible, oozing black blood. She remembered her own swollen eye, the one he'd given her, and how she hadn't been able to see anything on that side of her face, not even the edge of her nose.

William swung one of his big paws—for that's what they were, they were paws, huge and dangerous, just like the creature's—but Mattie was already moving, darting to his right side where he couldn't see her.

*Even a mouse has power,* she thought. *They can scurry so fast that you almost don't see them, nothing but a flash out of the corner of your eye. And William can see nothing, nothing at all.*

Mattie darted to the right and then forward, and then turned again before William realized what happened. She put both hands on his back and pushed as hard as she could.

William stumbled, dropped the rifle to the ground, cried out, "You damned little bitch!" but he didn't fall.

She almost panicked then, almost ran before he turned and

grabbed her, but William had taught her—over and over—that if she started a job then she should do it right, that to give half-effort was a sin.

William started to turn toward her, his left eye blazing, no ice remaining to freeze her heart.

She ran at him, her arms out, and he hadn't gotten his balance yet, and this time he did fall, his hands grasping for purchase, opening and closing on nothing but empty air.

He fell forward, his upper body pouring over the edge of the cliff, his legs still on the ground in front of her, and for a moment he was balanced there like a seesaw—half of him suspended in air, and the other half clinging to cliff.

"MARTHA!" he roared.

"I'm not Martha. I'm Samantha," she said, and she kicked him forward.

It was only an inch or two, just enough force to upset the balance, and then it was like the air reached out and pulled him away, and he was screaming, screaming, screaming.

Mattie stood there, swaying, her whole body trembling. Then she fell to her knees, to her stomach, and crawled forward on her belly to peer over the edge.

It was a long way to the bottom, a very long way, and even William couldn't survive that. But if he did then his body was broken, and he couldn't move, and nobody would be there to help him and he would die there, lonely and afraid.

Mattie's heart swelled with a fierce gladness, a happiness she had never known.

"He's gone," she said. "He's gone."

And then she was weeping, and her body was shaking, and she

didn't know what to do because the boogeyman was killed, she killed him and he would never haunt her steps or her sleep ever again and she was free.

She inched backward, pushed herself up on her hands and knees, and then managed to get to her feet though every part of her was trembling. Her eyes went black for a minute, like she was about to faint, but she breathed deep and managed to stay upright.

C.P. was still lying in the snow, but he wasn't facedown anymore. He'd turned to his side, and his eyes were open.

"C.P.!" she said, and hurried to him.

There was blood in the snow but not as much as she expected, just a little blot of red against white. "I thought you were dead," she said, and then she was crying again.

"Hey," he said, flapping his arm at her in a gesture that was probably meant to comfort. "Don't cry. It's okay. I saw what you did. You were so brave. The bravest girl I've ever seen."

"You don't think I'm a coward anymore?" she said, sobbing.

"Ah, well. I never should have said that. I can be an absolute jerk sometimes."

"Okay," Mattie said, crying harder.

"I mean, you don't have to agree with me," he said. "Listen, do you think you can help me get this pack off for a minute? I feel like a turtle stuck on its shell."

Mattie wiped her face with her mittens and then helped him ease the strap off his right arm. He pushed off his side then, leaving the pack behind in the snow as his left arm came free. Mattie saw the place where the bullet had entered his left shoulder then, the blood staining his coat and the stuffing leaking out of the hole in the jacket.

He followed her gaze and said, "It's actually not that bad, I think. I don't want to be stupid manly about it but I'm pretty sure that guy didn't hit anything vital. He was aiming for my heart, I'm sure, and with that giant elephant gun he would have made my heart explode without a doubt. But I don't think he could see too well, with that fucked-up eye. And I think this puffy coat probably saved me, too—it makes me look a lot bigger than I really am. It seems like the bullet just skimmed through the top of my shoulder, but I'm not going to take my jacket off and check it out right now."

"We should bandage it," Mattie said.

"No, we should get the hell out of here before something else happens," he said. "That guy might be gone, but the monster is still in the woods. And if you're right and it's picking us off when we're injured . . . well, as the injured person I vote we get out of its territory as soon as possible. The bad news is that I don't think I can carry that pack now with my shoulder the way it is, and it's way too heavy for you."

"It doesn't matter," Mattie said. "We won't need the tent. We're not going to sleep. We're going to keep moving until we're safe."

"Okay," C.P. said. "I'm on board with that plan. But let's put Griffin's camera and notebook in that sack you have with the food, all right? I still want to take those with us."

They transferred the camera and notebook to Mattie's bag. The camera did make the bag heavier but not too much. C.P. offered to carry the sack but Mattie shook her head.

"I can manage, and the strap would irritate your shoulder."

Then she remembered William stumbling forward, the rifle

clattering to the ground. "The rifle!" she said, and went back toward the cliff's edge.

It hadn't fallen off the cliff with William, as she feared. Mattie picked it up. It was heavy, and she didn't know if it still had ammunition inside, but if it did then they might need it.

She brought it back to C.P., who checked to see how many shots were left.

"Looks like ten. He probably had extra ammo in his pockets but we're not going to climb down to check. You still have those keys, right?" C.P. asked.

Mattie felt for the string around her neck and pulled the key ring out to show him.

"Damn, I really hope we find that guy's car," C.P. said. "I have never wanted to not walk so much in my entire life."

"We should go back to the stream," Mattie said. "It's not far from here, and we'll know for sure that we're heading in the right direction. And we won't be under the trees."

C.P. cast a wary glance at the tree branches hanging over them. "Right. But we'll have to go through the woods again to get there."

Mattie had thought of this, had realized that the creature could have crossed the stream and picked up their trail again already. She listened hard, and heard the sound of birds.

"It's not here yet," she said. "There are birds nearby. Let's hurry."

They climbed back up over the boulders and into the woods, C.P. moving very slowly.

"I really want to say it's just a flesh wound," he said, "but it hurts, goddammit. I will never believe anything I see in a movie again."

"What do you mean?"

"In movies guys are always getting shot, but in conveniently non-vital places. And they're always like, 'It's nothing,' and then spend the next hour sprinting around and punching bad guys like they've had no blood loss whatsoever. Well, I'm here to tell you that even this little wound makes me want to sit down for at least an hour, and also I want two meatball subs and a beer, not necessarily in that order."

Mattie didn't know what a meatball sub was, but she understood the impulse to sit down. The rush of fighting William and winning had passed and now she was more tired than she'd ever been, so tired she thought she could close her eyes and fall asleep standing up.

She felt her eyelids drooping and realized she was falling asleep, falling asleep while she was walking, which was something she hadn't thought possible.

"Stay awake," she said.

"I'm trying," he said.

"No, not you. Me. My eyes were closing."

"Mine are, too," he said. "What if we just stood here and took a one-minute nap?"

"No naps," she said. "Move now, nap later."

They were moving slower than they had been earlier, but it still didn't take very long to reach the stream again. Mattie felt a wash of relief as they entered the clearing. The creature couldn't hide from them here. They would have warning if it was coming.

Then C.P. cried out, "No! No! For chrissakes, no!" and she saw what he was yelling about.

Jen hung from her intestines in a tree on the other side of the stream, her torso an empty cavity like a blank eye.

"Don't look," Mattie said, though she couldn't stop staring herself and her voice didn't sound like it was attached to her body. "Don't look. You can't do anything for her. Don't look. Come on, C.P. Come away."

He let her lead him like a child, her hand pulling his. The rifle slid out of his other hand.

"The rifle," she said. "Get the rifle."

"What good will it do?" he said dully. "That guy had the rifle. He shot the monster. We heard him shooting it. But it still didn't die."

"We don't need to kill it," Mattie said, picking up the rifle herself and wrapping his hands around it. "We just need to keep it away from us so we can live."

"It doesn't seem fair," he said. "That we can live, and they didn't."

"No," Mattie said. "It doesn't. Come on. Don't think about it right now. Just take a step. Let's go. Come on."

They went on like that for some time, Mattie coaxing, C.P. shuffling along like a sleepwalker. All the while she was listening, listening for the sound of birds chirping above the bubbling of the stream, listening to make certain it never got too quiet.

The stream bent around toward the southeast, just as C.P. said it would. Mattie couldn't hear the river yet, but she hoped to very soon. The river meant they were closer to the base of the mountain, to town, to places where there were no monsters.

*William came from a town, once, and so did you. Your monster came right in through your bedroom window.*

No, she wasn't going to think about William. She wasn't going to drag his ghost with her all the way to her new life.

The quiet came all at once, a hush that swept through behind the wind.

*But why?* Mattie thought. *We're leaving, moving farther away from its cave, and neither of us look as weak or injured as Griffin or Jen did. It has no reason to hunt us.*

"Don't stop," she said in an undertone. "It's here."

C.P. looked at her, but his eyes weren't focused. He'd gone somewhere far from her, someplace where his friends were still alive and happy and not hanging from trees in the forest.

"What's here?"

"The creature," she said. "It's near. The woods have gone quiet."

The dazed look receded, and he glanced around. "I don't see it."

"You never do see it," she said. "Stay near the water, away from the trees. If it wants us it will have to come out and show itself."

"I don't want it to show itself. I never thought I'd say this, especially given why we came here in the first place, but I do not want to see it," C.P. said. He gripped the rifle a little tighter.

There was the sound of branches breaking, the sound getting closer and closer.

"It's coming," he said.

"I know."

"I think we should run."

The creature roared, the sound filling up the air all around them, pressing against their ears, vibrating inside their heads. Mattie couldn't run. She couldn't even walk. The roar made her legs weak, made her hands tremble, made her chest feel like it was caving in.

C.P. must have felt the same way, because he staggered and stopped, his face pale.

The roaring ceased, and Mattie stood there for a moment, trying to find her breath again.

The creature burst from the trees on their side of the stream, its speed impossible to track. Mattie only had a sense, as always, of something enormous, something fur-covered and powerful. There was a flash of one dark eye, a blood-covered maw, teeth, claws. Then C.P. was on his knees, screaming, and the hand that held the rifle was gone.

And so was the rifle, and so was the creature.

She didn't think. She pulled the long scarf off her neck and took the bloodied, ragged stump where his hand used to be and wrapped it tightly in the cloth. There was blood everywhere, blood soaking into the scarf, blood on her hands and on her trousers, so much blood.

C.P. passed out.

"Oh, no," Mattie moaned. "No, no, no. Not you, too. You can't sleep now. The creature will come and take you and then I'll be alone. Come on, come on, C.P., wake up. Wake up now."

She shook his shoulder, but he didn't respond. Her scarf was already soaked through with his blood but they didn't have any bandages.

She quickly unbuttoned her coat and pulled off her sweater. Underneath she wore an undershirt and this she removed, too, flushing because her breasts were exposed even though C.P. couldn't see. She quickly pulled all of her layers back on, shivering. Then she dragged C.P. closer to the stream, unwrapped the scarf, pulled up his coat sleeve and put the stump in the freezing water. Blood flowed away into the water.

She was only thinking about cleaning it and binding the wound more tightly with her undershirt, but the shock of the freezing water made C.P. open his eyes and sit up, shouting incoherently.

"Stop," Mattie said. "Just leave your arm there."

"Are you crazy? I'm going to get hypothermia," he said, and then he looked at his wrist, and turned his head away. "Nope, actually, I'm going to be sick."

Mattie quickly bound the stump tightly with her shirt. The blood still flowed, but it seemed a little more sluggish now. Maybe it was her imagination.

She stood, and tugged at his arm. "We have to go."

"Jesus, doesn't losing a limb entitle me to five seconds of rest?" he said.

"No. It's still here. It's watching, waiting to see what we'll do. And if you lay down or pass out it will take you, just like the others."

He didn't argue anymore, just let Mattie pull him up.

"Can you walk?" she asked.

"Not by myself," he admitted. "I'm a little dizzy."

She slung his uninjured arm around her shoulder. He was heavy, so much heavier and taller than her. She didn't know if she could drag him. "Don't fall asleep on me."

"It came for the rifle," C.P. said as they started forward, moving slowly.

"What?" Mattie said. She was trying to concentrate on her steps, to match her rhythm to his so that walking would be easier.

"It took the rifle. That guy shot it, right? So when it saw me with the rifle it wanted to make sure we couldn't hurt it again," C.P. said.

It made sense, but Mattie wasn't looking for explanations. She only wanted to get away. She didn't know how long the creature would follow them.

"We need to walk faster," she said.

"I don't think I can. I think you're going to have to leave me, Samantha Hunter."

She glanced up at him. His eyes seemed to be rolling in every direction at once.

"Don't you dare," she said. "Don't you dare pass out. It's you and me and we're going to make it to the bottom of this mountain so you stay awake, do you hear me? Stay awake."

They shuffled along, and Mattie felt the creature watching them from the trees, waiting for its chance. Its gaze seemed to press down on her, stopping the breath in her lungs.

*Just stay focused on the stream, on putting one foot in front of the other, on keeping C.P. upright.*

"Hey," he said, and he sounded more alert. "Hey, am I hallucinating or is that a road?"

He gestured with his stump, wincing when he caught sight of the bloodied shirt wrapped around it.

Mattie saw it then, too—a dirt road that wound along parallel to the stream, almost hidden by the trees.

The trees. There weren't many of them, but to get to the road they'd have to cross through the trees.

"The vehicle. Remember the key?" he said. "Oh my god, we're saved. Let's go find it."

The stream was wider here, and there were almost no rocks to step on to keep their feet dry. C.P. plowed forward, tugging Mattie along with him, splashing through the water.

A branch cracked behind them.

"No," Mattie said. "Don't follow us. Stay away."

They climbed up the little incline on the other side of the bank.

The trees weren't as thick here. They could see the road in between the trunks.

"We have to run through," Mattie said. "Because the trees are its hunting ground. Can you run?"

"I can do anything if there's a car waiting on the other side."

"We don't know there is for sure," Mattie said. She didn't want him to get his hopes up and then have them dashed if William had hidden his vehicle so well that they couldn't find it.

"It's got to be," he said. "That's a car key around your neck, and there's a road. That guy had a way of getting up and down this mountain quickly."

"Okay," Mattie said. "Okay. Let's run."

They took off, pushing through the snow, both of them barely upright.

The tree trunks were closer, closer, closer, and then they were inside them and Mattie saw the road on the other side, maybe ten feet away. Nine feet, eight feet, seven feet. They were almost out.

The creature roared again, louder than before, and the sound wanted to break her but she could taste her freedom and so could C.P. He grabbed her hand and they ran, breaking free of the woods, their feet touching the dirt road.

"He cleared this," C.P. said, looking left and right. "That's the only reason we could see it from the stream. He must have a truck with a plow on it."

Mattie didn't care what kind of vehicle it was as long as it was near, but she didn't see anything.

"It's not here," she said.

The roaring had stopped, and there was no warning crunch of branches breaking.

"Just because we can't see it doesn't mean it's not here," he said. "It's probably that way, closer to the cabin."

The cabin. Everything in her life seemed to circle back to that place, no matter how hard she tried to get away from it.

And the creature was following. If they went back in the direction of its cave, it might decide to eliminate them both with one swipe of its paw.

"Maybe we should just follow the road down," Mattie said. "On foot. It will still be easier than hiking through the snow."

"Let's just look," he said. "Just a little ways in that direction."

Mattie glanced back at the trees behind them. There was an enormous silhouette there, waiting.

"It's watching us," she whispered.

She saw him find the silhouette with his eyes, saw the blood drain out of his already pale face.

"But it's not attacking," he said, his voice trembling. "It's just watching. So let's just follow the plan."

He took her hand again, and squeezed hard. They walked up the road, toward the cabin.

"It can't be too close to the cabin. Otherwise you would have heard the sound of the engine every time he went somewhere."

Mattie knew he was trying to sound calm and normal, to pretend that the shadow in the trees wasn't following them with unnatural silence.

*It's watching and waiting. It's trying to decide if we're still a threat.*

She heard the creature's breath suddenly, heard the huff of its exhale.

*It's going to attack. It's not going to wait any longer.*

"There it is!" C.P. shouted.

The creature paused.

And there, parked in the middle of the road, was a huge black truck.

"With a plow, just like I said!" C.P. shouted. "Get the key, come on."

Mattie tugged the string holding the keys off her neck and handed it to him. He ran toward the truck, but Mattie stayed where she was. She turned to face the shadow in the woods.

"We're leaving now," she said, and her voice was so small, so faint. She tried again. "We're leaving, and we're not coming back. So the mountain can be yours now. There's no need to follow us."

The shadow shifted, and Mattie thought she saw the gleam of eyes.

Not two eyes. Four.

And then the shadow drew a little closer to the road, and though she still couldn't make out exactly what the creature looked like, she was certain of one thing.

There wasn't one creature, but two. A smaller one on the back of the larger.

*A parent and child?* she thought. *Is that why it chased us even when we were no threat? It was trying to keep us from its child?*

"What are you doing?" C.P. shouted. "We're leaving right now!"

Mattie turned away from the shape in the trees, ran to the truck, climbed inside. She felt the creature (*creatures*) watching as she went.

C.P. had already put the key into the ignition, but now he looked at the stump where his right hand used to be.

"I can steer with one hand, I think," he said. "But I need to hold the wheel while you put it in drive. Can you do that?"

Mattie stared at him blankly.

"The stick in the middle," he said. "I need you to press on the button on the side and pull it back until it's next to the 'D.'"

He grasped the wheel with his left hand. "Okay, I'm ready."

Mattie followed his instructions, and a moment later the truck was rolling forward.

C.P. started laughing. "I can't believe it. I can't believe it. We're actually getting away."

Mattie didn't laugh with him. She stared into the trees, looking for the gleam of eyes, but the silhouette was gone.

C.P. pulled the truck to a stop in front of a low, brick building. There was a sign on the front that indicated it was a state troopers' barracks.

"I think we should take you to a doctor first," Mattie said.

"This was closer," he said. "And they know how to call an ambulance, believe me."

Now that they were off the mountain the energy seemed to have drained out of him. He closed his eyes. "I'm just going to rest here for a minute, okay? I'm really tired."

A second later he was asleep, breathing deeply. Mattie looked at him. She looked at the glass door. She was going to have to go in by herself.

She climbed out of the truck. It seemed like it was a long way down to the ground, and she walked slowly toward the door, her heart pounding.

*It's okay. They're going to help you. They're going to help. They can't give you back to William anymore.*

She pushed open the door. There was a man at a desk. He had very short dark hair and he wore a uniform. She saw him take in the blood splashed on her trousers, her black eye, the bruised marks at her throat.

"Miss? Are you all right?" he said, hurrying around the desk.

"Yes," she said. "But my friend needs a doctor."

*My friend*, she thought. *I have a friend. And somewhere, I have a sister. I'm not alone.*

"Please," she said. "Please help him."

"We'll help him, don't worry," he said. He lifted a radio to his mouth and said several things that Mattie didn't really pay attention to. "What's your name?"

She took a deep breath, felt the years fall away.

"Samantha. My name is Samantha."

*Photo by Kathryn McCallum Osgood*

**Christina Henry** is a horror and dark fantasy author whose works include *The Ghost Tree*, *Looking Glass*, *The Girl in Red*, *The Mermaid*, *Lost Boy*, *Alice*, *Red Queen* and the seven-book urban fantasy Black Wings series.

She enjoys running long distances, reading anything she can get her hands on and watching movies with samurai, zombies and/or subtitles in her spare time. She lives in Chicago with her husband and son.

### CONNECT ONLINE

ChristinaHenry.net

AuthorChristinaHenry

C_Henry_Author

AuthorChristinaHenry

goodreads.com/CHenryAuthor

Ready to find
your next great read?

Let us help.

**Visit prh.com/nextread**